BUCK NAKED IN ANOTHER WORLD VOLUME 1

© Kotani Madoka 2019

Originally published in Japan in 2019 by MAG Garden Corporation, TOKYO. English translation rights arranged through TOHAN CORPORATION, Tokyo.

Seven Seas press and purchase enquiries can be sent to Marketing Manager Lianne Sentar at press@gomanga.com. Information requiring the distribution and purchase of digital editions is available from Digital Manager CK Russell at digital@gomanga.com.

Seven Seas and the Seven Seas logo are trademarks of Seven Seas Entertainment. All rights reserved.

Follow Seven Seas Entertainment online at sevenseasentertainment.com.

TRANSLATION: Garrison Denim
ADAPTATION: Matthew Grune
COVER DESIGN: Nicky Lim
LOGO DESIGN: George Panella
INTERIOR LAYOUT & DESIGN: Clay Gardner
PROOFREADER: Kelly Lorraine Andrews, Stephanie Cohen
LIGHT NOVEL EDITOR: E.M. Candon
PREPRESS TECHNICIAN: Rhiannon Rasmussen-Silverstein
PRODUCTION MANAGER: Lissa Pattillo
MANAGING EDITOR: Julie Davis
ASSOCIATE PUBLISHER: Adam Arnold
PUBLISHER: Jason DeAngelis

ISBN: 978-1-64505-543-3
Printed in Canada
First Printing: July 2020
10 9 8 7 6 5 4 3 2 1

BUCK NAKED in ANOTHER WORLD

NOVEL 1

STORY BY
Madoka Kotani

ART BY
Mochiusa

Seven Seas

Seven Seas Entertainment

TABLE OF
Contents

Before I Knew It,
I Was in a Developing Village on the Frontier

"I'LL ASK YOU AGAIN—what can you do for us?"

So there I was, buck naked and hogtied like a guy stuck in some hardcore bondage role-play. Don't jump to conclusions on me, though. I'm not into that stuff, and it's not like I'd have the cash for it anyway.

It was dawning on me that I was stuck somewhere a whole lot stranger: another world.

But how? I clocked out from my part-time job and started toward this bar by the station for a quick drink on the way home... but after that I couldn't remember a thing.

"I'm, uh, in pretty good shape. I've done all sorts of odd part-time jobs, so I can handle just about anything you throw at me." I don't know how I stammered all that out to the young woman in front of me. She seemed like the leader. I did not want to piss off the leader.

C'mon, think, Shuta, think! But the scratching sensation of sand inside my mouth was really damn distracting.

"Oh? I don't know what a 'part-time' job is, but you'd best not disappoint me."

"I'll do all I can."

"Hmph. This village doesn't have the means to accommodate anyone who can't pull their own weight, but we need all the man-power we can get."

The young woman motioned toward me with her head. On cue, the muscle-bound man beside her stomped over and grabbed me. After meathead dragged me through the dirt, he tossed me unceremoniously inside of a barnyard stable.

● ● ●

My name's Yoshida Shuta. I'm Japanese, and I turned thirty-two this year. Back in my old world, I hopped from one part-time job to another to get by. Did it in high school, and did it in college too.

My life didn't start going downhill until *after* I started college.

See, I actually had fun working part-time. Everything I earned I got to keep, and it was always better to have more cash. Even back in high school I knew that was the life for me, but after squeezing my way into a third-rate college and getting all that extra free time, I was convinced. The more I worked, the more money I got, so I thought, why waste time studying? I barely saw the inside of a classroom so, naturally, I flunked every class.

My parents were beyond pissed when they found out, and they eventually made me drop out of school because of it. It only made sense considering they had to get my two little sisters through college too.

After dropping out, I worked all kinds of jobs to get by. The stories I could tell from all the stuff I did (until I got to this world, at least) would be more than enough for good conversation over drinks.

I'd run the gamut of your typical part-time jobs: convenience stores, fast food joints, home improvement centers, liquor stores, restaurants, newspaper delivery, you name it. I was with demolition crews, at thrift shops, a mailman, even a set-builder for theaters, and it didn't stop there. A little construction work here, some civil engineering there, a smattering of freelance writing (fine, calling it "writing" might be a stretch), and even this one gig putting on performances while pounding mochi.

Since I was a college dropout, though, everything I could get boiled down to either menial or manual labor. Mostly I just heard about temp jobs from other people and got to working for them. Once my part was over, so was the job. That's why none of the work I got lasted too long.

Despite all that, there was one thing I *did* stick with for more than twenty years: karate.

At first my parents forced me to take classes when I was a kid, but it slowly became part of my life through elementary school and junior high. I kept it up till I had to start studying for high school entrance exams.

The thing was, I'd quit just in time for the huge martial arts boom. Catching the end-of-year matches on TV made me want to pick it up again, so I ended up joining the karate club while I was in high school.

It was a different style of karate than before, but I didn't care. Now that nobody was making me do it, I was actually having fun. And while the club I joined in college was pretty casual, I still got the chance to mingle with people who practiced all sorts of martial arts, karate included.

Still, my main focus was definitely on my jobs. Karate was just a way to blow off steam between shifts.

By then my parents had pretty much disowned me and kicked me out, so I got taken in by one of my old karate teachers and became a kind of assistant instructor for him. Good times.

Now here I was, stuck in some barnyard stable that—let's not mince words—smelled like ass.

The last job I worked was at an upscale restaurant washing dishes. Compared to that job, this place seemed like even more of a pigsty.

Let's not forget that I was stuck here in my birthday suit. Couldn't I at least get something to wear? I ran into a little incident after I got to this world, hence the buck-nakedness. I was wandering around in the nearby forest when one of the villagers found me. Or rather, they *caught* me, and then took everything I had. And I do mean everything.

The person who captured me had tawny, light brown skin, and—well, maybe "person" wasn't the right word for him. He looked like a demonic monkey. There were other villagers nearby who looked more like me, and they kept calling the guy a "goblin."

I'd woken up in some kind of fantasy world.

As I gingerly moved my aching body, my eyes slowly adjusted to the darkness. Rays of sunlight still peeked through the plentiful cracks in the walls of the rundown stable.

If I remembered right, I was captured sometime early this morning, and then brought before the village chief just before noon. All that while, I hadn't been given the tiniest scrap to eat.

Hungry as I was, I still couldn't quite digest the situation. Anyway, the more pressing issue was my full bladder. But this was a stable for animals, so I decided I might as well piss and try not to feel weird about it.

Man, it's chilly, I thought as I took another look around. I was lying on a pile of hay; the prickly stuff was strewn all about the stable. I was dying for a drink, but the only thing I could find was some water in what looked like a food trough for animals. Probably not good for humans, so I'd have to think on whether or not to slake my thirst with it.

Not that I'd have much of a choice if they left me here forever... but then, getting a bad case of the runs from foul water could spell death for me in this world. It was a terrifying prospect, to say the least.

On top of all that, I still didn't have the slightest idea how I'd ended up in this place.

I thought back to what the village chief asked me: "What can you do?"

You could say I could do just about everything, with all the jobs I'd taken…or maybe nothing at all. I could do karate, but I wasn't really that strong. It wasn't like I'd ever beaten the crap out of someone. As for all the stuff I made in my old jobs, with those I had the convenience of modern tools and computers. Here, I had nothing.

Since there were goblins in this place, it wasn't a huge leap to assume that this really was another world. So how far along was this world's technology?

If I really couldn't do anything for the village, I could easily see them killing me off. Just like the chief said, this place didn't have the means to accommodate anyone who couldn't pull their own weight. The only thing that I had to contribute was my body, then, forged through a lifetime of karate and physical labor.

Great. None of that made me less thirsty. Or cold. They could've given me my clothes, at least.

I wonder what they're gonna do with all the other stuff they took from me? Now that I think about it, I don't even remember what else I had when I first got lost here. Wonder if they'll give anything back.

The door to the stable opened with a loud creak.

"Time to eat. Come with me." It was the same goblin who captured me while I was wandering the forest.

He untied the ropes around me, and I finally made my way out of that cramped stable. Waiting outside was the muscle-bound man who had thrown me in the stable in the first place.

It seemed like he was in charge of keeping an eye on me. After a brief exchange of grunts between him and the goblin, the meathead followed after us.

"This way," said the goblin, and I followed.

Man, it's bright out here. I used one hand to shield my eyes from the sun, and the other to hide my crotch. The wind was brisk, but at least the sunlight was a bit warm. I'd wager it was spring in this world, or maybe fall.

A smattering of houses with walls built out of mud came into view as I followed—houses with chimneys, which meant that they probably had all the furnishings of real, proper houses.

Just as I thought when they first dragged me here, this village probably had a few hundred people living in it. The village itself was surrounded by forest, with only enough trees cleared out for the settlement proper. Small plots of farmland clustered near the houses, along with tiny stables like the one they tossed me in.

"Hey man, what's your name? I'm Shuta," I said to the goblin. He stopped, turning to take a brief glance at my face. I couldn't tell how old he was, but even though the guy was a good head or two shorter than me, he was absolutely ripped. Imagine a miniaturized junior heavyweight pro-wrestler and you're on the right track. Deep wrinkles lined his face, but I guessed that was just a goblin thing. It made it a lot harder to figure out how old he was.

The goblin ignored me and kept on walking.

"Aw, c'mon, man! Don't be like that. You do have a name, right?"

No response.

I decided to hold off on the questions for now. Even if I really wanted to just know where I was and what was happening, I didn't know what these guys would do to me if I pissed them off by talking too much.

Come to think of it, the talking itself was weird. I was in a different world, but I could still somehow communicate with these people.

We finally arrived at our destination, just behind the village chief's manor. It was no outdoor café or anything, but it had a wooden porch and an earthen stove, where they must've done some cooking.

"Sit." He was certainly a goblin of few words. I obeyed, sitting myself down on the wooden balcony. A young girl stood near the stove, ladling a thick, stodgy substance into a wooden bowl. She looked wary.

"Hey, thanks a lot," I said, flashing a smile as she handed me the bowl...at which point she darted away, unfortunately.

Great, she hates me...or maybe outsiders are rare, and she just doesn't want to be involved with me too much? I peered at what was in my bowl. The sludgy substance seemed to be some kind of porridge. I couldn't be sure, but from what I could see, it had red peppers (I thought), some beans, potatoes, oatmeal, and bits of what *looked* like bacon (I hoped).

"Eat. When you're finished, time for work," the goblin said as he took his own bowl from the girl. I snuck a glance at what he got. Weirdly, he not only got less than me, but it looked like I got more of those bacon bits as well.

When I finally brought my wooden spoon to my mouth, I found the porridge didn't have any flavor to it. Fine by me. I didn't need gourmet cooking on an empty stomach. It only took about ten spoonfuls before my porridge disappeared.

"I'm guessing there aren't any seconds, right?"

My question was ignored, of course.

After I finished eating, they finally handed me some clothes... kind of. Not my old clothes, but a raggedy old hemp loincloth. This wasn't even what the other villagers wore—they all had *full* sets of clothes.

They gave me one more thing besides the loincloth: a small hand axe.

"Chop these logs. When you do, pile them up over there," the goblin told me as he pointed toward a mound of wood. So that was my job here. Chopping firewood.

"What should I do when I'm finished with that?"

"Do all the ones here, then separate them so they can be used in the village. Then do the ones next to this pile, and the pile next to that one."

I tried not to wince at the mountains of logs before me. *Yeah, this isn't the kind of job you can finish in one day. It's gonna take at least a week to get it all done.*

I offered up the brightest, most apathetic smile I could muster. "Heh. Uh. You got it."

● ● ●

Hey, folks. Still Shuta here. You know, that guy who got sent to another world and gets to chop firewood for a living? All I've got is a loincloth and a hand axe. I suppose you could call that my work uniform.

It was the middle of spring, and yet another day of me working my way through a pile of logs. The goblin woodcutters gathered lumber, and my job was to chop it up so the villagers could use it as firewood in their homes all through winter. Simple, yeah, but exhausting.

My first day trying it went something like this: First, I set one of the larger pieces of wood on a stump and tried chopping it with my axe. I wasn't used to this kind of work, so the blade got stuck in the log and wouldn't come out. I lifted my axe again, log still stuck to it, and brought it down against the stump. That got the thing cut in half.

None of my cuts were even when I started, and my chopping technique was sloppy at best. It only took about five minutes for the palms of my hands to go numb, which was a sign of the calluses to come. Another five minutes, and the friction caused my skin to become hot. Five more minutes, and my arms were starting to give out, then my shoulders. The feeling of exhaustion finally crept down my lower back, and then I was down for the count.

The only reason I got that far was because of all the part-time jobs I'd done before—specifically, the one where I pounded mochi with a giant wooden mallet over New Year's. It took two hands to swing that mallet, and I eventually learned to make it easier on myself by relaxing my body whenever I took a swing.

That said, it was different enough to give me trouble. I was supposed to use one hand to swing the hand axe, and that was rough stuff. Still, that's how it had to be done, since it was crucial to give the arm I wasn't using a break before alternating back to it.

I didn't know that on my first day, though—I used *both* hands. It made swinging easier, but it wasn't as efficient.

Day two came, and work got a bit easier as I figured out the one-handed technique. I realized if I kept brute-forcing it, I'd only slow things down in the end—call it the intuition of a manual labor vet.

By the time day three came around, I'd finally gotten the hang of my work, and I was on my way to becoming firewood-chopping pro.

"Well, well, well. Just like you said, it seems you possess some amount of physical strength after all," the village chief said as she observed me at work.

Why thank you oh so much, Your Majesty.

I'm not trying to brag or anything, but even if I couldn't be perfect, I still felt like I'd done enough in my life that I could handle just about any work they threw at me.

It's my "60 Percent Rule." You get 100 percent in anything, good for you, you'll be satisfied with that perfection. What keeps you going is aiming for 60 percent. I'd treat that 60 percent as 50 percent for next time, then aim to give another 10 percent more to reach 60 percent again. Rinse and repeat.

"Thank you for your words of praise," I replied, making myself sound as humble as possible.

"I didn't want to start you with farm work all of a sudden. Couldn't have you eating all the crops, after all," the village chief said with a reserved giggle.

Honestly, the village chief was kind of cute. She had to be only a year or two into her thirties, with long, waist-length blonde hair.

I remembered reading in some book that humans in the past only used to live until around fifty or so. That's why they'd get married and have kids so young, climbing the stairs to adulthood faster than I could even imagine. Really, it wasn't so strange to see a thirty-something woman in charge of a village.

Anyway, she seemed satisfied with what she saw of my work. She winked at the meathead guard in charge of keeping an eye on me before returning to her manor, and he bowed his head as he saw her off.

Back to work, then. The worst part of it was that no matter how much I worked through the log piles, they never seemed to diminish. The goblin woodcutters just tossed new wood on the piles, day after day.

The guard watching over me was always around, but he never lifted a finger to help. He would only ever take his sword out of his sheath to swing it around. How efficient of him—intimidate me and get some practice in. What a guy, right?

On the fourth day, I wound up with an injury from the constant rubbing of my loincloth. I noticed a stinging sensation first, and it turned out my skin had actually split open a little. I hadn't been able to wash my loincloth in the last few days, either, so when I saw the young girl working at the village chief's manor, I tried talking with her about it.

"Excuse me, do you have a second?"

She didn't say a word. She was still completely on edge around me, and I couldn't blame her. I was almost completely naked aside from the scanty loincloth.

"I want to wash this thing I'm wearing, but is it all right for me to use water from this well to do it?" I cranked up the politeness. Friendliness hadn't gotten me anywhere with the goblin, so this time I tried to be as well mannered as I could manage.

Nope. In fact, over the course of our little conversation, the expression on her face had gone from anxiety to absolute terror. She lost no time fleeing back inside the village chief's abode.

"Um, so," I turned to my meathead guard, "about the well water..."

"No." He continued to sharpen his sword.

"But I haven't washed it once since I started wearing it. It's unsanitary. Maybe I could wash myself a little too?"

"No."

"Then what should I do?"

"Suck it up."

Ice cold. Dejectedly, I got back to work. The chafing from my loincloth was getting nasty, and it made me itchy, too, so I just stopped wearing it while I worked. Better to chop wood in the buff.

"Wonder what's on the menu today?" I asked myself aloud.

Lunchtime was when I got my first meal of the day, and it was the thing I most looked forward to since coming to my new world.

Besides the porridge they gave me the first day, I also got to eat baked potatoes, fried fish, broiled snake, and vegetable stew.

Meat was high-value stuff here, meant to be food for only the most hoity-toity, upper-class people. Even though I was on the bottom of the social totem pole, I still got to eat *some* meat... though it was only a few scraps of bacon. More often I'd get things like snake and fish, but I couldn't help craving some fatty, delicious cuts of the good stuff. I was out chopping wood from sunrise to sunset, after all, and even though it was simple labor, I worked myself to the bone.

It had been a little over a week since I was forced to become a woodcutter. The first few days my muscles hurt so bad I could barely move, but there's nothing like mortal terror to get you past the pain. Now, chopping wood was no big deal for me.

There was one sad thing about all this, though. See, wearing the loincloth made me so unbearably itchy that I stopped wearing it altogether. The chafing was a nightmare too. But the real problem started when I left it on a nearby tree branch to dry in the sun. I was wiping the sweat from my brow when an errant gust of wind snatched my loincloth from the branch and sent it dancing through the air.

"Ahh! My loincloth!"

I threw my axe to the side and chased after it, my exposed trouser snake bouncing to and fro.

When my guard saw me running, he drew his sword and brandished it at me.

"Where do you think you're going?!"

"My only piece of clothing is flying away!"

"Get back to work!"

"But it's all I have! Sure, it itches like crazy when I wear it, but it gets so cold at night! I'll freeze without it!"

"I told you to get back to work!"

Ice cold. No negotiations. He pointed the blade right at me, heading me off.

He's going to kill me. You learn things when you take martial arts as long as I have, and one of those things is murderous intent. This guy was brimming with it. He was completely prepared to kill me at any moment.

We glared at one another. Taking a quick look to the side, I saw the wind dragging my loincloth through the dirt, toward—oh no, I couldn't see it directly, but that was definitely the direction of the open door to the village chief's manor.

"EEEEEEK!!"

And that sounded like a shriek from the young girl working for the village chief.

"I *said* to get back to work," the man commanded.

"A-all right, I got it."

"Good."

"Look, I promise I wasn't gonna run away or anything. I just wanted to get back the only piece of clothing I had, that's all! If I catch a cold because I lost it, it's your fault!"

The man just thrust his sword in my direction again. Dejected, I picked up my hand axe and went back to chopping wood.

They didn't give me lunch that day.

Whenever I finished work for the day, I was given about five baked potatoes as payment. Although lunch was usually decent, dinner was always just cold leftovers. Since I hadn't been given anything for lunch that day, though, I was more than happy to eat whatever I got.

Oh, did I mention I never got any breakfast? Two meals a day. What a sad way to live. Speaking of food, that day's dinner came with a bottle of some sort. It was filled with some pretty unpalatable wine, the kind with bits of grape skin floating around in it. Drinking raw water was risky in this sort of world, so I guessed this wine was supposed to be a replacement for that. More wages from the village chief.

"Well, well. It looks like you're actually doing the bare minimum for work around here."

"Thank you for your words of praise. I must also extend my deepest and most profound gratitude for your additional gift of wine," I said, prostrating myself in the nude as I looked up at the village chief.

It wasn't like I was over the moon because of some crappy wine, but I didn't get any proper drinking water here. I had to be thankful to get *something* to drink, even if it was made out of the dregs of leftover grapes.

"Yes, it seems you're handling things well. Gimul! From now on, give this man a bottle of wine when he finishes his daily work."

"Are you sure?" asked my guard.

"I just said it was fine, did I not?"

The look on the meathead's face made it clear he wasn't happy to hear this. *So that guy's name is Gimul, then.*

Every day, I returned to the stable before sundown. Whatever animals used to live there, now it was just me. Home sweet home.

Well, I guess I did share the place with a few roosters. They'd be outside pecking away at their feed during the day, but my rooster roommates were there to greet me when I headed back to the stable. I was still itchy all over and couldn't really get a good night's sleep, but what could I do about it?

Just as I was thinking that, the girl who (I assumed) worked at the village chief's place as a servant came with a bucket of luke-warm water for me. Gimul—you know, the meathead guard—was there as well, of course. They still didn't trust me not to do anything horrible, then.

Gimul did the talking. "Here's some water. Clean yourself with this sponge."

Taking a glance at the girl, I saw she had some kind of tattered rag with her. She held it at arm's length, pinched between two fingers, like when you would hold something disgusting away from yourself. But the disgusting thing in question was...

"Oh, my loincloth!"

She thrust it toward me, basically begging me to take it away from her already.

"Thanks a lot," I said. "What's your name, by the way?" I mustered my friendliest smile again—but the cute girl just pinched her nose and ran away. I hadn't taken a bath in days, so I must've been downright rancid.

I wearily turned to Gimul. "Thank you very much."

"Get back to the stable. Also, you won't be chopping firewood anymore."

"Wait, hold on. Does that mean I'm...I'm fired? Am I going to be executed?"

"Hmph. We'll see," the man said. Then he kicked me back into my tiny stable and slid the bar on the door into place, locking me inside for the night.

I picked up the sponge and began to scrub myself in the darkness with the lukewarm water. With the remaining bit of water I washed my loincloth before setting it out to dry. No more working in the buff for me starting tomorrow.

Yoshida Shuta, thirty-two years old—and I finally finished my part-time job as a woodcutter.

My payment: crappy wine made out of bits of leftover grapes.

● ● ●

My days always started early in this new world. As in, before the sun even came up. That's when my rooster roommates would start crowing their heads off.

"*Cock-a-doodle-dooooo!*"

Morning-to-you-toooooo. With a stretch, I navigated the darkness to put on the only clothes I had—a loincloth. Hey, better that than nothing, even if it still made me itch like crazy around the waist. Still, I definitely wanted to get my hands on some genuinely decent duds soon.

Right then, I heard the sound of the bar on the stable door being removed before Gimul threw it wide open.

"Get up. You're not coming back here from today onward."

Before I could think, he was on me, grabbing me and dragging my hide out along the ground like it was nothing. A true gentle giant.

"If I'm not coming back here, does that mean I'm sleeping outside now? I guess that's fine since it's been getting warmer, but it gets so lonely at night. I'd want to at least take my rooster pals with me, you know?"

"Shut up."

And shut up I did.

The roosters in question poured out through the open stable door one after the other, not caring in the slightest as they hopped over me to get out. *Could you not just jump over me like I'm a corpse, guys?*

It was like all that time we spent together meant nothing. Ah, love. So one-sided, so fickle.

"So, what should I be doing now? You said I wasn't chopping wood anymore, right?"

"Follow me. Starting today, you're going to be taking care of the livestock."

"Wow, taking care of livestock!" I grinned, adjusted my loincloth, and stood myself up. "About time I had some better work to do."

It was still cold in the morning, but I would warm up by moving around a bit. I wanted to hurry up and get to tending those animals.

"So now that I've been chased out of the stable, where will I be living?" I asked Gimul, following behind him.

"There's a barn, bigger than that stable. That's going to be your new home."

Yes! Movin' on up!

The stable was just a little over fifty square feet, and now I suddenly got to move into a huge barn. *And with animal pals, too! Like cows! Or, oh! Maybe horses?*

Uh. No, actually. Pigs. It was pigs.

There were a few dozen of the little guys, oinking their bacony hearts out, and they *stank*. The stable may have smelled like ass, but the rankness here was a magnitude of ass that put the stable to shame.

"Pig crap," said Gimul. "Clean it." Leaving me with those words, Gimul moved a short distance away to keep an eye on me, just like before.

Does this guy even have *a job? Judging by the sword at his waist, I'm guessing he works for the village chief, but I've never actually seen him do any work. What a guy.*

Just as I was thinking that, a large, older lady made her way over to me (though it was hard to believe she was a lady at first glance.)

"So, you're the new manure guy, then?"

"Yeah, nice to meet you. My name's Shuta."

"Forget the formalities. Just grab that shovel and scoop it into those barrels until they're full of manure. When you're done, take the barrel to the mound out that way."

"Mound? What mound?"

"You'll know when you see it. Now get to work!" The old lady smacked me on the butt with the wooden stick she was holding. Hard.

"Ye-OUCH!"

"Less yappin', more pig-crappin'!"

This old lady was as hardass as they came. I scrambled to the shovel and got to work filling the barrels with the pig dung scattered around the barn. All that wood chopping really helped build my strength for this sort of work. Even so, my back started to give out in no time flat.

The barn was even bigger than I expected it to be, with each story around the size of a four-unit apartment. Over thirty pigs lived there, oinking and squealing away. I realized this world had no sense of hygiene—the barn was damn filthy, with flies buzzing all over the place.

It was a crap job (har har) that I wouldn't want to touch with a forty-foot pole, but if I wanted food, then I had to get scooping.

The lady watched me for a bit. Once she seemed satisfied, she wrung out one of the cloths in her wooden bucket and began wiping down the pigs.

No matter how clean you make them, they're just going to get dirty again when they lay down in the muck, I thought, piling the last of the pig manure into the barrels. That's when I got my next job.

"No slacking off, you. Go gather up the dirty hay and toss it outside."

"Hay?"

"Did I stutter? Hay! Replace it with new, clean hay. Don't just stand there, move!" the lady snapped. I scrambled to do as she said.

As I've mentioned before, I've done all sorts of part-time jobs. You usually got these older ladies from hell in smaller, family-owned workshops. They were as strict as could be and wouldn't stop nagging. I wouldn't really know what I was doing at first, but they wouldn't waste time giving me an earful at the slightest newbie screwup.

One time, I landed a job making school uniforms in a down-town tailor shop. They were looking for people with experience, but since no one else applied, I ended up working alongside a bunch of housewives and other ladies who lived near the work-shop. They all had some experience working at that shop, making me the only newbie.

I wasn't the most skilled person with my hands; nothing I made was sellable, and I got reprimanded for pretty much every-thing. All this after the old guy running the place had gone out of his way to ask me for help since they were swamped.

After a week, though, the complaints stopped. Turns out that a factory full of mostly older ladies likes having someone like me around to do the heavy lifting.

It seemed like the lady in the barn was treating me about the same, making me do all the physical labor like shoveling the pig dung and cleaning out the dirty hay. The only thing she didn't make me do was actually take care of the pigs.

I remembered reading somewhere that pigs were actually pretty smart animals. Even smarter than dogs, some people say. Maybe that's why they gave me the cold shoulder, since I was at the bottom of the village's social totem pole. Kept under watch by Gimul and constantly chastised by this older lady, I was lower than anyone who took care of them. Hell, the *pigs* probably had it better than me.

For the record, we're not talking the soft and smooth pigs back home. I'd describe these guys more as a mix between a pig and a tusky, thick-and-bristly furred boar.

Me? Well, I had a loincloth. Lucky pigs.

Just as the lady told me, when I started hauling out the dung barrels, I found the "mound" right off the bat. It was a mass of mud, dirty hay, and poop fused into one giant hill of compost. I was afraid I'd get another walloping from the lady's stick if I didn't hurry, so I dumped out my barrel and diligently went back for the next one.

My back started pleading for mercy after about seven trips, so I stretched out and gave myself a few raps on the back to try and alleviate the pain.

"No slacking off!"

"Sorry about that, ma'am."

"Who're you calling 'ma'am'?! I've got a wonderful name, and you better use it! It's Gintanen!" she shouted, and gave my arms a quick, sharp whack.

"I'm sorry, Gintanen!"

That's gonna bruise. I knew this kind of pain from all of my

31

years of karate. It felt like the aftermath of blocking a middle-kick to the body.

Lunchtime was still my one shining light. I worked more muscles in the barn, and I was all the hungrier for it. Instead of being taken behind the village chief's manor to eat like usual, Gintanen appeared with a basket of food.

"You're allowed to eat eggs from now on, so you better be grateful."

"Thank you!" Now I got both baked potatoes and boiled eggs for lunch. "Thank you so much!"

I couldn't even remember the last time I had eggs. I wasn't big on them back in my old world because, you know, all the cholesterol. I think I remember reading that it actually didn't really matter how many eggs you ate a day, but who knows with these things? Eh, whatever. These were going to be my first new-world eggs, so I couldn't give a damn either way.

There were a total of three boiled eggs and three potatoes. *I must be in heaven.*

"Hey, you," Gintanen suddenly spoke up. "What's your name? Even the pigs have names. You must have one too, yeah?"

The pig who was related to most other pigs in the barn was called "Pampi," in case anyone was wondering. *That's a pretty cute name you came up with there, Miss Gintanen.*

I told her my name when I introduced myself, but it seemed like she didn't remember.

"I'm Shuta."

"Shooter, huh. Humph! Think you're all that, do you? Hurry up and finish eating!" Her mood suddenly took a turn for the worse, and she gave me another hard whack on the head with her stick.

Dejected, I wolfed down my last egg, which promptly got stuck in my throat from trying to eat it too fast.

After finishing the pig dung, my new job was to mix the compost.

"Mix it real well, then cover the whole thing with dirt, top to bottom," Gintanen explained to me—or ordered, rather.

"Then what?"

"Get some water from the river and get the pigs something fresh to drink."

"All right, got it. And after that?"

"After that, we're finished. You better get moving, though, or things are gonna get messy."

"Messy? What's that supposed to mean?"

Gintanen put her hands on her hips, her bountiful chest bouncing slightly.

"It's gonna pour soon. So get moving."

I glanced at the sky. Enormous, ashen dark rain clouds spilled over the northern mountains. So, hell, I grabbed my shovel and got moving on that compost.

While mixing compost wasn't exactly a cakewalk, it was kind of similar to what I'd done as a civil engineer, so it wasn't anything I couldn't manage. I just wished it hadn't been so long since I'd done it. I don't know if it was an insurance problem or what, but at some point people just quit hiring freelancers like me to do construction work, civil engineering jobs, any of that junk. They looked down on us part-timers, I think, especially if there were any workplace accidents. If you were wondering why I was so rusty at manual labor like compost production, there's your answer.

After mixing the compost for a bit, I heaved some dirt over the top of the pile. The stench of fermenting compost was ungodly enough already, and the fresh dung and filthy hay dragged things still lower. I stunk something fierce up until the day before, but this smell turned the air itself rotten and clung to everything. It was the kind of job absolutely nobody would want to do, so hey, why not make some shmuck from another world do it instead?

With the compost mixed, I got to work replacing the water in the barn's troughs. Seeing as Gintanen was likely to kill me if I poured the reeking old water out in the barn, I hefted every one of those rectangular wooden troughs myself, and let me tell you—they were *heavy*. They weren't even filled to the brim with water and they were still too much to take all at once.

So I didn't. Dumping the water in the barn was out of the question, sure, but I could take a small bucket and scoop it from the troughs bit by bit. Once I removed enough water by bucket, I dragged the troughs outside and poured out the rest.

I kept an eye on the black clouds as I worked, racing against the rain to get all the old water out of the troughs. When I finished,

I grabbed a long wooden laundry pole and hung buckets on each side, hoisting the whole thing on my shoulders to get fresh water from the river.

A river, even though there was a perfectly good well nearby. I asked Gimul about going to the well and—

"You can't."

"Why not?"

"Because."

"Then where do I get water from?"

"The river."

There was a river on the outskirts of the village, apparently. Not...very close. But the well seemed like it was reserved only for a special few. Just delightful. With a bleak smile, I shouldered my laundry pole and hurried off to the river.

I was actually quite familiar with these long poles, thanks again to all that karate. Your fists are your main weapon, but you've got to learn to use more than that—forks, even poles.

The long poles I was used to were about six feet long, a little taller than your average guy. You could use them to control a confrontation in all sorts of ways: downward swings, thrusts, overhead strikes, and even a quick trip to knock someone still.

Good for immobilizing your opponent, easy to deal more fatal damage. Out of all the weapons I tried in the dojos, it had to be my favorite.

I never thought that a laundry pole like this would become an everyday part of my life, though. After about ten trips to the river and back, the thing was really digging into my shoulders. God, I wanted a handcart or something, but of course I didn't have one. Maybe nothing like that even existed here.

While on my umpteenth trip to and from the river, I happened to notice Gimul sitting down in the shade of a tree. He was drinking from a bottle—a very familiar bottle.

The bottle of wine from the village chief. My reward for all my hard work.

"Gimul! What do you think you're doing?!" I tossed my pole to the side.

"I'm wetting my whistle. Obviously."

"But that's my wine!"

"Yup."

"Then you'll repay me, won't you? Tell me how. Now!"

"Shut it."

Gimul left the bottle on the ground and stood, drawing his sword.

Oh. He was serious. Maybe he was buzzed, or maybe he really just didn't give a damn about me, or hell, maybe both. He readied his sword, gripping it tight with both hands.

He's really going to do it. Really going to kill me. Again and again the thought raced through my head (*really going to kill me, really going to do it, really going to*), but I stepped forward. I had to get the right distance between us, roughly the same length as Gimul's height and length of his sword combined...because I had a weapon perfect for fighting within that range.

With my bare feet, I lifted the long pole off the ground and sent it flying upward. I snatched it out of the air, ready to fight for my life.

• • •

Hi there—still me, Yoshida Shuta. Third-place champ of my junior high karate tournament back in the day, once the proud owner of a worn and tattered first-degree black belt.

All right, meathead. Bring it.

I fell into a basic stance with my pole, standing opposite Gimul. I kept my grip light, using about the same strength it would take to wring out a rag.

Gimul bulged with muscles. They filled his tunic like an overstuffed sausage sleeve—but I wagered those muscles were just genetics. Tons of people from all over the world look ripped. Looking ripped is the easy bit.

Not that I could talk. I packed on a few pounds as I reached my thirties. Still, I had enough muscle for a fight thanks to my classes. It was time to put them to good use.

(While I'm on the subject, the karate tournament I got third place in? There wasn't...actual...fighting. It was more about executing your forms, so I was pretty much petrified.)

However, after seeing Gimul take all those practice swings with his sword, I could tell he was a total amateur. See, I once played an extra on a movie set—nobody important, some guy who got slashed with a sword—but I'd actually gotten proper swordsmanship training for the part. Gimul's posture certainly looked badass, but I suspected that he sucked at all the actual murdery parts.

"You know what you'll get for opposing me, right?" Gimul snarled, swiping the air menacingly.

"Doesn't matter what I did then or what I'm doing now, does it? You were going to kill me either way." I had no doubt in my mind—this man intended to cut me down where I stood.

He drew closer. I caught on and jumped backward. No way was I going to let him get into a range he preferred. *No way* was I was going to die here. Though it wasn't like I wanted to start some little rebellion either.

Okay, what to do, what to do in order to Not Die. Disarm meathead. Then what? Get him on the ground, subdue him, and... and...keep hitting him till he stopped moving? Yell for help? If someone came by after I got him under control, it would look like I was the one attacking him.

Gimul was by no means a good man, but the fact he had a sword likely meant he was part of the village's top brass. Which meant I might be screwed. Maybe I could just steal his clothes and sword and make a run for it?

As that flurry of thoughts slashed and tore at me, Gimul shouldered his sword and made his move.

I'm no scholar of Western sword fighting, but it was easy enough to see that he had put everything into this one slash. I dodged to the side, brought myself closer to him. You don't fight from a distance with poles.

Fierce as Gimul was, his blade missed. It cut nothing but air, whooshing softly, swinging at a bad angle. He really was an amateur. I brought my pole down hard on that big, muscley sword-hand of his.

"You bastard!" Gimul roared; his right hand dropped from the hilt. He was using both hands to wield his sword, though, so he was still ready to take another swing at me.

This one was broad, horizontal. Amateur! The sword grazed my loincloth, but the momentum from his attack spun him around so his big dumb back was perfectly exposed.

I hooked my pole through Gimul's legs and sent him tumbling to the ground with a pathetic yelp. Then I flung his sword aside with my pole and followed that up with a few strikes to his elbows. No matter how much muscle your opponent has, going for their joints always works.

I wasn't trying to break any bones. Just his fighting spirit. I took another swing at his right elbow, since that seemed to be his dominant arm.

Gimul cried out, cradling his elbow as he lay face up and helpless. I pressed my pole to his throat.

"Don't move. If you do, I'm shoving this thing straight into your Adam's apple."

"Don't you dare think you'll get away with this."

"You're the one who tried to take my stuff. You're the one who tried to *kill* me."

"You have no proof. You're nothing but an outsider, and now you're going to die," Gimul growled as he fought through the pain and glared up at me.

A pole to his throat and he still hadn't lost the will to fight. That's why I hate people from the sticks. I'm a country kid myself, and I still have a lot of that in me, so I know better than anyone how much we're capable of enduring. Even when I started karate after moving to the city for college, the other guys from the sticks would push through nearly any agony while the guys from the city gave in at the first twinge.

Not saying that the country kids have it right, either—just that harsh farm life makes it easier to deal with pain. Basically, we're a pack of total masochists.

"Then I can take you down with me," I said. "Maybe I'll even get away with that sword of yours."

I pushed my pole still harder against Gimul's throat, and—

"What the hell is this?! Murder!"

And there she was—old lady Gintanen, screaming her throat sore at me. Like she always did, I suppose. "The outsider is trying to kill Gimul! We feed you, we give you work, and this is how you repay us?!" Gintanen shouted, jabbing her finger at me. "Ungrateful swine! Drop your pole this instant!"

As she spewed venom, a throng of goblins and older men gathered around me, armed with everything from wooden hoes to shovels to swords to whatever other farming tools you could use to beat an uppity stranger to death.

If I played my cards right, if I kept my eye on them and timed my dodges, I could take them. Maybe. They all looked just as amateur as meathead. Well, there was one person with a small machete-looking thing with some good moves, but he stood at the farthest edge of the crowd. Perhaps the guy was a hunter.

Now. If I won, I'd have to make a beeline to...where? All I knew was this village, and nothing more. And, again, that was if the crowd didn't farm-implement me to death there and then.

There was no guarantee that my training would translate to actual battle experience, so I threw my pole aside and raised my hands in the air. Nothing to do but surrender.

At which point Gimul launched off the ground, smashed his fist into my face, and knocked me out cold.

Welcome to my crib, folks. Up until this morning, I was living it up in a barn, but now I get a whole cell to myself. Pretty nice digs, eh?

My loincloth was a casualty of my fight with Gimul. I thought I dodged him, but nope. Just a hair off, and that was enough. So it goes...

Instead of a loincloth for those chilly nights, I made due with the fresh hay spread across the cell floor.

Makes you want to just count your blessings, doesn't it? Hooray.

So there I was in the village jail cell—as in, the *only* village jail cell, because of course it was. Just my luck.

It did, however, come with a toilet, and after everywhere else, that felt a bit like special treatment. The only other difference between the cell and my other brief homes was that this place was underground.

My new home: dark, damp, and reeking of—well, there was a toilet, so you can imagine. Even calling it a toilet was generous. It was a bucket. A wooden bucket in the corner of my dank cell.

"Looks like you don't have the best luck either, huh," I called out to my cellmate. She had to be under twenty, and her hemp tunic put my ratty old loincloth to shame. "Getting dragged down here away from the sunlight...nothing but misfortune."

She said nothing.

"My name's Shuta. What's yours?"

No response. She wouldn't even look me in the eyes.

"That village chief sure is a nasty piece of work, locking a girl like you in here," I said, chuckling.

Looking closer at the girl, she was just as cute as everyone else seemed to be. Was that just how girls looked in this world—drop-dead gorgeous? Then again, old Gintanen flew in the face of that. Pretty, sure...pretty terrifying. More pro-wrestler than runway model, which is...still an aesthetic, I suppose.

The girl working at the village chief's place wasn't exactly a supermodel either, but she looked sweet. Not that she ever acted with any genuine sweetness.

Meanwhile, my cellmate sat on the floor with her hands around her knees, staring in my direction. Nah, that undersells it—she was keeping an eye on me. She was completely free to move around, though I wasn't given the same luxury. Thick, foot-long chains clamped around my hands and feet. Life here was going to be a real hassle. I didn't even want to think about what I'd have to do when I needed to crap; peeing was nightmarish enough, thanks. The girl seemed not to care too much about it, though—she did her business, and the only thing she seemed to mind was if I looked anywhere near her.

I sat cross-legged on the floor, staring up at the ceiling. Stone architecture—a tower, probably. When I was going back and forth between the old rooster stable and the village chief's manor, I remembered seeing a three-or-four story tower. This had to be the place, and it was a jail. A spiral staircase stretched upward in front of me. The clacking sound of footsteps echoed down several flights of stairs.

Footsteps that were getting steadily closer. I focused my attention on the spiral staircase, and soon enough the village chief made her grand appearance.

"Seems like you really went wild this time, didn't you?"

I swallowed. Gimul was at her side, his face completely smashed in. But I hadn't beaten him that badly, had I?

"You quarreled with Gimul while taking care of the livestock. Do I have that correct?" she asked me.

"Yes, that's right," I said quietly.

Making excuses would get me nowhere now, and there was no point in denying the truth.

"That's when Gintanen happened across you two and had you captured, yes?"

"Right. Then Gimul punched me out."

"You look just as bad as him, you know. Take a look in the mirror," she added, giggling.

Har har. Get it? Because there's no way you'd find something as luxurious as a mirror here. Still curious, I tried touching my face... and regretted it. My nose hurt like hell. Smashed in, probably, or maybe even broken. I jerked my hand away just to stop the pain.

"What happened to Gimul's face wasn't me." I said quickly. "All I did was trip him. I didn't do anything else."

"I'm the one who punched my son," said the village chief calmly.

Gimul slumped his shoulders. The girl in the cell shrank against the wall. They were all terrified of her.

"Your...son?" I asked.

"Yes, my son. Stepson, to be precise. My late husband was the chief of this village. I was his second wife. Gimul was his son— something for me to remember him by, if you will."

"I see." That was the only reply I could give.

"A violent boy, though, and I wouldn't be surprised if drink drove him farther this time. I've already punished him on your behalf."

"So his face..."

"How shall I put it? The rules of this village go something like this: If you steal, we take your fingers. If you kill, we take your life."

And if you smash someone's face in, the village chief might smash your face right back, which is what happened to Gimul. Truly this was a woman to be feared.

"I've said my piece. You're cleared of all charges and free to leave."

Finally. One of the woodcutter goblins was with the village chief. He fumbled with the lock for a second before getting the door open.

"Thank you for helping me," I said to the village chief.

"There's no need to thank me, but I won't apologize for anything, either. We're even now."

Her son-in-law and me, both smashed to hell and back. Balance in all things, I guess.

"I've been meaning to ask, were you once a warrior?" the village chief said. "My son had a sword. Yet you took him down with only a stick."

"I wouldn't say a warrior, per se, but I guess I've been through some of the training."

"I see, I see. Looks like we have ourselves quite the find after all." Her dry laugh echoed throughout the stone tower.

"So," I glanced at my cellmate, "who's she, anyway?"

"Oh, her? I brought her here to take care of you. But never mind that. Come, follow me."

At the village chief's prompting, I stood up and left the cell. Which was nice, but it felt like they were forgetting something.

"Ah, I almost forgot. N'aniwa, take those chains off for him," the village chief ordered the goblin.

How was I supposed to pronounce that? Nan...nani what?

Freed from my chains, I pushed past a dejected Gimul. Oh, he hated that, you could just see it in his eyes...but he couldn't do a damn thing. Served that douche right.

The bright light of the outside world greeted us outside the tower.

"I'll go ahead and show you where you were *supposed* to live starting today," the village chief said.

"You mean the barn with the pigs?"

She turned around for a moment. "No, of course not. Who in the world told you that?"

I glared back at Gimul, following just behind us. He averted his eyes. The girl from the jail cell walked beside him; she looked pretty shocked when I looked her way. She frantically shook her head, as if to say she had nothing to do with this.

"Gimul, then," the village chief sighed.

"Yeah."

"Well, you have nothing to worry about. I was thinking of welcoming you as an official member of the village soon enough, after all."

"For real?! Thank you! Thank you so much!"

"And if you're going to be a member of the village, someone your age is going to need a wife," she said. "I've selected this girl. Marry her."

The girl behind us? "Wait, what?! I just met her! We haven't lived together, we haven't really talked, I—what about her? What about what she wants?"

"What are you making such a fuss for? You're of age. She's a woman. Starting a family now is only natural."

I didn't know if I really *needed* a wife, though. I'd never had a steady job, and my old house was a rundown apartment. I never cared where I lived, to be honest, and I could take care of my, uh, "needs" by myself. Then again, I wasn't about to turn her down. If relationships and free will didn't exist in this world, maybe I needed to get with the program.

"Thank you for your consideration. My wife and I will do our best to contribute to the village."

My new wife froze up. It hit me then that I didn't even know her name. I wondered if she'd warm up to me.

"About this house..."

47

"It's over there, on the outskirts of the village. It used to belong to one of our hunters."

"What happened to them?"

"Oh, he died. He went into the forest last winter, and it seems a wyvern got him."

"A, um...wyvern?" Why Vern? And would Vern strike again?

All right, yeah, stupid joke. I knew what a wyvern was well enough—one of those flying lizards you find in any generic fantasy setting. Huge, deadly, famous, and basically public domain.

"So a wyvern killed him?" I continued.

"They killed each other, actually. They call you Shooter, don't they?"

"Shuta, yes."

"A good name for an archer. Starting tomorrow, you'll receive your own bow and become a hunter."

"Huh?"

"Surely a Shooter has hunted before, correct?"

No, it was Shuta, Shuta. Though "Shooter" did sound pretty rad, right? But no, I was over thirty, and that was some goofy junior high gamer-name stuff.

"Yeah, I've hunted," I said, responding to her question. It was with one of my uncles. The guy hunted ducks. In elementary school, I was absolutely terrified of all his hunting dogs.

When I stayed at my aunt and uncle's place over summer and winter break, I was always at the bottom of the pecking order. My uncle was top dog there, my aunt was second-to-top-dog, then the literal dogs, and finally me. Hunting dogs are only friendly with their owners, I'm sad to report. They're pretty smart.

The problem was that when we shot ducks, we used guns—not a bow and arrow.

However, I also used to work in an apparel shop where my manager was a former Self-Defense Force paratrooper, and he took all the employees to airsoft places on our days off. Once when we were in the mountains, he'd run us up and down the cliffs there as a kind of "rappelling" crash course, so I was also familiar with mountainous terrain.

I even caught and ate some snakes when I was out there, so I bet I could at least do that here in the new world. (If you're curious about the taste: tiger keelbacks were delicious, striped snakes were mediocre, and rat snakes...don't bother with rat snakes.)

"Good. I'll have all the proper equipment sent to you by tomorrow morning, so I'm expecting you to work hard for us."

"Thank you again for your kind consideration."

The village chief laughed heartily. "You have a home and a wife now, so I'm expecting you to man up and protect your family." She paused for a moment. "By the way, this girl just so happens to be the daughter of the hunter who died. Make sure you take care of her!"

"Oh, uh! Right! Got it!"

From a tiny stable to a literal pigsty, and now, a real house with proper walls and everything—finally, I had a decent place to sleep in this world. It even had its own thatch roof, meaning I wouldn't have to worry about the wind or rain anymore.

And a wife. I just...had a wife now. That was normal in this world, I suppose, but it felt weird. I mean, what about her? How did she feel? You weren't just *given* wives back home. Marriage was mutual. You turned in a registration and everything.

"So, what's your name?" I tried.

Still no response from the girl. No, she didn't seem happy with this at all.

The village chief had declared us husband and wife, though, so I at least wanted to try getting to know one another. We'd be miserable otherwise; I couldn't imagine not even knowing her name. "I already said it before, but I'm Shuta."

"You're...Shooter?"

"Hey, you can talk after all! Yeah, I'm Shooter."

No matter how many times I introduced myself as "Shuta," the people in this world kept calling me "Shooter," so I decided to just roll with it. What, was somebody going to charge me with having a false ID? And you know what? It did sound pretty cool the more I heard it, just like a badass wandering stranger.

"I don't want to just call you 'you' all the time," I said. "Are you sure you don't want to tell me your name?"

"I...I'm Cassandra."

"Cassandra, huh? That's a pretty name."

We stood facing each other in the late hunter's house—her father's old home. I supposed Cassandra must've grown up there. It was much more spacious than the old rooster stable, probably just over 140 square feet. There were two long, narrow beds inside, and an earthen stove sat near a wall. All said, it reminded me more of a studio apartment than a house. Not that I was complaining. It even came with a bucket to take care of your "business" in the corner and a large tub beside it.

And to think at one point I had to go in the stable and scrub myself down with only the meager amounts of water they rationed me! One week later, here I was with a house *and* a wife. For the first time since arriving, I felt a sense of relief.

"Cassandra," I said, "I know you must be pretty shaken up about being married off to me all of a sudden." Who wouldn't? I mean, I felt weird about it too. I came back from work into another world, got hogtied by a goblin, pressed into chopping wood every day, and now at the end of it all I had a new house, a new life, a new wife.

"I know we can't just act like husband and wife right off the bat or anything, so let's try and get to know each other better a bit. Maybe someday we'll be the real deal."

Cassandra was just overflowing with enthusiasm...that is, if looking hangdog miserable was how you showed enthusiasm in this world. Probably not, eh? Great start to a joyous marriage.

"Let me get you my father's old clothes."

Oh. Um. House or no house, I was still buck naked right now. I gratefully accepted the clothes of my late father-in-law.

I Wonder if My Wife Isn't Warming Up to Me Because I'm Naked?

Hey, everyone, Yoshida Shuta here at the old hunter's shack. Oh yeah, and feel free to call me "Shooter" if you want.

My new wife Cassandra just handed me her late father's clothes, probably because I'd been running around in the buff since Gimul sliced off my loincloth. Hey, I'd take anything at that point.

Including a fur vest. Just a fur vest. "Um, Cassandra? Did your dad wear pants?"

"I sold them to scrape by. All I have now are his vests."

Three fur vests, to be precise. I wore one and stuffed the others in a small wicker chest of drawers. She wasn't joking. There were no pants.

Well, nothing I could do about that. Might as well wear what I got and show off my interdimensional junk to the whole world. I was kind of bummed not to have any underwear, so I took an old raggedy hand towel and tied it around my waist for a makeshift loincloth. The end result? Depressing. The hand towel was in even worse condition than my old loincloth, and it was so short there was barely any point to wearing it at all.

"How's it look on me?" I asked Cassandra, strutting my stuff like a hobo supermodel.

"It, uh, looks...incredible," she said while averting her eyes.

"It does, huh?"

"I'm sure my father would be proud."

"Thanks. I'm happy to hear it." Very polite, super sweet, absolutely a lie. This wouldn't look good on anybody. Still, I tried giving a short bow to show my appreciation...but the towel was too short. The ratty thing came undone, and out came the goods.

"W-well," I stammered, "the village chief's calling for me, so I have to get going."

"Be, um...careful..."

With my new wife's half-hearted farewell, I left our house on the edge of the village.

On our first night together as newlyweds, we didn't so much as hold hands. We slept in separate beds, the one that was hers and the bed that used to be her father's.

Cassandra was afraid of me. She curled up in her bed with her back turned to me, and all I did was lie alone in my own bed, sulking. On the first night of my marriage. Very romantic. Was the next step a child?

Now that brought some weird thoughts, having a kid with a pretty girl like her. I bet she could see those thoughts too, with me wearing such a small, ratty loincloth. Ugh, no wonder she was freaked out by me.

The next morning, a goblin named Wak'wakgoro waited for me outside. I couldn't see a difference between him and N'aniwa the woodcutter, but apparently they weren't even related or anything.

"The village chief prepared everything you need for hunting," he said.

"Thanks, glad to hear it."

"I heard you were a warrior before coming here. They say hunting's just another part of warrior training, so it must be your specialty, right? I'm looking forward to seeing your technique."

"I've gone hunting before, but I wouldn't exactly call it my specialty."

"But your name's Shooter! That means you know how to use a bow. I might be uneducated, but even I know that."

Out of all the villagers, Wak'wakgoro was the nicest one I'd met. He kept the conversation going on the way to the village chief's manor.

"Cassandra's a good girl," he said. "She's been through a lot since her father passed last winter, but she's got you now. About time some good news came her way."

"Yeah, I guess so."

"Come on now, any man worth his salt knows how to be a good family man! Get your act together!" he shouted and punctuated it with a smack on my bare ass. Shuta Jr. bounced back and forth between my thighs.

A family man. As a thirty-something-year-old hopping from part-time job to part-time job, I never even really thought about marriage. Hell, I hadn't even thought about dating anyone.

After dropping out of college and getting disowned, I stayed with one of my old karate teachers in Okinawa. Their house had a dojo that I slept in, and in exchange I was sort of an assistant karate teacher. I couldn't afford to feed myself with just that, though, so I also did all sorts of jobs—plumbing, making fireworks, whatever I could get. That left no time to think about dating and relationships.

Any man would try to seek some way to satisfy his more carnal desires every once in a while, but not me. It was a religious thing. Well, kind of. Well, not really. It wasn't that I had offered my chastity to the god of martial arts or anything, but more that I was a religious scholar attending the seminary school of hardcore hentai.

Porn mags are something else—just one glance and bang, your heart's pounding. The only problem was that my karate teacher's high schooler granddaughter found my stash, told everybody, and got the sacred texts tossed to the curb. Which is stupid, by the way. I mean, I was an adult keeping my stuff in a private place (under the bed), so what did it matter?

That was reasonable. My getup now—fur vest, raggedy dick-wrap—was a wee bit more objectionable.

"Anyway," Wak'wakgoro continued, "can't you at least put some clothes on?"

"I've just got fur vests in the new house," I said with a sigh and a quick, self-conscious crotch-cover.

"That so? Then I'll let you have one of my loincloths later. I've been wearing it for pajamas at night, but it's better than having nothing at all."

"Thanks, man."

"How old are you, come to think of it?"

"Me? I just turned thirty-two."

"Thirty-two? You sure don't look it! I took you for more of a youngster, but I guess you just look way younger for your age."

Weird thing to say, but I'd take it. "Thanks. I get that a lot," I lied, stroking the stubble on my face I hadn't been able to shave since I got to this world.

"Funny, I wonder if you're about the age Cassandra's father was."

"Uh. How old is Cassandra going to be this year?"

"I think about sixteen or seventeen, something like that."

Uh! Uhh! Yikes? Is this a crime? I thought to myself. *I feel like this is a crime? Oh god, I'm Dad-Age here. I'm Cassandra-Dad-Age. That's! Not great!*

"Well, you humans live longer than us goblins, so I don't think it's anything you need to worry about. It's not that strange to see some big age differences between husbands and wives for you guys."

"You sure?"

"I am. The village chief is gonna be thirty-one this year, but she was nineteen when she got married to the old chief. Guy was a grandpa pushing fifty."

"And the current village chief was the old one's second wife, I hear?"

"Yeah, she came here from another village. She's infertile, sorry to say, and that was her second marriage too."

"Ah, that's rough." I supposed the old village chief married her so someone would be there to look after his son. She really was a looker, so the whole thing seemed like such a shame. It hit me then that, given her age, she might be closer to being a "big sister" to Gimul rather than a mother. An unrelated-by-blood and very pretty big sister that turned big meathead Gimul into a meek mess? How earthshakingly unshocking: the meathead had the hots for step-mommy.

"But what I told you is our secret, okay?"

"Oh, uh, natch! I got it, Wak'wakgoro."

There had to be a trick to getting the pronunciation right on these goblins—it was driving me wacky.

By the time we reached the village chief's place, she was already waiting outside for us.

"You will be a hunter starting today," the village chief proclaimed, lording over me as I prostrated myself before her. "As such, you shall be provided with the tools to fulfill that work. These tools have only been bestowed upon you because I have recognized you as a member of our village. You are never to use them against another person."

"Deepest of thanks. I understand and obey." I was catching onto all that bowing, scraping, and groveling.

The civilization in this world seemed to be around our Middle Ages or so, maybe even before that. It looked like a Renaissance hadn't occurred yet, with sprawling rural countryside as far as the eye could see.

The difference between this world and my old one was that my Dark Ages didn't have forks. These ones were shaped differently than the forks I remembered, though, with just two prongs. More like "skewers" than forks, you could say.

Anyway, in this primitive world my hunting gear was a spear and a bow. I'd be like one of my ancestors in those old Japanese hunter-gatherer communities, wounding prey with bows and arrows before finishing them off with spears.

Besides the weapons, I also received a leather pouch and a pair of boots. I was rocking it barefoot right then, just asking to ruin my feet somehow. Those boots were going to be a lifesaver.

"From today onward, you will be working under Wak'wakgoro and the other hunters. After you learn the lay of the land, you'll begin hunting on your own, and you'll earn a proper share as a hunter of our village."

"Understood. I'll be the best hunter I can, for the sake of my wife, and for you too!"

"Good. Get to it, Shooter."

"Yes, ma'am!" I said, and bowed just an inch lower.

I donned my new hunting gear behind the village chief's manor, making sure to give my feet a quick scrub before slipping on those boots. They gave me socks to go along with them, but there was a strange gap between the big toe and the rest, sort of like traditional Japanese socks. There was no stretch to the material, either.

When I worked as a walking instructor, I learned that socks were sort of an extension of the skin on your feet. See, the more you change your socks, the less wear and tear it puts on the soles of your feet. I didn't know if the village chief understood that as well, but I couldn't have been more thankful for the ten pairs of socks she gave me.

I slipped my high-laced boots over my brand-new socks, feeling fancy. Boots were supposed to be a high-value commodity here, after all, with people replacing the soles of their boots so they could be used for years to come.

Around my waist the hunter's pouch hung from my belt, and under the belt I tucked my old raggedy hand towel to prevent chafing. The pouch itself was filled with a canteen of water, some hard rye bread, and two dried-out pieces of cheese, all prepared by the girl working at the village chief's place.

On my back, I wore my bow with a full quiver of fifteen arrows. The shape of the quiver meant it could probably be used a variety of different ways, but we'll get to that later.

Finally, I carried a spear, which doubled as a walking stick, as well as a small machete for cutting through thick foliage. It was dangerous to carry it around with the blade exposed, so I kept it in a leather sheath.

"Hey, look at you!" Wak'wakgoro exclaimed. "Finally looking like a proper hunter!"

"I mean, I am one starting today, so I'd hope so," I said with a smile.

"Except most hunters cover up a bit more," he said with a cackle.

I was letting it all hang out, as usual. Being naked didn't seem to matter as much here as it did back in my old world. Other people wouldn't so much as flinch at the sight of my dangly little dude. Sure, my new wife Cassandra and the girl at the village chief's manor would look away, but they must've just been embarrassed because they weren't mature enough to handle it. Yeah. Yeah, that had to be it.

"Shooter," said Wak'wakgoro, "you just gotta trade any extra prey you take out to get yourself some clothes."

"Oh yeah, of course. Just because I'm wearing this doesn't mean I'm not civilized. I'm embarrassed. Who wouldn't be?"

"Y'know, sometimes I just don't get what you're saying."

With Wak'wakgoro as my guide, we made our way to the forest. The other villagers only stared at us in silence. No one said a word.

"Everyone seems to be giving us a pretty wide berth," I noted. "No 'hellos'? No 'good lucks'?"

"We're hunters," he said sadly. "They hate hunters in this village, and always have."

They kept staring at us. Now I just wanted to look away.

• • •

Hunters know their own hunting grounds; the places get etched into their souls. My uncle wasn't just an expert duck hunter. He also knew every nook and cranny of his ground, knew the tiniest details about his prey. The same went for his hunting

61

dogs. They were all thoroughly trained, and every one of them could navigate the roughest terrain in pursuit of prey.

Whenever my uncle went to a new hunting ground with his friends, he'd have a local hunter show him around, treating him like an honored guest in unfamiliar territory.

A hunter is the master of his grounds, the king of his wilds.

My prior hunting grounds happened to be a little more... computerized. But it was a video game about hunting monsters, you see, so doing the same thing in this world seemed like a perfect match. Wyverns? They were nothing to me...I mean, in video games.

Wak'wakgoro and I made our way through the lighter woods to the east of the village until we pushed our way into a darker, more foreboding forest.

"The locals call this place the 'Apegut Forest,'" said Wak'wak-goro.

"Apegut?"

"Mmhm. Apparently they call it that way because they found the guts of some kind of giant ape around here."

Oh, so this world had gorillas now? Or maybe we were talking yetis, a bigfoot, or some other relative to the great apes.

"How do a bunch of ape intestines get slathered everywhere? Does that mean something killed it, ate it, and just flung pieces all over the place?"

"Probably something like that," he said, sighing through his hooked nose. "There's a wyvern nest located deeper in the forest."

"And that's what Cassandra's father died facing."

"That's the one. But Shooter, listen up."

"Yeah?"

"Don't try going all gung-ho on me here. I don't care what they call you—any hunter only just setting foot in this forest wouldn't be able to take one down. Not now."

All of his humor, all of his friendliness, had given way to seriousness.

"Of course. I'm only a part-time warrior, and like you said, I just got here. I'll be listening to everything you say until I've got a better grip on our hunting grounds."

I didn't even know what a wyvern looked like, and I didn't care to find out. As a matter of fact, every moment spent not in the presence of a wyvern seemed like a teensy victory. My video-game wyverns were huge flying dragon-things. What kind of idiot would try hunting that with a dinky bow and arrow? Even a rifle seemed barely adequate.

"Good to hear. Our target is something else."

"Got it. So, what's your specialty when it comes to hunting?"

You hear the word "hunter" as a blanket term, but anyone who hunts animals has their own area of expertise, whether that be birds, deer, wild goats, foxes, rabbits, whatever. My uncle's specialty was wild birds—ducks, turtle doves, pheasants, you name it. Wild boars and bears were said to be some of the nastiest targets, real violent bastards. The safest way to hunt them was to lie in wait and take them by surprise before finishing them off. Even then, there's always the danger of losing your hunting dogs to an attack.

"Me? *This* is my specialty." Wak'wakgoro stuck out his pinky with a hearty laugh.

"You...I don't get it, what do you mean?"

"Females. I especially like 'em young. I'm not talking about human ones, though."

"Goblins, then?"

He was a goblin himself, so I guess it wouldn't be strange for him to specialize in going after all the little loli-goblins.

Wak'wakgoro gaped. "Wha—I—no, what are you talking about? I can't just go around nabbing goblin girls, the village chief would have my head!"

"Then what do you mean?"

"Kobolds, Shooter! The females usually travel around with kids, and if you attack a group of them, there's a pretty good chance the females will get left behind."

Oh, duh. Fantasy world. "Females" could mean just about anything. "What are kobolds like?"

"C'mon, you serious? They're like little monkey people, but with yappy jackal heads."

It sounded like the kobolds he was talking about weren't much different from what I knew from in folklore, games, and the like.

"So you capture them?"

He went on, "They breed like rabbits, and they're a pain in the ass, always ruining our farmlands."

"Kobolds are pests, then."

They were, and Wak'wakgoro treated them that way. My good goblin friend used the captured kobolds as bait...by killing them.

It felt crappy, but the kobolds put the livelihood of the whole village in danger. My uncle used to capture the weasels that would attack his chickens as well, so it wasn't like I didn't get it.

"They attack the livestock, too. Nothing good comes of kobolds, and the awful things are dumber than a box of rocks."

"They're beasts, after all. What happens after killing the kobold?"

"We use them as bait to lure out the real prize—lynxes. Their fur is some real high-quality stuff, and you can sell them for a good price to merchants."

"Lynxes?" Was that a magical thing? No, wait, they were like those big cats from my world. "Doesn't that mean we can't get any meat from the kobolds?"

"Nah, kobolds aren't my real target. I hunt my fair share of deer and rabbits, for meat. They're good eating, and you can find them all over Apegut."

"Deer and rabbits, gotcha."

"Deer around here aren't all that big, so you can take them down even if you're all on your own. Now come on, follow me." He gave me a pat on the back, pulled out his machete, and started hacking through the foliage, trekking deeper into the forest.

There I was, hiding myself in the thick overgrowth of the forest. According to Wak'wakgoro, herbivores passed through all the time. Not just deer and wild pigs, either—kobolds.

"How good are you with a bow?" Wak'wakgoro asked.

We took our bows off our backs and readied them to fire, should our target cross our paths. As for being any good at one, well...I played a role in an Enka folk singer's performance as a hunter back when I was job-hopping. The bow I used then was made of carbon, but I never ended up *firing* the thing.

"I used to have a longbow before, so this one feels a bit different," I said, which was almost not a lie.

"Gotcha. You are a warrior, after all, so I get that. Don't underestimate a nice shortbow, though. Doesn't matter if you're experienced or not, it only takes a little getting used to and then it's a breeze."

Bows were for bleeding your prey dry, and the spear was to put them out of their misery. Handling poles was my forte, so the spear would be no problem. The shortbow, on the other hand...

"I'd love to practice firing it sometime."

"Yeah, I bet. Let's meet our quota for the day and I'll be happy to help."

Bugs feasted on my way-too-bare skin as we waited. And waited. There, rustling...and it was just another rabbit. How long had we been out there? We left the village in the early hours of the morning, but it must've been nearly noon.

Wak'wakgoro was more than willing to shoot the breeze with me, but he wasn't so talkative as we hid in the forest underbrush. We decided to eat our lunches a bit early. The rye bread just made me incredibly thirsty.

All of that on top of getting profoundly itchy in the forest thickets. The bug bites weren't helping, and worse, I was basically naked. The rocks and pebbles on the ground dug into my butt, and the grass rubbed against my skin, leaving tiny cuts. It was driving me nuts! I'd have to ask Wak'wakgoro or Cassandra for some advice on how to be even a little less uncomfortable next time. At the time I just smeared mud on my skin as a kind of makeshift solution.

"You're pretty resourceful, huh," Wak'wakgoro said, raising his eyebrows and watching me apply my earthy anti-itch cream.

"I learned it back when I went camping with a portable fire pump."

"A fire what?"

One time when I worked at the apparel shop, my manager made us take part in a surprise attack on another airsoft team who were camping in the mountains nearby. I went marching through the mountains decked out in full combat gear, carrying a fire pump and a two-liter water bottle.

Bugs were just as hungry for my sweet flesh back then. We had this stuff called "bug juice" that was supposed to act as a repellent, but did absolutely jacksquat. Instead, we slathered mud over any exposed skin as a countermeasure. It didn't protect us all day, but it kept the bugs from eating us alive.

"A fire pump," I said, "is a magic tool you use to put out fires."

"Wait, you're a warrior *and* you can use magic?"

"Nah, not casting magic, just using magic tools. Anyone can do that."

"*Kobo!*"

Aaaaand kobolds. Everywhere, fuzzy yappy kobolds. Must've approached us while we were talking. I almost yelped, but Wak'wakgoro's hand shot over my mouth. They didn't seem to notice us at all. They were probably en route to find food or water or something.

Wak'wakgoro poked me with his elbow, signaling that I should be ready with my spear. Not like I could be the one using the bow yet. As he whispered and signaled instructions, Wak'wakgoro readied his bow and took aim. His movements were fluid and precise, a thoroughly entrancing technique.

"*Koboooh!*" The boss of the group of kobolds, noticeably bigger than the rest, let out a howl to signal his comrades to gather around him.

I grinned. Yeah. This first hunt was gonna go well.

The goblin huntsman Wak'wakgoro cut a gallant figure. His bowstring stretched taut as he nocked an arrow from the shadowed bushes, and—snap!—let it fly. The arrow dug into a female kobold.

"*Kogyehhh!*" A high-pitched screech rose from the wounded kobold. Wak'wakgoro kept calm, grabbing another arrow he had left by his feet. Released it. Had to be five seconds, maybe less.

The pack panicked. A second arrow found its mark as well, and the children close to the target went running back to their mother.

The boss kobold swung its stick, scanning its surroundings... and freezing as it saw the brush where Wak'wakgoro and I hid.

"All right, go get 'em, Shooter!" Wak'wakgoro roared as his third arrow pierced another kobold. I picked up my spear with one hand and charged.

While we were hiding in the bushes, Wak'wakgoro told me that once he let loose with the arrows, my job was to rush in with my spear. Though kobolds were extremely cautious creatures, they weren't very attentive. If they found something that piqued their curiosity, they would become completely fixated.

Not too surprising, if you think about it. I mean, we're talking dog-headed monkeys here.

Kobolds were fairly weak on their own, so they formed packs to live together. Sure, they could use tools to protect themselves, but if they ever picked on somebody they couldn't take, they'd panic.

Wak'wakgoro told me that kobolds only showed the bare minimum when it came to intelligence. Basically, whenever they faced something genuinely dangerous, they were just smart enough to fly into a panic about it. Sure, they could be sly and cunning if a fight was going their way, but their brains clicked off the moment the tide turned against them. Which is totally unlike any *other* intelligent species, right? Right. Let's just...keep telling ourselves that.

Anyway, that's why I leapt out of the bushes and started really raising hell. If I gave the kobolds time to react, they might decide to try and fight back. The wilder I acted, the less likely that was.

"*Bogo bogeh!*" the boss kobold howled. It must have been some kind of order in koboldish (or whatever you call it), because several other kobolds lunged toward me as the young and the females ran away.

I took a low stance and drove my spear straight into the chest of the kobold leading the charge. The blade slid into its flesh, wet and sickening. Nothing like karate.

I pulled it out right away before the blade stuck in the contracting muscles—I've heard those things happen when humans get shot or stabbed in all kinds of ways.

Warily I closed the gap between me and the kobold leader.

"The boss is coming your way, Shooter!" Wak'wakgoro cried.

The boss kobold (incidentally, wearing a *much* nicer loincloth than mine) rushed at me, brandishing a razor-sharp wooden stick.

Mud and dirt sprayed in all directions as the boss kobold's spear struck the earth. The guy was fast and looked pretty strong to boot. I didn't have to take him down, though. All I had to do was make him afraid of me.

"Take this, you damn, dirty ape!"

Times like these, you gotta be assertive. And although kobolds weren't just primates, everything about them reminded me of something just barely past monkeys on the evolutionary ladder.

With a mighty shout, I thrust my spear toward the boss kobold. He dodged. I didn't care. More kobolds appeared on either side of me, but I had my spear ready and waiting.

"*Ratten koboh!*" the boss kobold howled as they made their retreat, dragging a kobold I'd killed with them. The children and females scampered after them.

Once again, Apegut Forest was silent.

"Nice going. Just what I'd expect from a warrior like you, Shooter," said Wak'wakgoro. He switched to his spear, and he looked carefully out at his surroundings as he turned one of the kobolds over with his foot. I just took a long, ragged breath. It was over.

"We bagged ourselves a grown male and a younger female. Usually I'd only be able to take down a female by myself, you just got us twice the bait."

"I've never done something like that before," I said. "I was actually panicking a little, to be honest."

"You serious? You handled yourself pretty well out there."

"How would you deal with a whole group of kobolds when you were hunting alone? Like, assuming you managed to take one down with arrows first, what would you do next?"

"I'd switch to my spear right after my first arrow and rush straight for the head honcho. You wanna try and hurt them before they get a chance to think up anything sneaky. I don't bother with anyone else."

Made sense. Hit the big guy, strike fear through the entire pack, and get them running away all on their own.

Wak'wakgoro beamed devilishly before unsheathing his machete and starting to slice up one of the kobolds.

"So there's no point in really going for them, then."

"Yup. You went after the head honcho's lackeys too, but it's not about numbers. It's all speed."

"That was my bad. Sorry."

"Next time, I want you to just focus on the boss. They're usually tougher than the rest, so it'd be a pretty even match even for a goblin like me. I'd at least be able to mess him up if we took them by surprise. An injured kobold is basically helpless, so when you get the ball rolling it usually ends the same way."

The last (and only) time I was in a fight this big was when I worked at a Japanese BBQ restaurant. A couple of drunk customers got into a scuffle. I jumped in and got them to stop with a few good hits, but I ended up getting fired because of it. Huh. I wonder how that manager's doing?

Wak'wakgoro ran his machete across a kobold throat. Fresh blood gushed from the wound. He grabbed the body by the ankles and began dragging it across the ground

"What are you doing?"

"Spreading the scent of blood. Grab our stuff, we're gonna get our trap ready."

I gathered our equipment and followed.

The trap was a simple snare, the kind with a rope that would loop around our unfortunate victim's leg and hoist them into the air. Any flimsy rope wouldn't be enough to handle something like a lynx, so we were working with a sturdy wire. It was a primitive kind of snare, made to tighten around whatever sprung the trap.

Maybe that was the limit of technology here, or maybe better traps cost too much for a tiny village. I'd have to ask, because a bear trap would be a damn lifesaver.

"Seems like a pretty well-thought-out trap," I said.

"It may be simple, but let's say our prey gets caught and starts thrashing. That wire's just gonna dig deeper into their leg."

"And we're setting up a bunch?"

"We have to. That's the trade-off for them being so simple. We set 'em, cover 'em, tie the front of the trap to a stake or tree branch, and boom! Snap! Thrash, dig, all that good stuff!"

"You're really an old hand at this," I said, admiring Wak'wakgoro's work as I helped him get the traps together.

"I should hope so after all these years. Don't get me wrong, I'd love a good bear trap instead, but the governor has to approve or we'd be breaking the law."

Convenient—he answered my question before I could even ask. The answer made sense, too. Animal rights groups back in my world argued that bear traps were inhumane, which got those things tied up in red tape there too.

"That's why we're only allowed to use those when we're hunting big game," Wak'wakgoro continued, "like wyverns."

"Gotcha. Where does the governor live?"

"In the village chief's manor, obviously."

"In the—?"

"The village chief *is* the governor. She's been granted knighthood, which makes her the leader around these parts."

"Really? That true?"

"This is the frontier. Who else would be the governor?"

Damn, so the village chief was a real-life knight? My mind hurtled back to some...unique manga about proud lady knights being unladylike with some very *robust* orcs. Was that a real knight thing? It'd be super tacky to ask, right? Right?

"Uh. Hey, man, why're you holding your crotch? Hello? Wire? Kobold traps? Let's go?"

"Nothing! Nothing weird's happening, everything's fine, let's go!"

Look, Shuta Jr. is a sensitive guy, you know? Way too sensitive, if you ask me, especially when it came to my overactive imagination.

After we set up snares in a couple spots, the look on Wak'wakgoro's face said everything before he spoke a word: we'd done a good day's work.

"That'll be it for today, so let's head back."

"We're leaving already? We're not going to nab some rabbits or something?"

"Only if we see 'em on the way back. We really just have to wait for a lynx to trip our snares. It'll take some time for the scent of the blood to spread throughout the forest."

Our work finished, Wak'wakgoro went back to his normal, talkative self. He asked question after question. "You slept with Cassandra yet?" was a big one. And, while we were at it, "How many kids you want?" Along with the extremely specific but much appreciated, "If you want to enjoy that newlywed life for a bit, would you like me to show you to the priest, get you some decent birth control stuff?"

I did my best to keep it casual. "No messing around yet, we're gonna try it out as friends first. Oh, but I have seen her going number two before. I know it doesn't count, and it's nothing to be embarrassed about since we're married, but she did *not* seem happy about it. She was angry the whole time, matter of fact!"

When I finally came home, I found that my new wife wasn't exactly on the edge of her seat waiting for me.

"I'm home and ready for dinner! Saw that smoke coming up from the chimney, so I figured it's almost ready!"

"Eep!"

When I pushed the front door of our little cabin open, I saw Cassandra staring up at me from her bed, eyes wide with shock. She froze, curled up tight with both hands between her thighs for...some reason?

"Ah! Um! Welcome home..."

"Yeah, I'm back. You, err...that smoke...you weren't cooking?"

"N-no...I was heating the water so you could wash yourself."

"Oh, that sounds great. I could use a good wash. Think I'll just go ahead and get going."

I let all my hunting gear drop to the floor. I took the wooden bucket and poured the scalding water into the bath cauldron. Cassandra stood up from the bed. She watched me. As I reached to undo her father's old vest, she approached me. Cautiously, she reached out to take it.

Our hands touched and—she pulled back suddenly and dashed to a corner of the room. Cassandra's fingers were moist for some reason. A bit sticky, too. She shifted, looking away from me and pressing herself into the corner.

Weird wet hand, skittish run to the corner...I didn't know this culture, but it was clear that she wasn't warming up to me at all. She must've hated that order from the village chief to marry me.

Day two of newlywed life. Thirty-two-years-old, and just now it hits me that my wife probably isn't warming up to me because I'm naked!

● ● ●

The next morning, I found Wak'wakgoro waiting for me outside my house in full hunter attire, spear in hand.

"Morning, Wak'wakgoro. You heading out somewhere?"

"Catching lynxes in our traps, I hope—and you're coming with me."

"Think we'll get one so soon?"

"Who knows?" Wak'wakgoro replied with a snort. "The smell of blood should be spreading through the forest by now. Lynxes love blood. They've gotta be close by."

"Right, got it. Then I guess I'll be off now," I said, bidding farewell to my wife.

"Um. Be careful out there."

Cassandra saw us off. Before long, Wak'wakgoro and I were in our hunting ground once more.

The lynxes in the forest were usually solitary, Wak'wakgoro told me, and they tended to have their own territories.

"Yesterday we placed our snares on a spot where a bunch of their territories intersect with each other. Usually the males try to avoid that, since it leads to some pretty nasty fights between them."

"Cats," I said suddenly. "They're like a bunch of housecats."

"Bigger, sure, but you're not wrong. Male and female lynxes, on the other hand, tend to have territories that overlap each other, but that's because they gotta get that sweet pussycat lovin'." Wak'wakgoro grinned. Ah, shit. "So," he said, "how're things going with Cassandra?"

"Slowly." Even that was overstating it. She always looked away when I smiled.

"At least she's warming up to you."

"C'mon, have you looked at us?"

"I've known Cassandra for a long, long time, man. This isn't a big village, you know? Trust me."

My wife seemed unhappy at times, but she was damn cute. I hoped Wak'wakgoro was right.

We were on our way to our snares when Wak'wakgoro suddenly stopped me.

"Something wrong?"

"These footprints—they're fresh."

And gigantic, too. These cat-like footprints had to be the size of a girl's hand, maybe bigger.

"These are some pretty big prints. Is it a lynx?" I asked tentatively.

"Gotta be. Outside of bears and wyverns, they're the biggest animals around here," Wak'wakgoro said, gazing out at the trail of prints. Man, these things were huge, even for fantasy-world junk. Lion-sized, tiger-sized, maybe bigger.

With a nod, we crouched and stalked along the trail. Wak'wakgoro fell quiet again—back to hunter mode, I guess. The lynx could be anywhere.

I gripped my spear tightly—no point in using the bow until I knew what I was doing, so I wanted to have something ready in case we found the lynx. Getting caught flat-footed by something so fast would be trouble.

After following the tracks for a bit, Wak'wakgoro stopped. Crouched low.

"These prints haven't dried yet," he whispered.

I was on edge now. The lynx must've been stalking close to our snare traps. Sure, they smelled the kobold blood, but they were playing it safe for now. *Clever girl.*

All at once Wak'wakgoro bolted upright and readied his spear. "Shooter, there!"

I whipped out my own spear just in time—a massive, snarling cat-like creature beast rose before me. It was just enormous, big as a tiger, and its roar was as much like a pussycat's as a wolverine's. The lynx leapt from the bushes and swiped at me with a muscled front leg, its obsidian claws glinting in the sparse light. One hit from that would've been it.

I rolled out of the way, pausing only to land a glancing blow on its flank. Fast as it was, it was *big.* You could telegraph those movements, wait for when it readied the next move and there— right there, that's your window.

Rising from my roll, I spun around. The lynx charged. I aimed a solid thrust as it came at me. No time to put power into it, not with such a short distance, but I didn't have time to complain. The tip of the spear vanished into the black inside of the lynx's mouth. The shock of impact shuddered through my right hand. I let go of the spear and jumped back to avoid the death-spasms of the lynx's razor-claws. The spear dug into its mouth, the point gleaming red through the back of its skull. It thrashed absently, agonized, before falling to the ground, where it twitched and seized.

"You okay, Shooter?"

I took a deep breath. "That, uh. Wow. Close, huh? I'm okay. Not hurt, at least."

"You took out that lynx with just one blow."

The lynx was still breathing. This was a younger one, Wak'wakgoro told me. He drew his machete and, without hesitation, slit its jugular to put it out of its misery.

"Judging by its fur, I'd say he's somewhere between three and five years old. That's a good profit, long as we carve him up nice and proper. Bit smaller than I thought, though. The spots on a more mature lynx would be a lot bigger."

"I guess it's lucky for me that it was a young one, then. I'd hate to face off against a full-grown adult."

"You're right about that. Being a hunter means weighing your risks. Get greedy and get killed. Play it safe and you can hunt another day. We wouldn't want to send you home to Cassandra in a pine box, you know?"

I bowed—it was good advice from a veteran hunter.

"Since I sometimes hunt male lynxes, other males start to move in this way from the deeper parts of the forest. Of course, all I do then is hunt *them* down, and the cycle continues. Man, I'm looking forward to seeing what we get tomorrow!" Wak'wakgoro said. He slapped me on the back, laughing.

We never imagined we'd get our lynx while on our way to check those traps. It was one lucky haul. We strung up the lynx between our two spears and decided to head back for the day.

After coming home, I started skinning the lynx with Wak'wakgoro. Cassandra was shocked when she came home and saw us.

"Your husband's a real catch, Cassandra. This guy just took down a lynx in one strike! Just what you'd expect from a vet in the warrior business!"

"That's amazing…"

All I could do in the face of all these compliments was sheepishly scratch at my head, maybe give a few quick bows of gratitude.

"Make sure and take good care of him, will ya?" said Wak'wakgoro. "He's gonna make it big someday, I tell ya."

"I will."

I was feeling pretty good from all this praise I was getting, so I turned to look at my wife—maybe today was my lucky day—and she promptly turned to look away from me in kind. But no way was I going to let that discourage me!

Wyvern Hunters

IN MY WARM BLANKET, alone in my new bed, I dreamed.

I was walking through the shopping district in front of the train station, dressed in my usual kind of outfit—a long-sleeve shirt with a t-shirt underneath, the Official Workpants my employer made me wear, and my trusty backpack. Faintly I could make out my favorite bar before me, and that's when I realized that this was probably *it*. The last moments of my old life.

I'd been thirsting for a drink after work, so of course I picked my favorite cheapo dive. I didn't *hate* drinking at home, but using my meager part-time wages for a cheap "After Work Special," chatting up a pretty waitress, just unwinding...perfection.

So there I was, about to step inside the bar, and that was it. That was all I remembered. Did I die or something? Get hit by a car? The bar stood before me. The narrow roads of the shopping district blurred with heavy traffic. No one veered off to hit me. And the bar...I didn't go in.

I turned around, as a matter of fact. And that's when my dream ended.

My name is Yoshida Shuta. I'm thirty-two. Also, I'm stuck in another world learning to hunt.

After trading "good mornings" with my wife, I grabbed my gardening hoe and headed out the door. She asked me to tend to the vegetable patch out front, and I was happy to oblige. There'd been no one to help take care of it when she was living alone, and so the whole thing was in bad shape.

Cassandra said it was near the end of April. The good weather rolled in at February's end, when the mountain snow began to melt. It was supposedly too late to start plowing now, but it wasn't like Cassandra could've done anything about that on her own. Back when she was alone, she planted potatoes—they were easy to get a hold of, cold-resistant, and didn't need too much water.

I swung my hoe into the earth, working to till nearly barren soil. Cassandra had four plots of land for farming out front. Since one of them already had potatoes in it, I decided to tend to the one in front of the potato patch. If I was going to make Cassandra's life easier, I wanted to do it as soon as possible. That meant working at this every day. That's what it means to be a man, after all.

As I tended to the dry soil, I heard a familiar voice call out, "What do you think you're doing so early in the morning?" It was Wak'wakgoro, of course, bow strapped to his back and ready to go.

"Morning. That time already?"

"Lynxes are nocturnal, so the trap could've snagged one by now."

"Yeah, it'd be nice if we could deal with one that already got itself caught."

And with that, I had to leave the field half-tended so I could check on the snare traps.

"Hey, I'm heading out again!" I called out to my wife. "Stay here until I get back, okay?"

"Shouldn't I tend to the fields?"

"I'll take care of that when I get back. You just sit tight and try not to burn the house down. It's not like I expect you to be hammering away at an anvil while I'm gone or anything."

"Hmm. Blacksmithing? I've never done that before."

Wait, was she taking my joke seriously? Or was this some kind of comeback, like saying that she already handles the laundry and cooking just fine, and I shouldn't underestimate her? Maybe this was her way of telling me that? Like a, "I may not be the greatest, but I do my best!" kind of thing. Which is cute, I'll admit. Good weapon of choice.

"I'll come help out when I'm back," I said.

"Thank you. Be careful out there."

I said my goodbyes to Cassandra, and Wak'wakgoro and I headed into the forest together.

"So you think you can forget about me and just start flirting? You dog, you!" Wak'wakgoro ribbed me as we walked.

"You call that flirting? We haven't even held hands yet. Everything's still so...awkward."

"Hold up, you two still haven't gotten it on? You swing the other way or something?"

"Nah, I'm straight as an arrow. But man, every time I try and look at her, she seems freaked out or something."

"*You're* naked, my guy."

"Hey, don't downplay the vest."

"You're *almost* naked."

Ehh. Fair. I scratched at my crotch and continued down the path.

Wak'wakgoro told me that he didn't use hunting dogs, since trying to train them and keep them fed was time he didn't have. All of the village's hunting dogs were managed by a goblin named Saki'cho, the leader of the hunters.

"Goblins aren't usually held in the highest esteem," said Wak'wakgoro. "No matter which village you're in, we're usually only allowed to be farmers, woodcutters, or hunters."

"Damn. Sounds like you guys have it rough."

"The really talented goblins all leave town and go off to become mercenaries or adventurers, livin' it up and relying on nobody else."

"And you didn't?"

"'Course not. What the hell kind of person abandons their family?" He snorted indignantly. "Say I leave town. What happens to the rest of my brethren? Their families and mine? Hunters already have it bad enough as is. If we don't bring in any game, then the villagers see us as a bunch of freeloaders. And it gets *really* rough in winter."

According to him, the heavy winter snow blocked off the deeper parts of the forest. That meant hunters settled for hunting deer where the snowdrifts were less dense...and these deer were hell to catch. They gathered in a vast, wide-open area, where there weren't many spots for the hunters to lie in wait.

"Then how do you survive when you can't hunt?"

"Side gigs. Make boots, or sharpen spears, fashion arrows, whatever. Winter is the time for blacksmithing, I tell ya."

"Wow, you even smith stuff?"

"The old dwarf smith in the village keeps pretty busy, so hunters like us try to stay self-reliant. Here, take a look at this." Wak'wakgoro took an arrow from his quiver and showed it to me. "You can make your own arrowheads out of stone."

From what I've heard, stone arrowheads are way better for taking out animals than ones made of metal—these things really dig into animal hide. Iron arrowheads may have become the standard once they were easy to mass-produce, but those weren't for animals. They were for people.

That aside, it surprised me to learn how insecure the life of a hunter was. Coming upon our first snare in the Apegut Forest drove it home.

"It managed to grab the bait without setting off the trap," Wak'-wakgoro said with a sigh. He crouched to search where the snare was placed, but only made a face once he found tracks in the dirt.

"No good," he muttered. And our first lynx hunt yesterday went so well. These tracks showed that the lynx dragged the kobold body away from the trap, probably back to its nest.

BUCK NAKED IN ANOTHER WORLD

The second trap had gone off without catching anything, either.

"Well, shit," Wak'wakgoro muttered.

"Yeah. Bad luck."

"It happens when you go hunting every day. You can live off a big haul for a while, but luck turns as it wants. We got lucky last time. We aren't lucky today."

Being a hunter was pretty similar to a part-time job in that way. There was something comforting about that familiarity, whether it was good or bad. The only significant difference was being buck naked all the time in this world, which I generally avoided back home.

"Is there any way to lure out the lynx and wait to get the jump on them?" I asked.

"Once they're done raising their kittens, sure. Right now they're too cautious."

"Gotcha."

Smart. My uncle said something similar about never messing with a mother bear when she had her cubs around. Bears were dangerous even for the most experienced of hunters, so I didn't even want to think about a massive pissed-off mama lynx.

On our way back home, though, we ended up bagging ourselves a fox. We were almost back to the village when I spotted it.

"Let's get 'em, Shooter!" Wak'wakgoro roared.

He whipped the shortbow from his back, nocked an arrow into his string in one fluid motion, and I hurried to follow along with my own bow. Our target was close, probably just thirty feet away. Two arrows sped toward the petrified fox. My arrow missed its mark, but Wak'wakgoro's struck home.

"What, do they call you Shooter ironically? C'mon, man!"

It was my first time using a bow. Sue me.

"Um. It's hard to cook when you look at me like that."

I always thought that the best part of married life would be eating your wife's delicious home cooking. Up until now, I lived alone in a cheap apartment on a shoestring budget, either cooking my own meals or grabbing discount side dishes from the supermarket. Just having someone else cooking for my sake was heaven.

"Err, sorry about that, I didn't mean to stare. Are we having baked potatoes again?"

"Potatoes don't have much flavor on their own, so I was thinking of cooking some beans as well. I don't know. Does that sound good to you?" Cassandra pulled a pot up onto the counter and let out a long, heavy sigh.

The village chief had ordered us to be husband and wife, but there was no way Cassandra could just accept that without a second thought. I couldn't blame her, but I also couldn't help but be happy about it.

"Nope, totally fine by me. Is there something I can help with?"

"A hunter's wife," she lectured, "is supposed to cook for him while she's home. A man does the cooking for himself when he's out in the field."

Huh, I didn't know that was even a rule. I put on my best smile—I really didn't want to give Cassandra creeper vibes—and backed away to give her some space. That's easier said than done when you live in a tiny shoebox of a house. The best I could do was sit on my bed, watching my wife as she worked.

Cassandra finished getting the stockpot ready, placing the bones inside and slowly bringing it to a boil to make broth. She tossed in some chickpeas along the way, a couple carrots from the fields, and a few onions we'd gotten from the neighbors. She gently ladled the soup as it bubbled and simmered.

"Since I'm making the broth from fox bones," she said, "I can't guarantee it will taste that good."

"Yeah, I guess foxes aren't all that delicious, are they?"

"O-oh! Ack, I didn't mean—I know you went through all that trouble to catch it for us, so I wasn't saying—I didn't mean that—um!"

She didn't look upset at me at all. She looked flustered, in fact, as she tripped over her words to explain herself.

"It's all right," I said gently, "I didn't take it that way at all. I'll make sure to bring home some tastier meat next time. Besides, I'd love to eat anything you made."

"Well, um, erm! Thank you! Thanks for saying that." She blushed, gazed at the floor, and I thought that newlywed life might not be so bad after all.

● ● ●

Shuta here, dealing with a terrible case of updog! What's that? What's updog? Not much, dude, how 'bout you? Well, not much is up besides my wiener—and I'm not talking about the dog.

I went out hunting again with Wak'wakgoro, but when I got back home, Cassandra was nowhere to be found. There were no pens or paper in this world, so she couldn't leave me a note or anything.

The laundry hung drying near the front door, and boiled beans and eggs sat hot and ready on top of our well-worn table. It seemed like a lot of food for just one person, so I assumed some of it was for me. I also told her I was just going to check on the snares before I left, and she knew I hadn't brought a meal for the road.

Cassandra didn't seem to be coming back no matter how long I waited, so I gave up and ate the food she left in glum silence before going to sleep. I was feeling lonelier than usual, so I laid myself in my wife's bed and went to sleep smelling her scent—hence the updog.

"Um, Shooter?"

When I finally woke up, I saw Cassandra, confused and frightened at why my flag was at full mast. Standing next to her was an older man, covered in a dense, thick layer of hair. Who the hell...?

The man stroked his beard. "How 'bout you put on some clothes?" He tossed me a loincloth.

"Ha. Uh. Good morning, everyone. Cassandra, who would this be?" I launched out of bed and nearly leaped into my skimpy loincloth. I couldn't just leave my flexin' little guy exposed.

"This," said Cassandra, "is my father—"

"Your *father*?"

"My father's *nephew*."

Good to know that my *dead* father-in-law hadn't climbed out of his grave, at least. This guy was about my height, but a little wider around the waist. His chest hair nearly burst from the gap in his V-neck tunic, a tangled mess that ran down to his thick arms. He looked like a bear who'd figured out facial hair.

"I'm Cassandra's cousin, Ossandra," he said bluntly. Aw, cool, their family had a name thing going!

I offered him a handshake with one hand while covering my crotch with the other, but wouldn't you know it, all he did was stare back at me! Rude people, I swear.

"I came because I heard Cassandra got herself a husband. That's you, then?"

"Yup. The name's Shooter, pleasure to meet you. I'm following in the footsteps of Cassandra's father, working as an apprentice hunter," I said with a quick, sharp bow of my head.

"You used to be a warrior, too," he said, "or that's what they're saying. Well, you seem pretty well put-together. Here, I've got a wedding gift for you. Food too."

"You didn't have to do all that for us," said Cassandra.

"Thank you so much for this," I said, bowing still more deeply.

Ossandra's wedding gift to us was a new weapon—a short-sword. Useful, and I could pawn it off if things got tight, but I still would've appreciated some pants.

Except it wasn't for me. "This is a present for you, Cassandra. You toil day in and day out. You deserve a reward for that."

"Ossandra..."

The two of them turned and stared deep into each other's eyes.

Very, *very* deeply into one another's eyes. Make-a-husband-the-third-wheel deeply.

"So!" I said tightly. "What brings you here today?"

"Ossandra is a blacksmith," Cassandra replied.

"Huh! Great! And?"

"You mentioned the other day that I should learn how to smith, right? I thought it would be faster to just introduce you to Ossandra. I can only do simple things like putting arrowheads on arrows, after all."

"Huh?"

A blacksmith? She—oh. The joke I made yesterday. She'd taken it completely seriously.

"Hunters need to make sure their equipment is all taken care of," said Ossandra, "and that includes things like their spears and arrowheads. You're thinking ahead. I admire that."

"Th-thanks?"

"But if you don't put on some clothes, you're going to burn yourself in the forge."

"Yeah, maybe. I get that a lot." Not like I could do anything about that without clothes.

"What, you like being naked?"

"No, I just don't have anything to wear except vests. I'm good on vests. I've got vests for days," I said. Cassandra handed me one of them and I slipped it on.

"If you help out at the forge, I'll pay you. You can use the cash to buy yourself some clothes."

"Hey, that sounds great! I'd be happy to!"

That was how I ended up going along with my wife's cousin to work at the blacksmith's forge. When I asked if she was coming with us, she turned me down.

"No, I've got chores. I'll try not to 'burn down the house,' as you said."

Yeesh. All right, so maybe we still weren't on the same wavelength.

There I was, standing out behind a blacksmith's forge with nothing but a hand axe, chopping wood in the buff. *Déjà vu.*

It was hot, which was why I'd forgone wearing clothes again. My vest would reek to high heaven if I got sweat soaked into it, and Shuta Jr. kept bouncing out of my tiny loincloth whenever I really got into the axe-swing of things. At least being naked made it way easier to move around.

Ossandra would carry the wood away with a look of thinly veiled shock on his face as he watched me work in my skimpy outfit.

"How's the hunting coming along, anyway?" he asked me at one point.

"I managed to get myself a lynx the other day, but that was it. We didn't catch a single one after that, even after setting up a bunch of traps."

"Not surprised. Those guys are pretty hard to take down."

"I've been going out hunting with a veteran hunter named Wak'wakgoro."

"Huh, that so."

"We didn't get a lynx, but we at least managed to nab a fox on the way back home yesterday."

"Good. A fox pelt would make that loincloth look half-decent."

I didn't know about that, but if people *thought* it looked better then maybe it was worth a try. I'd ask Wak'wakgoro if I could have the fur once he was done skinning it.

From what I heard, a forge needed a ton of wood to function. Blacksmiths got their own wood, then chopped it up to turn into charcoal. I made a deal to help out with that for a bit, and in exchange Ossandra would teach me how to sharpen my spear and even eventually to make arrowheads. Now I had a place to work when prey died down.

As an aside, it turned out that despite his looks, Ossandra was only a little over twenty years old. *Damn, how is he younger than me?*

"Is it really okay that we're not doing any smithing today?" I asked.

"There's five of us here at the forge. They said it was all right to train you for the day."

"Seems like you must keep pretty busy, then."

"You said your name was Shooter, right?"

"Yeah."

"You gonna stay in this village forever?"

My axe split another log. I stopped to turn and look at him. Ossandra stared back at me, wearing a stone-serious expression on his bearded face.

"Hm. I mean, I'm married here, after all..."

I hadn't really given any serious thought to what came next. Here I was, a Japanese guy from another world—and this *had* to be another world instead of the past or future, what with all the goblins and wyverns. Who knew if I would be able to find a way to make it back to the world I came from?

I thought of the dream from that morning. Maybe it was me reliving everything up until I wound up here, or maybe it was the last moments before my death. If I *had* died, then that would mean I was reborn in this world. If I hadn't, then surely something transported me here.

Reborn, though? Really? I still looked the same as I had back in my old world, and all of my memories were intact. If I somehow bit the big one before coming here, then I'd been reborn as a middle-aged man. And reborn...without clothes? Wow, what a blessing. If I'd been reborn, I didn't even get to be a baby. Just a naked thirty-two-year-old. Thanks, God! Love it, so good!

"If you're staying," said Ossandra, "then you better get ready for what's coming. Hunters get a lot of flak in this village, so it ain't easy being one here. Life was nothing but one hardship after another for my uncle."

"They're shunned, then." I considered what the reason could be as I swung away at the wood. I was used to the work, so I could let my mind wander a little.

The first reason hunters might get shunned: inconsistent work. If they didn't bring anything home from the hunt, then it was like Wak'wakgoro said—they were perceived as nothing more than freeloaders living off what the village provided for them, providing nothing in kind.

That feast-famine setup was the reason why hunter-gatherers eventually learned how to farm. Agriculture allowed people to live much more stable lives. Sure, they probably had their share of bad harvests, but stockpiling food solved that problem.

Also, if life was already tough for a given family, it must've been that much harder to find someone to marry their children to. I didn't know if marrying for love happened in this world, but I'd bet it was probably taboo at best, maybe reserved for actual developed towns. In villages like this one, village chiefs or parents probably played matchmaker—just like what happened with Cassandra and me.

I could see, then, why no parent would want to marry their daughter off to a hunter. On the other hand, there also might not be anyone willing to marry the daughter *of* a hunter, like Cassandra. Which probably got hunters treated even more like parasites to be shunned.

On top of that, there was the tendency for goblins to take jobs as hunters. Not many parents would want their daughters marrying goblins, from what Wak'wakgoro said. Goblin discrimination. They must've been the lowest position on the village totem pole. It just seemed to be a thing in fantasy worlds. Even hobgoblins got more respect, if only a sliver.

"I'll help if you want to leave," Ossandra said as he gathered up some of the wood.

"Leave the village, you mean?"

"Right. I doubt anyone here would be happy to see an outsider like you sticking around, and I'm sure they wouldn't care if you up and left."

"What about Cassandra? If I left her here, things would just get worse for her."

"True. This isn't something to consider lightly. If you ever decide to run away, I can at least get some money ready for you. If you're staying, you best be ready to work if you want to earn everyone's trust. Warrior, stranger...this is your path to choose."

Leaving me with those words, Ossandra disappeared into the forge.

I gave a lot of thought to Ossandra's words. Sure, I was born in the sticks, but I was never ostracized, especially since my grandparents had been such social people. My grandma was so well known where we lived that they made her the vice president of the local fishing co-op. Back home life was easy.

Not that people weren't shunned at all. There was at least one family who everyone avoided. Maybe *they* were shunned. Never thought about it till now. They had a girl who was about the same age as me, but we never played together much. She was usually with her younger sister, so my sisters and I never really talked with them. Maybe now I knew how it felt to be in a family like that, marrying somebody above my station, even if only a little.

It was going to be rough if I kept living here—I'd need a strong will. I'd have to build up my status in the village, to really show the villagers that I was worth keeping around.

Once, in my old world, I had this part-time job at a marketing firm. They mainly proposed new ideas to clients or found ways to improve projects in progress. Consulting, basically.

It was a small company, so my days there consisted of trying to drum up business alongside this young guy, the representative director of the firm. He told me there were a few tested ways to get a client to agree with our ideas.

First, you hook them on the idea, and then you show them that it's achievable. I'd make a slideshow doing just that (with this awful program that I hate using; you're probably familiar with it), and then the director would clean up my rough draft. Clients always went for the ideas that grabbed their attention.

The next step would be to earn the client's trust by getting to know their top brass. Department heads, managers, whoever— get those guys on your side and you could get even the most outrageous ideas approved, easy peasy.

Now, who was the top brass in the village? Bingo—the village chief. First things first, I had to get her to accept me. With a governor on my side—and a knight at that, with all the power and privilege that entailed—no one would even try to ostracize me. Even if people had a bone to pick with me, they wouldn't dare say it out loud if I had enough prestige. And hell, if I got the village chief on my side, then she wouldn't tolerate it either.

If I was going to make that happen, I needed actual results. A consulting firm's goal was to bring in sales, whether for the client's business as a whole or for individual projects. If I was going to apply the same logic here, I'd either have to somehow broadly improve the lifestyle of the village, or I'd have to bring in something *big* as a hunter. That would mean really busting my ass to get better, maybe even good enough to take down a lynx or two without breaking a sweat.

I wiped the sweat from my brow. A whole lot of options, and none of them perfect. Still, it was a beautiful, cloudless day. A refreshing breeze blew in as I worked.

Suddenly, I spotted a strange black cloud in what should have been a cloudless blue sky. It sped through the air too quickly—it couldn't be a cloud at all, not moving that fast—and it plummeted to the earth at breakneck speed.

Someone screamed out: "W-w-wyvern!"

My name's not Vern, chief, I thought—you know, like an idiot. The villagers poured from their homes, panicked and crowding.

"It's a wyvern!"

Sure was. And it was going after the livestock.

● ● ●

In my old world, wyverns were nothing more than the product of someone's imagination. Here the wyvern was living, breathing, and *big*. About the size of a small bus, matter of fact. Its maw gaped wide, revealing rows and rows of needle-sharp teeth, and hard scales lined its body from head to long, long tail—so long that the beast was half-tail. *King of the lizards,* I thought deliriously.

The lizard king intended to pick off cows from a spot near the center of the village. The poor things were just chewing their cud, safe and out to pasture, when the wyvern started tossing them screaming to the ground, sinking its razor-talons into their bloated bodies.

The wyvern was strong. Some villagers shouted and pointed at it, while others peeked out from behind shelter to watch. No one even tried making a move on the beast.

Not that I could blame them. Most of the villagers were farmers and their families—not the type liable to charge at the scaly lizard-bus of the skies. Only a veteran hunter like Cassandra's father could've stood a chance against it.

"What's all the ruckus out here, Shooter?" Ossandra cried, running out with an armful of charcoal.

"It's a wyvern, Ossandra! Look!"

The charcoal spilled from his arms. He stared for a moment in mute horror.

"A wyvern," he said finally. "But why?"

"I don't know, it just came flying in all of a sudden."

"How can this be happening?"

We all just stood there staring as the wyvern devoured its prey. That's when I saw them, a brave group of challengers, racing to fight the king of the skies. It was the hunters, and Wak'wakgoro led the charge. They were decked out in hunting gear, almost as if returning from a hunt—and they weren't the only ones charging.

The village chief, her son Gimul, and a bunch of others—all armed to the teeth—marched to battle the beast. Even N'aniwa the woodcutter was among them in the back lines.

The two groups darted between houses for cover, zig-zagging and weaving their way to the wyvern. Wak'wakgoro and the hunters split into two smaller groups. The first group carried countless bows and quivers, and the second bore spears. Made sense. One would rush in to attack directly, and the rest would lay down covering fire.

The wyvern seemed to ignore them completely, ripping and tearing at its beefy feast, slurping down entrails, all that nasty stuff. I heard that larger mammalian carnivores only ate their prey after tearing out their throats to finish them off, but I could still hear the cow under its claws crying out as the wyvern ate. It was a vicious old lizard, through and through.

The village chief's group met up with the bow-carrying hunters, and they began debating furiously over their next move. The village chief wore a simple breastplate over her usual flowing dress, probably because that was all she had time to don before checking out the commotion outside. A longsword dangled from her waist, the typical weapon of your traditional female knight.

I had only been able to stare on until now, dumbfounded, but watching her clicked my brain right back on. I couldn't let this continue. I *wouldn't* let this continue—no way would that wyvern capture the village chief like the female knights from my porn mags. That'd be bad enough, but the wyvern might not even let her say the same lines they did before eating her! If I wanted to make a name for myself in this village, then now was the time to put my spear skills to good use.

Not that I really needed a reason to protect a pretty lady.

"Spear..." I muttered to myself and turned to Ossandra. "Do you have any weapons in the forge? Preferably something with reach."

"We do, but what are you going to—"

"Just let me borrow it for a bit—a polearm, even, anything like that."

"If you want something long, we should have spears, halberds, perhaps some two-handed maces," he replied, bewildered.

"Sure, sure, just go get one for me!" I said, pushing him along.

"Are you actually thinking of taking that thing?! That wyvern's a full-grown male!"

"The village chief is going to get ravish—devoured by that wyvern, and I'm not just going to stand by!"

I burst into the forge, almost knocking over the dwarf blacksmith, and scanned the room.

"Ossandra, who the hell is this?" the dwarf shouted.

"He's my cousin's husband, boss. He said he wanted to borrow some weapons."

No weapons in this room. I turned back to Ossandra.

"Weapons. Where are they?"

"The longer ones are in that room. The good spears are in the back, the decent maces are up front."

Ignoring the dwarf, I ran into that room. I grabbed the spear farthest to the back—no time to take a close look—and ran back outside.

Ossandra came after me. "Don't do anything stupid, you'll break Cassandra's heart if you get yourself killed!"

"Hah! Sure I will. We haven't even hugged."

"Her father was killed by a wyvern, too, you *must* know that! Do you really want her to go through this again?"

Okay. You know what? Enough was enough.

"Listen, man," I snapped. "I may have stared directly at her while she took a big ol' dump back at the house, but we're nowhere close to being a husband and wife yet. If I die, how about *you* marry her? You think I haven't noticed the way you look at her?"

"I haven't, uh! I—no, but, well, I mean—"

With him babbling nonsense, I unsheathed my borrowed spear and got myself ready to make a break for it. The wyvern raised its head high over the shreds of cow and unleashed an earthshaking roar. The very air trembled. Dread carried on sound waves.

The roar was the last straw for Wak'wakgoro and the other hunters. The group providing cover fire pulled their bowstrings back in unison.

"Damn, I better get going if I wanna show off my spear work! I'm not just going to let myself get shunned by the village forever, after all," I said, flashing a wild grin at Ossandra.

I took off after the wyvern, and I was goddamn terrified. Can you blame me? The only things I'd ever faced in a fight were a couple of drunks at a restaurant, a guy who got to second place in nationals for karate, some indie pro-wrestlers, and Gimul. Try to imagine *that* version of me getting asked to fight a tiger with chopsticks or something wild like that.

But at that moment, something in my brain chased my fear

into the recesses of my mind—adrenaline. Just like when it kick-started my body in karate matches, adrenaline writhed to life and all of my fear, all of my doubt melted away.

The battle was already underway as I ran toward the wyvern. Wak'wakgoro and the other hunters were almost perfectly synchronized, sending their first volley of arrows flying toward the beast and, in no time flat, the hunters providing covering fire loosed their next volley.

They weren't aiming at any particular spot, since the wyvern was so large that you could hit it as long as you aimed in its general direction. The second group of hunters took up their weapons and charged toward the monster.

The wyvern let out another bellowing roar that resounded across the village. My legs turned to jelly; I collapsed on the spot. There went the adrenaline—that golden, invincible feeling disappeared completely. I fell about fifty yards away from the wyvern. The king of the skies towered over me. Funny. It looked even bigger closer up.

I was scared stiff.

• • •

You know, everything in this world was a bit (read: *very*) ridiculous.

A brave goblin who had gone to attack the wyvern went flying with a single swipe of the monster's tail. Everyday people with everyday lives just don't see people going full on ragdoll physics through the air. Now I had, and not because I used to work as a stuntman. No, there was a goblin hunter whose name I didn't even know tracing a perfect arc in the sky before my very eyes until—well, I didn't look to see that part.

The next man took advantage of the goblin's sacrifice and charged with his spear. The wyvern flapped its wings as it back-stepped. The gust sent the man flying backward. The wyvern (clever guy) took the chance to rip into the man with its powerful maw. His dying scream froze my blood.

God, it was merciless.

The rest of the hunters faltered, spreading out to surround the wyvern at a distance. The archers stopped providing covering fire, not wanting to hit their fellow hunters. Not that it mattered. The arrows hadn't pierced a single scale.

Swords drawn, the village chief's group joined the hunters surrounding the wyvern. I managed to get myself back on my feet and caught up with them. I talked so big back at the forge, but I just ended up freaking out, falling on my butt, and making myself look pathetic. I'd be laughed at for weeks if we made it out alive, I was sure.

"You have to retreat, please!" Gimul begged the village chief.

"I'm in charge of this village. I will not back down. I will not *allow* myself to back down."

"Then I beg of you, at least stay on the backline!"

As they bickered, the hunters loosed another wave of arrows. The wyvern never dropped its guard, not even for a second. It spun, deftly snapping its tail at its attackers.

One brave soul had the will to slay the monster, a single goblin who seemed a step above the other hunters. He wore leather armor over his fur pelts and wielded a mace in each hand.

The village chief barked her order, "We have only one goal—strike the blow that drives out the beast!"

The goblin charged forward. He had to be Saki'cho, the leader of the hunters Wak'wakgoro told me about. I'd seen him when I fought with Gimul, too. As the leader of the hunters closed in on the wyvern, the other hunters took up their weapons, and I joined them.

"Oho, you're here too, Shooter?" the village chief teased. I ignored it for now.

Saki'cho whaled on the wyvern's stomach, pounding furiously with his maces before rolling out of the way. No dice. The wyvern snapped at the goblin, its razor-sharp fangs gleaming, as a hail of arrows came down on its vast wings.

The wyvern let out a high-pitched screech. *The wings*, I thought as it began to beat its massive wings. Those had to be its weak point.

Airborne now, the wyvern raised its deadly claws and set its sights on the village chief.

I'm no action star, all right? I mean, I've been a stuntman. That's not nothing. It also has nothing to do with a gigantic wyvern. I've been beat up by people charging at me on horseback for a shoot, but I reiterate that these people were not, as far as I knew, *gigantic wyverns*. But—ah, hell—if I wanted the village to owe me a favor, this was the moment.

The wyvern was big, but I only had to wait until the last second to dodge, just like I had with those horseback riders. Well, not exactly like that. In a way, this job was going to be way easier.

I threw my spear aside and sprinted with everything I had, making a beeline for the village chief, leaping into the air and—wham!—tackling her out of the way. The wyvern let out another roar, turning its claws toward me. The village chief fell flat on her butt from my tackle, and only looked on in a daze. I drew the shortsword Ossandra had given us as a wedding present. Maybe it was pointless, but I wasn't about to go without a fight.

Huh. That was really a possibility. Dying at worst, maimed forever at best. No wonder smart hunters stuck to ambushes.

Right when I'd given up hope, the goblin hunter clad in fur pelts swung his mace right into the wyvern's ugly, scaly face. With a sickening crunch, the weapon connected with the monster's snout, and it reeled back in agony.

Oh, thank god—I was saved.

"Get the village chief out of here, now!" the goblin hunter yelled. I nodded, grabbed the village chief's arm, and yanked her to her feet. Surprisingly enough, the village chief just followed along with me, all the color drained from her face. No way in hell was I letting that wyvern get its claws on her.

"I'm leaving the village chief in your hands!" the hunter shouted before turning back to face the wyvern. What a guy. He reminded me of my old karate teacher from Okinawa who took me in way back when. Not that I got to know my savior that well...because those were the last words he ever spoke. He wasn't careless, he wasn't stupid. He was just one man up against a creature with the strength to dominate the skies.

The next moment, the wyvern unleashed a thunderous roar. Raw and powerful, it emanated pure rage. There was a magic to it, I was sure. Something to make your head freeze up. When I turned back to look at the goblin, he was completely frozen in place, arms still raised as if mid-assault.

But it was over. The wyvern sank its dreadful claws into the goblin hunter, spread its enormous wings wide, and took off into the sky.

The magic from the roar seemed to wear off for Wak'wakgoro, who readied his bow as he shouted an order to the rest of the hunters: "Don't let it get away! Fire!"

All too late. The loosed arrows traced an arc through empty sky before falling to the ravaged ground.

The wyvern climbed higher into the air, circling the village just once before disappearing toward the mountains far away beyond the Apegut Forest.

For the first time, I was invited into the village chief's manor.

As for the village chief herself, she was so shocked by the wyvern attack that she couldn't even walk by herself. Gimul had tried to lend her a hand, but she refused him. In a hushed voice she insisted that I do it.

Probably because she lost control of her bladder out of fear. As she crumpled to her knees, watching the wyvern carry off the goblin hunter, a yellow puddle formed around her. I imagine she hadn't wanted her son to touch her after that. I didn't think it mattered—Gimul had already seen it, after all—but asking for my help instead of his was probably her last-ditch effort to keep some shred of pride.

But if it was a matter of pride, why was she okay with me touching her? Maybe because she didn't even consider me human, what with me sitting at the very bottom of the social ladder.

"Three dead, one gravely injured, and one missing. There was also one cow killed," the village chief said, falling back into her role and pretending that she definitely did not piss, and, in fact maybe *you* were the one who pissed. Anyway, our missing villager was the goblin who had been carried off by the wyvern, the leader of the hunters: Saki'cho.

The gathering included Wak'wakgoro and the hunters, the top brass of the village, and those who worked in the chief's manor. The only reason I was included was because I carried the village chief home.

I leaned against a wall in the corner of the room, fiddling with the shortsword Ossandra had given me as my marriage present.

"We need to decide on a course of action," said the village chief. "Wak'wakgoro, is it possible to rescue Saki'cho?"

"If you're asking if we can get him back alive," he said slowly, choosing his words carefully, "then no, that's impossible."

"Can we recover his remains?"

"It depends on if we can reach the wyvern's nest."

The thing was, the wyvern hadn't attacked us at first. It just wanted to much on some cow. It only got hostile when we

interrupted it, which was probably why it carried off Saki'cho—
to get a sort of revenge. The other villagers weren't thinking about
its motives, and just wanted to get him back. I got where they
were coming from, though, and I felt for that.

"Once a wyvern acquires a taste for people, it means they are
sure to attack again. Isn't that right, Wak'wakgoro?"

"Right." He forced his words through gritted teeth. "We can't
let it get away with this."

"It's an animal. Anyone could become a target, including the
children of our village. We must prevent that from happening at
all costs."

"Even if we gather all the people we can from the village and
surrounding settlements, I'm afraid it won't be enough. I've never
seen such a massive male."

Cassandra's father lost his life trying to use traps to take down
a desperate wyvern, one who was just encroaching on human
territory because it didn't have enough prey for the winter. If a
hunter was up against that kind of weakened creature, or a female,
or perhaps a younger wyvern, then maybe they'd have a chance to
win with traps and clever tactics.

But it was a completely different story when it came to a male
who'd already lived for a century, maybe more. A human-made
trap could only do so much against a beast like that, and when
a hundred years of hungry scales and teeth came flying at you?
What could anybody do against that?

The village chief sat back in her armchair. "Gimul," she said.

"At your service."

"Take a horse to town as soon as possible. Request adventurers. We need reinforcements."

"Understood."

It wasn't a problem that a single village could handle, and she knew it.

With a nod, Gimul made to leave the room. On his way out, he stopped and whispered to me in a low voice—just when I was mid-scratch on Little Shuta. "I have no right to ask you this, but make sure the chief...make sure my mother doesn't do anything reckless."

"Aye, aye, sir. She'll be good and protected."

"Tch. Don't get too full of yourself."

I didn't know if he was trying to ask me a favor or pick a fight, but I wished he'd make up his damn mind. At least he left the room, probably for the stables.

"As we wait for the adventurers to arrive," said the village chief, "we will remain alert. Post a lookout on top of the village tower to keep an eye on our surroundings. The minutiae are yours, Wak'wakgoro."

"Understood, chief."

"We will also hold funerals for those who perished in the attack. Melia, go tell the other villagers that we shall make arrangements as soon as possible."

"Of course, Miss Alexandricia," said a servant. She bowed and headed for the exit, but not before giving me a silent look just like Gimul had all those ages ago. I happened to be scratching my ass, I'll admit, but that hardly seemed necessary.

More importantly, I knew that the village chief's name was Alexandricia. It was...an impressive number of syllables.

"And as for you, Shooter—"

"Yes, ma'am?"

"You seem to be fine despite the fact that you're covered in blood. How are your wounds?"

"Huh?" Covered in *what*?

"Hm?"

So hey, I was covered in blood. I guess I hadn't noticed it because of all that adrenaline, but at some point I went from *not* having a huge bloody gash in me to having a very big, extremely bloody gash across my chest. Somehow. The wyvern hadn't even touched me! Also, *Oh my god oww holy shit it hurts!*

"I can only apologize," she said sheepishly. "That was my fault."

I was rushed to the only church in the village to see to my wounds. How had I gotten them? Simple.

When I pushed the village chief away from the wyvern, her sword ended up slashing me across the chest. So lame. I hadn't done a thing in the wyvern fight, and in the process I slashed myself open.

Hey, at least there was no prolonged hospital visit. This being a fantasy world, a pastor and a deacon at the church could apparently use holy magic to patch me up. The deacon in particular was supposed to be an expert at the stuff, curing lacerations and flesh wounds whenever the villagers needed his help.

I was rolled in with the other wounded hunters from the wyvern fight, and I found myself spread out on a bed in the church.

"I thought you looked fine before despite all the blood," said the village chief, "and it seems it really was only the one gash on you. I shouldn't have been worried after all."

Despite her words, I could see Alexandricia tearing up a little. This was a woman with enough mental fortitude to completely ignore the fact that she wet herself in front of me, but here she was shedding a tear over me getting hurt. There really were some cute parts to her, deep down.

"Well," I said, "the deacon's already patched me up, thanks to you."

"Yes. We're going to need warriors like you, so I'm glad to see your wounds weren't serious."

Very sweet. Then she was done, walking to the bedridden hunter right next to me, and using the same concerned tone on him. Just when I thought she was really worried for me, too. It was all lip service, another pitch-perfect performance from the chief of the village. Blegh.

"Seems like your wounds have all healed up," said the deacon. "You're free to leave now."

"Thanks for taking care of me."

"You may feel like a bit lightheaded from loss of blood, so make sure to eat plenty of meat to get your strength back. Also, it pains me to inform you that, well..."

"Yes?"

"Your vest was positively soaked with blood. Far too unsanitary to keep around or for you to even wear. We took the liberty of disposing of it."

Slashed open and once again in the buff, I started on my way home.

As I left the clinic that was connected with the church, I found Cassandra and Wak'wakgoro waiting just outside.

Wak'wakgoro jumped to attention. "Hey, they let you out already?"

"It wasn't a very deep cut. Closing it with healing magic pretty much did the trick."

"Gotcha. You're one of the lucky ones, then."

As Wak'wakgoro and I talked, Cassandra stared at me with an expression of concern.

"Why is she here too?"

"I told her to come. Well, kinda. When I told her that they took you to the church to get healed up after the wyvern, she got all panicked. Rushed right out to come see you."

"Sorry about that," I said, turning to her. "I didn't mean to trouble you."

"No, it was no trouble," she said, casting her eyes downward. Wow. She was actually worried for me this time!

I gave Wak'wakgoro a nod. "I'm sure she couldn't just sit around when thinking about what happened with her dad."

"Um, well," she started.

"Don't worry, Cassandra. Some wyvern won't do me in so easily. In fact, I wish all those other amateurs could've just stayed out of the way. Flailing all over the place, making it so much harder for the *real* professionals," I joked.

Cassandra wasn't laughing. "I see."

Annihilated by my wife. Wifenihilated. "Uh. Yup."

"Is Ossandra all right?" she asked. "He was with you for the fight, wasn't he? I heard some people were injured. Killed, even."

Of course she wasn't worried about *me*. I wasn't happy about it, but I tried my best to explain things as nicely as I could manage. "Yeah, he's totally fine. He was holed up in the forge the whole time. He did get hurt when he fell over after I grabbed a spear to, you know, risk my life to fight the deadly murderous wyvern, though."

"He's fine? Oh, thank goodness!"

Totally head over heels. I didn't complain. It was *great* that he was fine! I was only just a *little* terribly depressed! As for Wak'wakgoro, he took a different tone.

"Hey," he said, taking me aside, "you just going to let your wife worry for another guy like that? C'mon, man up!"

"I mean, they are cousins. They've known each other pretty much their whole life, so they're basically childhood friends, right?"

Back in my world, childhood friends falling in love with each other was a classic bullshit fantasy thing. All very well, except I was actually living in a bullshit fantasy thing, so who was I to get in the way? Even if something about it rubbed me the wrong way, I was certain that they harbored feelings for one another.

I put on my fake smile and tried to be Considerate for My Wife. Like an adult.

"I bet Ossandra's still at the forge right now," I said to her. "Want to go see him?"

"No, that's all right. More importantly, what happened to your clothes?"

"Oh, you mean the vest? The deacon said it was unsanitary and tossed it. I'm sorry," I said with an apologetic bow.

"It's just a vest," she whispered softly. "I'm glad it wasn't you."

How sweet.

Wait.

Hold up, was she being nice to me?

• • •

The funerals for the three dead villagers proceeded at the village's communal graveyard. We offered silent prayers to the fallen as the pastor recited his holy scriptures. But there were only a dozen or so people at the gathering. The dead had fought to protect us all, so you'd think more people would care, but it was only the village chief, the families of the victims, and fellow hunters. We hunters really were hated.

I guess there was another reason: the village chief had ordered all livestock to be returned to their barns, as well as for the villagers to not travel too far from their homes. But they could've at least showed up for the funeral. Even an outsider like myself and my wife came to pray for the departed. Absolutely heartless.

Also, Shuta Jr. was chafing all weird, so I had to shift his position a bit to focus on the grieving.

It was customary to wear crimson red scarves at funerals in this world. It was a sign of mourning, and people wore them until the departed were reborn into their next life. As I listened to the pastor read on, I listened for more talk of being born into new worlds. Maybe I'd ask him more about their fantasy mythos when I had the time. It could wait. For now I wanted blood. Wyvern blood, specifically, for the three hunters in caskets and the one carried off.

When the funeral services ended, I started heading home with Cassandra when the village chief called out to me.

"You—you look unsatisfied. Is it the other villagers? I bet you're upset that they didn't show up for the funeral rites."

"No, not exactly," I said. "It's more complicated than that. I'm sure they've got their reasons."

"Everyone has *reasons*. Today it's an old tale, one that says a wyvern pursues its prey with ferocious tenacity, even after death."

"They're worried the wyvern may come back for the corpses of the hunters."

"Mere rumor, but they fear it all the same."

Disaster spreads its tendrils through the atmosphere. And I guess proximity to damage is like being close to the disaster itself. Like pollution. Not to mention that the dead were hunters, and who cared about hunters? Maybe the villagers were happy to be rid of a nuisance.

"Why," I started, and realized it was too late to go back on my question, "does everyone hate hunters so much, anyway?"

"It was the efforts of myself and my husband, the previous village chief, that paved the way for the development for this village," said the village chief. "Hunters and woodcutters lived on these lands before we arrived."

"Is that right?" I asked, turning to Cassandra.

"Yes. My father hunted in the Apegut Forest even before this village was built."

"Eudora was an exceptional hunter," said Alexandricia. "The same thing can be said for Saki'cho and the other hunters who lost their lives yesterday." I supposed Eudora was Cassandra's father, then. "As far as the villagers who colonized this place are concerned, the hunters are strangers. Foreigners. I'm sure they'll blame the hunters for not finishing off the wyvern too."

The thought made me furious. "That's awful! What are we supposed to do against a monster like that?"

Silly question. That was the *point*. We were scapegoats.

"All I know is that things won't calm down until the wyvern is taken care of. In fact—" The village chief gave a short cough before tucking her hair behind her ear—an ear that happened to be unusually pointed. Oh god. She was an elf, right? *A hot elven knight who was also the ultra-capable village chief—kill me now, Alexandricia!*

"The other night," she continued, "the owner of the dead cow—Gintanen—filed a complaint with me. She stormed in and asked me who would compensate her, and what she was supposed to do about feeding the rest of the cows when she wasn't even allowed to let them outside."

It seemed that the village normally let the cows and sheep roam free to graze and eat whatever they could find. Now that the livestock were stuck in their barns, the expense of hay fell to their owners.

Even though the wyvern was the cause, the blame was spreading to the hunters too. Strangers or outsiders, the villagers hated them both. Hunters *were* both, to them. Old Gintanen was a great example of that type.

"As chief of this village, I have a duty to eliminate that wyvern."

"Yeah, I guess so."

"If I don't, then my command over the village will falter, and the people will rise against me."

"Sure, that could happen." I didn't know exactly how to respond, so I just said whatever came to mind as I looked at her.

At times like this, when she wanted something, the village chief tried to hide behind my back a little. It would have been cute if she was doing it because she trusted me, but nope. She was definitely trying to get out of my sight. *Still*, I thought, *it'd be a liiiittle cute if she grabbed my sleeve while trying to hide, right?* Except, wait, no sleeves. Or pants. Oh god, I was still naked. Oof. Maybe she could grab my scarf? Or even...Shuta Jr.?

That thought made Shuta Jr. act right up, so I covered him with both hands and tried to play it off with a smile. "I'll be sure to make myself useful in any way possible."

"Good. I'm expecting great things from you, warrior from another land. Now, have you seen Wak'wakgoro?"

"Yeah, he should be keeping watch on top of the tower. I think there's another guy up there with him, too."

The three of us turned to look up at the old stone tower, the highest building in the village. Weird to think that they'd thrown me in a jail cell there, and that it had been where I met my wife.

Nostalgic, even, to remember how I watched her take a dump. Or, uh, watched her take a dump for the first time, I guess.

Wak'wakgoro and the surviving hunters took turns looking out from the platform at the top of the tower. In the event of another wyvern attack, they would ring a bell to alert everyone. Wyverns were usually active during the day, so lookout duty began at the break of dawn and ended at sunset.

After tallying the dead and wounded, we found only eight hunters were still in good health, myself included. Five of them had shown up for the funeral. All looked coldly furious, ready to take vengeance upon the beast who caused this tragedy.

"I believe the adventurers from town will arrive later tonight or early morning tomorrow," said the village chief. "Could you pass that message on to Wak'wakgoro for me?"

"Has Gimul come back, then?"

"No, he sent a messenger pigeon before he left the town. He's coming back to the village as quickly as he can."

"Understood. I'll tell Wak'wakgoro." Cassandra and I bowed our heads as we saw the village chief off, but I couldn't resist asking one last question.

"Excuse me, but—you wouldn't happen to be an elf, would you?"

"Oh! Is it the ears? Sorry to disappoint you, but no—I'm half-goblin. Just a hybrid with human and goblin parents."

Well. *That* was unexpected. "Um, a-a hybrid?"

"He he. My apologies for not being an elf."

"No, no, it's all fine!" Or maybe it wasn't so unexpected at all.

She was unfailingly kind to the woodcutters and us hunters, after all. So, Alexandricia had goblin blood in her veins.

The adventurers arrived in town before the break of dawn. I expected a regular pack of tabletop-gaming heroes, but nah. Fully decked out in chainmail, they looked more like a squad of Vikings than adventurers to me.

They carried a whole assortment of weapons. I'm talking spears and halberds, strange polearms with what looked like crossbows attached to the ends, and even giant nets and bear traps. So much for permission from the governor; the king and adventurer's guild clearly gave these guys special dispensation to use as many bear traps as they wanted. Broadswords hung from their waists, weapons focused on durability over short-term deadliness.

They could almost be mistaken for a band of mercenaries by their appearance, and that probably wasn't far off. Mercenaries occasionally got involved in disputes between territories, after all. But just like hunters, adventurers made their real living slaying monsters like wyverns. The big difference was in strategy. Hunters took time to set traps, using their knowledge of the land to pursue their prey. Adventurers, on the other hand, relied on pure, brute strength. Also, while hunters took advantage of bows and arrows to snipe from a distance, adventurers were all about getting get up close and personal. How promising.

"You want to use the bodies as wyvern bait?" Wak'wakgoro roared.

The sun hadn't even truly risen as the leader of the adventurers finished explaining their secret plan to all of us. We gathered in front of the village chief's place as Wak'wakgoro continued, snarling with rage. "Are you trying to desecrate the dead?!"

His casual friendliness was gone. I could hardly blame him. The adventurers wanted to dig up our fallen comrades and leave them rotting in an empty part of the village.

"That's right," said a tall, middle-aged adventurer. "A hunter like yourself should already know how wyverns fixate on the prey they've killed. It'll come back for them. They always do."

"Sure, everyone says that, but how do we know it's true?" Wak'wakgoro snapped.

"Oh, it's true. We've got plenty of firsthand experience with this particular wyvern, so believe me. Believe *us*."

"But...but those are our fallen brethren you're talking about! We can't just hand them over to you like it's nothing! Village chief, tell them!"

Wak'wakgoro turned to Alexandricia, but she said nothing. She shut her eyes tightly, as if deep in thought.

"Is it because they're goblins? Is that it? And how are we supposed to explain this to their families? You come in and boss everyone around, but this cost falls on *us*—on the people who live here!"

The adventurer sighed. "I know we're asking for a lot. But this is the only way to guarantee we take down the wyvern. Just think, are we supposed to tromp into the wyvern's own territory and kill it? Do you know how many days we'd need to prepare for that? How long and drawn out the battle would be?"

"I know that. It's just...it's all so inhumane."

"The longer we wait, the more victims that monster claims. If our client—if your village chief—rejects this plan, we'll follow her orders and think of another, but..."

The village didn't have time for another plan. Not when we lived in constant fear of that ruler of the skies. It had been a few days since it last raided the village, and no one knew when hunger would bring it back for another meal.

"It's fine, ain't it?" A voice broke into the conversation as Wak'wakgoro and the adventurers glared at each other. It was a girl wearing a cloak with a longbow strapped to her back. "I'm sure the guys who bit it would understand. I'd be more than happy to give up my own dead body for something like this. I mean, it's not like a bunch of corpses are gonna complain. They're dead. Who cares?" She broke into raucous laughter.

Wak'wakgoro and the other hunters scowled at her. "Who the hell invited this drunken bum?"

"I thought we might be a bit short on help," said the village chief. "And she does have the skills to help us, here."

The goblin hunters whispered to one another about the girl. I had a lot of questions myself—who was this Cloak-a-hontas? Was she famous or something?

"Well, there you have it, village chief," said the middle-aged adventurer. "That girl agrees, so do you think you can convince the others? We don't want to do this either, but we need to take this wyvern down as fast as possible. I guarantee you it's the best plan we've got."

The adventurers turned toward the village chief. *The best plan they've got.* Hearing that from a group of fully armed adventurers meant something. Their years of battle were practically etched into their faces, and any exposed bit of their skin was covered in scars. They were right. Everyone could see it.

The village chief's words cut through the silence.

"Very well. I approve your proposition. I will find a way to convince the families of our fallen."

Wak'wakgoro balked. "But chief, are you sure about this?"

"Wak'wakgoro, we will not wait for the wyvern to steal our buried comrades. *We* should be the ones to unearth them. If anything should go wrong with this plan, I will take responsibility for the consequences of my actions. I'm willing to bet everything on this, whether it be my titles—" a bitter look crossed her face "—or my head." And with a wave of her hand, she dismissed us. The meeting was over.

It wasn't just the adventurers who joined us. Hunters from all the other settlements within the village chief's jurisdiction trickled in to join the assault against the wyvern. The village boasted a population of over six hundred people, but the other settlements were much smaller, each having no more than five to seven families.

Around ten hunters total came from the other settlements, none of which were very far away. Add that to the other hunters from the village, the adventurers, and me, and our wyvern extermination squad barely broke thirty people.

The just-buried bodies of our hunters were dug up once more and placed in the open field where the wyvern had gone after that cow. The village chief had gone to each family of the bereaved and explained the plan, told them why we needed their bodies—as bait. Surprisingly enough, they agreed without a word.

"Why do you think the families said yes so easily?"

I couldn't understand it, so I asked Cassandra as we stood together on lookout duty atop the stone tower. We stood with our backs to each other, staring out in opposite directions. I couldn't see the expression on her face, but I could hear the sadness in her voice as the breeze carried her answer to me.

"They're afraid," she said faintly. "If they refuse, you see, then they might not be able to live in this village anymore."

"Oh. Is...is that the reason you decided to be my wife?"

Cassandra didn't answer. I don't think she had to.

"I came in out of nowhere and just...wrecked everything for you, didn't I? I'm sorry."

"No, it's all right. I'm fine with this."

"Don't worry. Once we're finished with all this wyvern stuff and things start going back to normal, I'll make a better living for us. Put in some real work this time."

"Um. Please, just don't overdo it, all right?"

I turned to look at her, but even looking at her still seemed to make her so unhappy. Of course it did. I wasn't her childhood friend Ossandra. I didn't fit the trope at all.

Then, all at once, Cassandra clung to my arm.

"Whoa there. It's still the middle of the day, you know? If the village chief finds us flirting on the job, then—"

"No, it's not that! Look, over there—that black cloud of seeds in the air!"

A black cloud of what? But I looked to where she was pointing. Had to strain my eyes a bit, but eventually I saw it. Some black, grainy blip far off in the distance. A stealth bomber?

"I can see it clearer now—" and she wasn't quiet or reserved anymore, but pulling on my arm, shouting "—it's the wyvern!" What a pair of eyes. She really was the daughter of a hunter.

"Ah crap, seriously? It's started!"

I rushed to the alarm bell on the tower and swung the rope like mad, again and again, sending deafening clangs across the village. The wyvern extermination squad hurried to their positions near our trap.

In my heart, I made a promise to Cassandra: This thing was going down. Right here, right now.

● ● ●

Breath caught in my throat as I watched the wyvern soar closer and closer to the village. I snuck a peek at my wife beside me, whose face was filled with horror—the monster was gigantic. She latched onto my arm and wouldn't let go. It wasn't so bad a feeling, having someone rely on you. Kinda made you feel like you *were* reliable.

All right. It was time to figure out how to do everything I could in the battle without dying horribly. This was my chance to put them all in my debt...somehow.

"I'm pretty sure it's safe up here," I told Cassandra, "so stay and keep a lookout. If the wyvern tries to fly off, tell us where it's going."

"A-all right. What are you going to do, Shooter?"

"I'm going down with the rest. I'll show them what I can do with this here spear, yeah?"

"Um, all right, but don't do anything too reckless."

"What, are you worried about me?"

"I, uh..."

"Okay, I can't even deal with how cute that is, it's amazing, but how about we do this after we kill the ruler of the skies?" I flashed her a smile.

And there it was again, that familiar look of utter distaste. Just when I thought she was really worried for me. She was all about Ossandra. How did I keep forgetting that? We barely knew each other, after all.

"Right. Okay, uh. Bye." With that, I ran down the spiral staircase of the tower, hoping that somewhere in the long run I'd forget how shitty I'd made myself feel.

When I emerged from the stone tower, there it was. It touched down in a vacant part of the village, stretching its neck from side to side, glowering at its surroundings. No trace of fear in its eyes, in its movements, anywhere. The village was part of its own territory now, I suppose. Before long, it noticed the hunters' bodies. They were placed right where our last battle had occurred.

The hunters and adventurers of the wyvern-extermination

squad hid in the houses and haystacks surrounding the bodies. I'd seen them running to their positions from up on the tower, and while I technically should have still been at my post as a lookout, Cassandra was in charge of that now. I dashed to my hiding spot, the place I was assigned to hide if the wyvern hit us when I wasn't on lookout duty.

Deathly silence. The hunters and adventurers bided their time, waiting for their chance to jump out and begin the ambush. I could see a few hunters hiding behind houses, peering out from time to time to watch the wyvern.

I crept along with my back to the wyvern, slowly making my way toward my assigned haystack hiding spot. Inside of it was my hunting spear and shortbow, as well as the second spear I "borrowed" from the forge during the last attack. I kind of, technically, definitely forced Ossandra to let me keep using it, and I knew the dwarf running the forge was *pissed* about it.

Well, tough. If I was going to show off my spear work, I couldn't do that without an actual spear. My hunter's spear was all right, but it wasn't built for wyverns. It was short and easy to handle, but I needed reach. Longer weapons were my specialty, and a long spear was the easiest one to handle.

I crawled into the haystack and pulled my spear toward me, keeping an eye on the wyvern all the while. My heart pounded like crazy. Everything felt so much tenser than when I first saw that monster, but, I mean, of course it did. I completely underestimated it before. Just because my father-in-law had taken one down by himself, I thought I'd be able to do the same.

Now it was different. My whole body trembled, and it wasn't because I was naked in the cold. This was fear.

No matter how fast the wyvern was in the air, it moved more sluggishly while stomping to the hunters' rotting bodies.

I swallowed. Hard. It just tore into them. What a fine meal for the bastard. The once quiet air filled with sickening crunches, cracks, slurps. I grit my teeth—when were they going to set off the damn trap? The bodies of the deceased hunters sat on a wooden platform, and beneath it lay a huge pit. That platform worried me. I was afraid it would snap under its weight like a bunch of twigs, but it held. Despite its size, the wyvern was apparently much lighter than it looked. Made sense. You need to be light to fly. Hollow bones and such, like birds. That would explain why a simple reinforced wooden door was enough to hold it.

If the three corpses were taken off the platform, however, the wooden trap door would collapse and drop the wyvern into the pit below. Then the adventurers lying in wait nearby would throw spiked chains over it, ensnaring the monster.

And now it was time.

The wyvern hadn't shown the slightest concern for its surroundings while tearing into the corpses. When it lifted them from the platform, on the other hand...the trap sprung, and the wood collapsed beneath the beast, as if the devouring mouth of hell were opening beneath it.

With a dull roar, the wyvern plummeted into the hole. The adventurers' countless bear traps awaited it in the depths, all of which were lashed to spiked chains that coiled around the wyvern. It was the perfect plan.

The moment it fell, the squad sprang into action.

"Fire!" When the leader of the adventurers gave the command, the archers lying in wait at a distance rained arrows. At the same time, several adventurers wielding spiked chains threw their weapons high, arcing in the air and coming right down on the beast.

"Close in!" the leader barked.

At that, adventurers wielding those strange crossbow-fitted spears charged. The king of the skies was trapped in a pit while spiked chains dug into its body, and countless bear traps snapped shut on its legs. It let out an earthshaking scream.

The crossbow-spear users were in range now, firing bolts into its face as its head thrashed in agony. Strings dangled from the end of the fired spears—the bolts loosed when you pulled them. Interesting.

I dodged the wyvern's flailing tail and moved in closer. Now, when I say I've got some experience as a stuntman, I know that sounds impressive. The truth is, though, that people like me are invaluable when there aren't enough real stuntmen to go around only because we can take a nasty beating. I've been flipped around in cars, kicked by horses, fallen off castle walls, and been sent tumbling down a flight of stairs, so I was pretty confident in my ability to tumble out of harm's way if I had to. I don't know how effective I could be with stabbing proper, but getting a hit in before bolting? That I could do, if I had the guts to go for it. There were no rehearsals here, after all.

I let out a long, ragged shout to pump myself up as I ran. Maybe it sounded stupid, maybe not, but it was for *me*. A big badass barbarian scream to keep me going. I tightened my grip on my spear and thrust it forward with everything I had.

Face, neck, tail, whatever—I wasn't aiming for anywhere specific. I'm no veteran hunter, not some experienced adventurer. I'm a serial part-timer from another world. I only had one mission here: to get a hit on this thing anywhere I could.

My spear pierced straight into its belly. Hardly stuck around to see what happened then—just pulled out and ran away, as fast as I could. Other people nearby used the same strategy, getting a hit on the wyvern with their spears before beating a hasty retreat.

In a fit of pain and rage, the wyvern started thrashing at everything and everyone. It managed to get half its body up out of the pit and flap its enormous wings, sending several hunters toppling off their feet. I barely rolled out of reach and readied my spear at once. That was something I picked up from my time working on samurai films, where you had to break your fall while still holding your weapon. (Here's to the stunt industry, folks.)

I took a moment. Assessed the situation. Could I get another hit in? I took aim at the membrane on its wing and thrust up.

"The wyvern's coming out from the trap! Everyone, fall back!"

As I heard those words, I finished my second hit and once more rolled away from the wyvern. I beat a retreat with everyone else. The hunter next to me had fallen over, so I stopped for just a second to get them back on their feet. Right then, the wyvern crawled up out of the hole, bleeding and screaming with rage.

The roar it let out was unlike anything I had heard before—or, maybe I heard it *once* before, right before the monster seized Saki'cho. Just like then, everyone in earshot froze on the spot. The archers' last volley of arrows, fired seconds before the roar, rained down on the wyvern like hail.

It was the final straw. Unwilling to take any more abuse, the wyvern shook its body free of the gore-covered spears, arrows, chains, and other weapons. It struggled and stumbled, trying to get airborne, each pained flap of its wings sending pummeling gusts of wind everywhere. It limped along, readied itself, took a running start, and rose into the air...retreating into the distance.

It left behind only the mangled, rotting corpses of our hunters and countless pools of its own blood.

Alexandricia and Gimul were on standby inside the village chief's manor. When they finally came back outside, the adventurers were examining the trap hole, assessing the situation.

"It managed to pull all those wired bear traps off itself, but it definitely took some damage to its legs," the leader of the adventurers reported.

"Take a look at this," said the village chief. "Looks like it lost a talon."

"That thing's huge. I knew it was one of the biggest males I've ever seen, but I never thought it could be *that* big. My eyes weren't playing tricks after all."

The village chief nodded. "I saw one of the arrows strike it in the eye, too. It can't have gotten far."

"Did you see what direction it went?" the adventurers asked us hunters once they climbed out of the hole.

I hadn't, but my wife had.

"Um! It went to the left side of Apegut Forest. It didn't go back toward its nest." Everyone turned to stare as Cassandra explained. She was squeezing my arm as she talked, and—look, I know she wasn't finally warming up to me and that I was pretty much the only person she could lean on for support, but by God I was going to take what I could get.

"Then we'll put together a search party," said the village chief. "It can't have flown far after a beating like that."

"Yeah." An adventurer frowned thoughtfully. "Also, someone had the guts to land a blow on its left wing. Who was that?"

That would be me.

"Yes, a good move on their part," the village chief mused. "It was an agile, absolutely naked hunter, if I recall."

Yup, that's me. Right here. The only naked hunter in the bunch, and everyone was finally looking at him. Naturally.

"Oh," cried the village chief, "so that was you, Shooter! Certainly fitting for a warrior such as yourself." She just lavished me with praise. When the other adventurers heard her, their confusion over how I was (or more accurately, wasn't) dressed turned into wry, appreciative smiles.

"Hey, so that was you?"

"Quick thinking, man."

The pride on the village chief's face was clear as she continued. "He's one of our village's hunters, and was a warrior before he joined us."

"But he didn't finish it off," someone pointed out. "Wounded wyverns are way worse. It's gonna be pretty much impossible getting to it now."

And just like that, the villagers once more turned their scornful stares on me, as if they wanted to know why I hadn't just killed the damn thing. Cool, love to not be ostracized for literally twenty seconds.

"Er." The village chief cleared her throat. "Right. Then let's hurry to send a squad to find it."

"How should we search for it, then? Split into small teams?"

"Yes, small teams of three. One adventurer, one hunter from the village, and one hunter from the surrounding settlements."

The village chief could tell what the other villagers were thinking. It was time to bring the meeting to an end, and quickly.

● ● ●

"Hey, you. Come with me."

As we were deciding how the search parties would be split, one of the hunters from the other settlements singled me out. It turned out they lived on their own, and usually ended up going solo on their hunting missions.

Their name was Nishka. They wore their violet hair short, which is *very* fantasy universe and usually gives you an active, sprightly vibe. Also, they had an eye patch, maybe from a hunt?

They had a badass look for somebody who had to be in their late teens. They wore an old yellowish blouse with a leather vest over it, and something that looked like...medieval fantasy hot pants? Medieval fantasy *leather* hot pants? And the way they wore their gloves and leggings made it seem like they were wearing a garter.

God, fine, they looked stupid hot. *She* looked super hot, because, if it wasn't obvious already, Nishka was a girl. Though the village chief's ears may have ended in a slight point, Nishka's were even longer.

"Are you talking to me?" I asked.

"You see anyone else around? You're the one who ripped right through that thing's wing, yeah?"

"Yeah."

"You're kind of a weird one, huh," she said as she placed her hands on her hips. At that moment, her vest pushed her chest up with a jiggle that no mortal could ignore. This girl was just packed with, uh. Attitude. Huge, rockin' attitudes.

Nishka slid in close and wrapped her arm around me.

"So, here's the plan," she whispered, "we're gonna go out and take care of this ourselves."

Here was how she described it to me: After the search party groups were decided, they'd fan out into the Apegut Forest. Four or five of the village hunters were supposed to take point to act as guides, since they were most familiar with the lay of the land.

They'd have new weapons now, something called a "spike." Spikes were spears that had a spiral notch fashioned into their tips, and they were used to hunt only the biggest game. The spirals were laced with poison, and their tips would dig in the more the target resisted and tried to pull them out. Ugh, sure would've been nice to have those things earlier.

Not that we could've used them. Spirals apparently weighed a ton, so they couldn't be used with a quick, uninjured target. In the first battle they were secondary weapons, never even picked up. Still, unwieldly as they were, they were perfect for striking a final blow.

"Those things are too heavy to drag around," said Nishka "They're basically useless. Anyway...Shooter, was it?"

"Yup, that's me."

"Can you handle any weapon you get your hands on?"

"For the most part, yeah. Spears and halberds for sure, and probably swords, too."

I'd only used swords for kendo and staged fights, though. I took first place in a local sword-fighting competition once, but that was less a contest of deadly steel and more flailing around with inflatable toys.

"How about bows?" she asked.

"Bows? I can shoot a few arrows, if you really need me to." And miss the broad side of a barn.

"That's fine. I'll be the one finishing it off, anyway."

"Huh?"

"You look like you've got some muscles on ya, so I want you to take my bow. You blast it with arrows from a distance. I'll follow up and make sure they hit."

"But why would I be using your bow? Wouldn't it be easier for you to use that instead of me?"

"That's 'cause I'm gonna be focused on guiding the arrow to the target, dummy. Trying to make sure those arrows hit one after another after I've already shot 'em is friggin' hard. That's why *you're* gonna be the one firing the arrows for me."

"Uh...hmm." I had no idea what she was talking about.

With that, Nishka and I broke off from the rest of the group and headed into the forest ourselves. Just as Nishka said, the other hunters acting as scouts headed to the left of the forest, where Cassandra had seen the wyvern flee. There was apparently a lake somewhere in that direction, off to the west of the village.

The other hunters and adventurers didn't seem to be in any hurry. The monster would have lost a lot of blood from its wounds, and wyverns were diurnal. We had all night to find it. By morning, the search party's net would have closed around the beast.

"But they've got to lug around those huge-ass spears, so I bet that's just gonna make it harder for them to catch up to the thing," said Nishka casually.

"Why do you think that?"

"You serious? It's me, here. You know, Nishka? *The* Nishka! Somebody around here had to mention me, right?"

"I'm not from around these parts, so..."

"Tch, so that's how it is. Saki'cho didn't tell you anything about me?"

"I never got a chance to *talk* to Saki'cho."

Following Nishka's directions, we headed into the forest. We passed by the spot I'd set traps for the lynxes with Wak'wakgoro and moved on, trekking deeper and deeper into the trees. By the time the village chief noticed we went ahead, it would already be too late.

I was pretty confident in the work I turned in for that last battle, but I was also sure that the other hunters and adventurers were looking for their big break too. They might not be so keen on letting an outsider like me strike the final blow against the wounded wyvern.

Still, the long-eared hunter girl led the way, pressing on through the dense undergrowth.

"It's almost like you know where the wyvern went."

"'Course I know. This forest might as well be a garden to me."

"Really?"

"Of friggin' course! The hell do you think I am, anyway?"

"Rude? Foul-mouthed?"

"No, ya moron! What the hell are you on about?"

"A girl who somehow ended up a hunter, but you've got some good parts to you, too? And you're built like a brick house?"

"God*damn* I have no idea what crap you're spewing, ya—wait, are you covering your crotch?"

Hey, I was getting some good reactions out of her, so I couldn't help teasing her a bit. And even if she was a little annoyed, my karate instincts told me that she was still all wary hunter. This long-eared hunter chick knew her stuff. I could sense it.

"How 'bout I tell you what my other name is?"

Oh, other name? Like Shadowolf? Or Bloodgun? Very edgy, and oh, look at that eye patch. I couldn't wait to hear her DeviantArt-ass OC name.

Not that I said any of that out loud. "What is it?"

"They call me Scalesplitter. Nishka the Scalesplitter."

"Scalesplitter, huh. That's a pretty, uh, impactful name you got there." Presumably not for scaling fish, so I held off on making a joke.

"I've hunted as many wyverns as I've seen winters since becoming a hunter. Those adventurers have *some* experience, but I've done this song and dance solo. I know everything there is to know about wyverns."

"Which explains why you didn't hesitate to go into the forest."

"Yeah. It's my home turf. No one is better at handling the wyverns here than me," she said, flashing me a perfect pearly-white grin. It must've been different for her, then, to try hunting that thing in the village.

"So where do you think this wyvern headed off to?"

"Toward the lake. Your wife already told us, remember?"

"M-my wife?! Were you watching us back there?"

"Kinda hard not to. People tend to stick out when they stand arm-in-arm in public. Next time, try to keep it in your pan—er, I mean, cut down on the flirting, man."

I hadn't *tried* to flirt back there—Cassandra was the one who latched on to me when everyone looked at her. But, well, what was the point in protesting?

More importantly, this was (apparently) Nishka the Scale-splitter. The bow strapped to her back was about the size of your traditional Japanese longbow. Well-endowed as she was, I wondered if her chest got in the way when she was trying to shoot.

"That's no shortbow, am I right?"

"Heh! As if! A shortbow wouldn't do squat to a wyvern."

"Looks like this one could even pierce its scales."

"Bingo. We're gonna take it down with one shot while it's sleeping, and a shortbow isn't enough for that."

"Hold up, while it's asleep?"

Nishka flashed me another wide grin. "Exactly. Did you know that wyverns can use magic?"

"They can? Even though they're animals?"

"Doesn't matter. Human, animal, whatever. If it's alive, it has the potential to use magic. Basic laws of nature here, my man."

"Oh! Is it like how if a wyvern lives long enough, it'll turn into an elder dragon or something? Talk to adventurers, give quests, cast fireballs and such?"

"The hell are you talking about? You some innovative new kinda dumbass?" Nishka stabbed her spear into the ground and glared, exasperated. "Whatever. Look, that thing's enormous, and it needs to eat a ton of food to keep itself going. If it needs to fly, then it has that much more weight it needs to drag around."

"Yeah, that sounds about right," I mused, nodding.

"That's why it goes after things like wooly mammoths or giant apemen. But those things are friggin' huge too, so it can end up getting hurt if they fight back. That's when the wyvern goes off and casts some kind of healing magic on itself. Don't know how exactly, but we don't know even half the stuff these things can do."

Do a certain amount of damage and the monster runs off to cast a healing spell. Sounded pretty standard fantasy-RPG to me, even if I was wrong about my wyvern-dragon theory.

She continued. "There's a cave near the lake big enough for a wyvern to crawl into and hide. That's where this one goes to sleep and rest up."

"It almost sounds like you already knew about it before all this happened."

"'Cause I did. I know everything there is to know about this forest."

"That right?"

"When we started building villages and stuff around here, we started gunning for the same prey as the wyverns and all the other guys in here. They got short on food, so they started leaving the forest. Going after more. You get me?"

Leaving the forest, going after more food, running into my wife's dad. Killing him. Yeah, I got it. Nishka picked up her spear and started off again, so I hurried to follow after her.

"Now, you've got my bow. Just shoot it. Don't worry about aiming, just let 'em loose with everything you've got."

"Without aiming? That's nuts!"

"Normally, sure. But I'll be using magic to *make* it hit the wyvern. You just focus on using enough strength to pierce its scales. That makes it so we're both putting in the same amount of work. Doesn't sound too bad, right? You in?"

"Yeah, I'm in."

"Good! We're almost at the lake, so let's head downwind."

I swallowed, now on high alert as I followed after Nishka.

The injured wyvern was lying on its side near the bank of the lake. It occasionally let out a feeble growl, which was almost cute compared to the deafening roars from the battles before. *Almost* cute. Still terrifying.

"It'll need to rest before using magic to heal its wing," Nishka explained. "It's going to wait a bit before attempting the regrowth."

"How long will that be?"

"Half a day at most, maybe less. That's why we need to take it out now. By the time tomorrow rolls around, it could be fully healed. Be careful, now. These things get wary when they're about to go to sleep."

None of the other search parties had shown up at the lake yet. Nishka was right to call this place her own private garden. She knew shortcuts none of the other local hunters could hope to find. Just like how Wak'wakgoro went after lynxes, wyverns seemed to be Nishka's specialty.

"All right, no more talking. I'm leaving the bow to you, so get ready to fire when I give the signal."

"Where should I aim?"

"The eyes. We'll take away its vision, then aim for somewhere easier. After we pop an arrow into its other eye, we'll go for its lungs and brain."

"So we're trying to gouge out its eye in one shot. Can you do it?"

"This isn't a can-or-can't situation, man. We're going to do it, and that's that."

Nishka shoved her longbow and quiver into my arms. I took them with a nod.

"I'm damn good at wind magic, so just leave it all to me."

"You've got to teach that to me sometime."

"If we get the chance, maybe."

With that, we dropped to the ground and crawled through a grassy plain. We were downwind from the wyvern, so it wasn't able to smell us coming. It was a classic predator tactic, and Nishka the Scalesplitter was at the top of the food chain in this forest—if she wasn't all bluster.

We squirmed along, flat on our bellies, pushing forward with our hands and knees. Nishka inched toward a good shooting spot and I followed right behind.

I found a boulder I could use for cover and hid, pulling an arrow from Nishka's quiver. The tip looked like it had been hammered out of some kind of uneven rock. Obsidian, maybe? Nishka gave a satisfied nod as I examined it. I pulled out a few more arrows to have ready for a quick follow-up shot, just like I'd seen Wak'wakgoro do before.

Leaning against the boulder, I finally stood to peek around my cover. There were about one hundred and fifty feet between me and my target, though the size of the wyvern made it feel much closer. My gut instinct screamed that it could be just a hundred, maybe even fifty feet away. How was I supposed to line up my shot when I couldn't even get the distance right? Still, I kept a firm grip. Pulled the bowstring taut.

Do it, Nishka signaled with her hands.

I let go. An amateur could have seen the power behind my arrow, even as it whistled through the air and *way* off course. Nishka muttered something to herself beside me. Wasn't she supposed to be guiding this thing?

Then it happened: the arrow turned in mid-air, its point aimed right at the wyvern's face. It was like she said—I was in charge of the bow and arrows, she was in charge of hocusing and pocusing them on course. You could call us a sniper and his magical spotter.

The arrow made a visceral squelching noise as it lodged in the wyvern. Well, it didn't really make a noise, but my brain made one up to fill the odd silence. A brief silence, too, because the wyvern let out a gut-wrenching scream and began to writhe its head in pain.

"Next one, hurry!"

Obviously. I nocked the next arrow and let it fly. The king of the skies gave a roar that once more sent the very earth trembling as the arrow embedded in its head. Both arrows stuck firmly in each eye as the beast swung its head wildly, desperately, as it tried to survey a world it could no longer see. I readied my third arrow.

"All right, this time aim near the body. Doesn't have to be exact. Not yet, steady...now!"

I loosed the arrow at Nishka's command and again it found its mark, sinking into the wyvern. It got the lungs. The wyvern had left its stomach exposed as it thrashed about. Its belly was soft enough that the arrow lodged deep—much deeper than I expected.

The wyvern flipped over backward and collapsed with a thunderous boom. No flailing. Not this time. Before I knew it, Nishka dashed toward the barely breathing monster. She whipped her machete from her back and lunged for the wyvern's neck.

I didn't have time to worry about counterattacks, or failure, or any of that stuff. She just plunged the blade deep into its throat—this one last, greatest weak point—with all her might.

The king of the skies could offer no resistance. Its eyes gouged, its lungs pierced, the wyvern gave one last shuddering whimper before finally perishing.

A pool of blood spread out over the ground, spurting red and fresh from the wyvern's severed artery. Before I even had time to take it all in, Nishka came over and snatched her bow from my hands, along with an arrow from her quiver. She turned her aim toward the sky and let the arrow fly straight up into the air.

"What was that?" As I asked, a loud whistling noise sounded out as the arrow sailed into the distance.

"A whistle-arrow. That your first time seeing one?"

"Yeah, it was."

"It's a signal. Shouldn't be long before the other search parties follow it and get to us."

Nishka retrieved her quiver and slung it over her back, then took out her machete and stabbed it into the wyvern, already starting to carve it up.

"Oh god, that reeks."

"'Course it does. This thing doesn't even brush its teeth, whaddya expect?"

She seemed totally unbothered as she plunged her machete into its guts over and over again, her massive attitudes bouncing all the while. Carving out the intestines was the basic first step when it came to prepping an animal after a successful hunt. Guts start going bad as soon as they're out, so it's best to just toss 'em. We fished the bodies of the dead hunters out of the wyvern as well.

Nishka had clearly earned the title of "Scalesplitter." She was an old hand at carving up wyverns. Every dozen seconds or so came another huge splash of blood as she dug through the wyvern's intestines with her machete. Her pretty face was smeared with blood to which she was utterly indifferent.

She took a chunk of meat from the wyvern and offered it to me. "What, you hungry?"

I wasn't. I didn't know if I'd ever be hungry again.

● ● ●

The battle against the wyvern had finally come to a close. Three hunters lost their lives in the initial fight, and two more were gravely injured in the second, eventually succumbing to their injuries. As Nishka and I dug through the wyvern's intestines, we found the body of Saki'cho, the goblin leader of the hunters, bringing the total number of casualties up to six. The poor guy hadn't even been fully digested.

In accordance with village tradition, the bodies were covered in clean cloths and placed inside coffins. The victims were all hunters, either from the village or the settlements located close by. The fact that one of the victims in the second attack was a young man from the top brass must have been a hard blow for the village.

It was the second funeral I attended in the new world, and this time the whole village was at the graveyard for the proceedings. Well, only the people who had the time to come attended, but that number still came to over a hundred. Even the adventurers showed up.

I stood with my wife and Ossandra; the three of us put our hands together in prayer. Cassandra and Ossandra clasped their hands in accordance with their religion, while my palms were pressed flat in true Buddhist fashion. What I prayed for, how we prayed, none of that mattered. We were there to honor the dead.

I stepped forward to help bury the fallen on behalf of our village.

Nishka was there too, standing off to the side quietly. She was out of her bloodstained clothes and wore her normal yellow blouse, vest, and hot pants. She wasn't wearing her handguards or leather tights this time, but rather a pair of long boots.

As was customary, we all wore crimson-colored scarves. That day I learned the scarf's purpose. The color was meant to evoke the image of blood. We the survivors inherited the blood of those who passed on and would carry their blood to the next generation. We had to. Or we would truly lose the departed, forever.

Instead of the usual scripture readings and prayers to the victims and the Goddess, the village chief began to speak.

"Though we may have lost many, I was glad to see our whole village unite as one in order to eliminate the wyvern threat," she said, gazing at the attendees.

"'Whole village' my ass," Nishka snarled. "These guys didn't do jack."

She had a point. Everyone was only concerned for themselves during the first attack, at most just complaining to the village chief. None of the other villagers even showed up to the first funeral.

Japanese society had shown me that being ostracized meant being ignored by everybody outside of only the most important occasions. This village really outdid us there. The only thing uniting these guys was their devotion to being gigantic assholes. Oh, but here they were, showing up to the *second* funeral! Probably because they saw the young man who died as one of their own. The other hunters could eat shit, I guess.

"I also offer my sincerest regrets for the loss of so many hunters, these indispensable servants of the village," the village chief said, turning toward the hunters and our families. "Our work here is only halfway done. Hunters are essential to the development of our village—life would grind to a halt without them. That is why I will be looking to recruit new hunters from town, as well as more workers to assist in building up the village."

Was she talking about replacing the dead hunters with new ones? And on top of that, recruiting more builders?

"Hmph, so she wants to bring more deadweight?" Nishka spat, just loud enough for Cassandra, Ossandra, and I to hear. "We don't need more useless meatheads who're all talk."

Damn, that was a harsh way to put it. But then, as far as the hunters and their families were concerned, this just meant bringing in more people who didn't understand hunters or what we did for the village. More people who would treat us like dirt.

The village by Apegut Forest was on the very edge of developed society. Maybe someday it would end up a hub for the region. But that would only be after decades of building and trade. Right now it was nothing more than a poor village. The newcomers would be from towns, from bigger cities. They'd spit on us just like the other villagers.

Nishka nodded—she must've seen the look of disgust on my face. "Yeah, I feel you," she said. "The only ones who should act any kind of high and mighty are the ones ready to throw their lives on the line." Cassandra and Ossandra gave me a shocked look, but they said nothing more.

Which was probably for the best, because the real shocking bit was coming right...now.

"I will be sending personnel from the village to gather the necessary people from town. To that end...Shooter!" the village chief cried. "I wish for you to act as the escort for this mission."

"Hey, would you look at that?" Nishka said, grinning. "You're going to be carrying that deadweight." My wife and Ossandra were staring at me now as well.

"M-me?" I stammered.

"Yes, you. You haven't seen anything outside the village beside the forest, correct? Think of it as a chance to broaden your horizons. I'll make the necessary arrangements." The village chief's voice boomed with authority, and that was that. This was Alexandricia's great order, and she'd given it to me.

I Need to Put on Some Clothes If I'm Going to Town

ONE MORNING, when I was out tending to the fields, as usual, Wak'wakgoro came to see me.

"Hey, Shooter! I got something good for ya!" he shouted, giving me a toothy grin as he waved at me. He looked pretty cheerful, his red scarf fluttering as he approached. A dog obediently followed at his side, or, well, maybe a wolf? Whatever it was, its tail wagged.

"Morning, Wak'wakgoro. You're looking chipper as ever."

"'Course I am! I'm always ready and rarin' to go, my man. Wyvern's gone! We can finally do our jobs and get on with our lives, yeah?"

"For sure. But c'mon, man, you're the new leader of the hunters. Don't tell me you're not psyched about that."

With Saki'cho lost in the wyvern attacks, the village chief named Wak'wakgoro to replace him. At first I thought that would make things rougher for him, what with all the hunting dogs he'd have to feed, but that didn't seem to be the case. Apparently, not only was the lead hunter exempt from paying taxes, they got a hefty pay raise as well.

"Meat! My family, my siblings, we get some real meat now! Of course I'm gonna be in a good mood!" Wak'wakgoro said, giving his hunting dog a scratch between the ears. It didn't seem too attached to him yet, and only yawned in response. "Here, these are some fresh onions from our place. Bring 'em to Cassandra for me."

"Thanks, man, I will. Talk about a 'good' thing!"

"Oh, I'm not talkin' onions. Take a gander!" Wak'wakgoro broke into an even wider grin and handed me a fur pelt. "Rejoice, my friend! Remember that fox we hunted a while back? Well, they just finished skinning it, and I'm giving it to you."

"Oh yeah, that feels like ages ago! Ah, but look at the poor thing now. I think the fox shrunk in the wash. What a pity," I joked.

"Well damn, you don't seem all that happy about it! You like being naked that much, do ya?"

"I'm not *naked* naked. Just *sorta* naked. Everybody forgets about the vest!"

"The vest doesn't hang low enough, my guy. You're going to town, right? Then shut up and wear this so you don't embarrass the village."

"Well, *yeah,* it's not like I enjoy bumbling around in the buff. Happy to have it. Is this a fur loincloth, then?"

"Fitting for a hunter like yourself, right? And here, some clean cloth as well. Give it to Cassandra for underwear."

"Thank you so much for all this."

I bowed over and over to show my gratitude for the gift of new clothes.

Though we were called hunters, it wasn't like we went on expeditions into the forest every single day. Since I was about to go to town, all I could really do for the next few days was help my fellow hunters by gathering traps with them. If I tried to set any new ones now, I wouldn't be able to collect any prey I captured while I was away. That's why I was getting some practice in with my shortbow, trying to hit a stump. Trying very hard to hit a stump.

"What the hell was that, doofnuts? Your elbows are all over the place! You don't use brawn to shoot a shortbow! It's all in the chest."

The "fellow hunter" with me this time happened to be Nishka the Scalesplitter, of course. She yelled at me pretty much nonstop.

"You're supposed to be escorting those village big-wigs to town, right? Then at least learn how to use a friggin' bow!"

"I'm a beginner, so I kind of need you to spell things out for me."

"Hand it over, I'll show you how it's done."

Nishka snatched the bow away. After glaring at me and giving a dismissive snort, she nocked an arrow. She puffed out her chest as she pulled back the bowstring, and on her chest were two very valuable assets, puffing up her leather vest. Geez, how the hell did she shoot a bow with those things?

"First, you do it like this. Got it? Then you do...this!"

I could almost hear a "twang" as she let go of the arrow. It wasn't the arrow making the noise, though, but the sound of those planet-killer asteroids jiggling on her chest. (Fine, maybe that sound was in my head.). Anyway, the arrow sailed through the air and embedded itself in the stump.

"Now you do it," Nishka said, handing the bow back to me.

When I went to nock my own arrow into the bow, she came up behind me to correct my posture. I was totally expecting her to press herself up against me, but I got something even better. Since Nishka was shorter than me, her face came up just above my shoulders. Every time she breathed out through her nose, her hot breath tickled the back of my neck.

"All right, I'm gonna say it again: use your chest when you're drawing the bowstring. Don't use your arms, but your chest. Yeah. Yeah, just, like that."

"Mm. Yeah, that's pretty good."

Listen, I'd do anything she asked right then. I was in heaven! For, uh, a second.

"No, what the hell are you—? Get over here, stop hunching over!"

She'd pressed up against me a little too long, and if I didn't shift a little she'd know for sure that Little Shuta was having a bit too much fun. With another twang, the arrow trailed in an arc far from the stump.

"See, that's what you get for not aiming with your chest!"

"Err, yeah—I'm paying attention, but I sort of had to bend over."

"Had to—?"

For a moment Nishka was confused, seeing me cover my crotch with my hands. Then she flushed a deep, deep shade of red. "Y-you. *You!*"

"Okay, look, sometimes bodies just do things and it's perfectly natural, and also I'm super sorry about it, ya know?"

"You're popping a boner and you're married!"

"I can't control it, I'm sorry! It was the way your breath hit me, all kinda hot and tingly and stimulating? And such?"

Nishka covered her chest with her arms as she looked at me in disgust.

"I'm telling Cassandra, you horny animal!"

She aimed a swift kick straight at my groin, and I passed out from the pain on the spot.

Another hunter asked me to help them out by plucking some pheasants. Later in the evening, I was doing my work on a table out back when Ossandra came to visit me, looking a bit uneasy.

"Did you change your mind at all?" he asked me in a hushed voice, probably so as not to let Cassandra hear us.

"You mean about running away?"

"You still have time if you want to pull it off."

"I'd just be heading into unknown territory if I did. I don't even have any money saved up, so I think I'll stick around and wait a bit, see how I feel."

"I can always get some cash together for you."

"Sorry, I make it a policy to never borrow money from people."

"O-oh, uh. I see."

"Yup, there you have it. If that's all, then I guess we're done here."

"W-wait, there's no need to be that hasty..."

It seemed like Ossandra really wanted to chase me out of the town. Gee, could it be because of Cassandra? Who could say, what a mystery.

"I want you to let me take care of Cassandra while you're gone," he managed to ask me after tripping over his words.

"Oh yeah? Sure, I hereby bequeath her unto your capable hands. She was saying she needed some more apple cider vinegar, so I bet she'd be grateful if you brought her some."

It was incredible watching how fast Ossandra's mood improved from hearing me say that. I mean, I thought he'd be happy, but he was like a kid pretending to be chill in a free candy store.

Tonight's dinner was a stew filled with wyvern meat, potatoes, beans, kale, and onions. Pieces of the wyvern had been handed out to the rest of the village as a way to memorialize those who lost their lives to it.

Cassandra and I sat next to each other in silence as we poked at the pot of stew on the table. There were no chopsticks in this world, so I had to use that strange two-pronged fork and a ladle to eat.

Lovely memorial to the dead, I guess, but wyvern meat was godawful. It was way too tough and chewy, with just as much fat as it had flavor—that is, none whatsoever. We tried soaking it in wine overnight to improve the taste, but it hadn't even softened the meat. I was pretty sure the other villagers were thinking just about the same thing, but meat was a precious commodity. There wasn't much else we could do besides eat it.

"You've had this stuff before, I'm guessing," I said to Cassandra. When her father passed away, I was sure.

"Yes. I had so much meat delivered to the house I didn't need to worry about food for quite some time," Cassandra said, and paused to blow on her soup to cool it down.

Free food or no, life couldn't have been easy for her back then. There'd been no one around to help her tend the fields, and she even sold off her father's clothes just to get by.

But she was happy now, right? She had an extra pair of helping hands with me here, and I was learning how to work the fields by watching other people do it. We planted beans, potatoes, and even some herbs that could be harvested without much work. As long as I wasn't hunting, though, that meant eating into our reserve food stores.

Then there was Ossandra, the friend Cassandra had known since childhood.

"Hey, Cassandra? Are you...happy?"

Shouldn't have asked, I bet, but the words came tumbling out my mouth all the same.

Cassandra timidly looked up at me. "I don't have to worry about food, and you're even providing for me. I suppose I'm the happiest I've been."

"Oh. Uh. Then I guess I have to just keep on aiming to be a better hunter?"

"Yes, please do. You'll be heading out into town tomorrow, so make sure to eat properly and rest up for your trip."

Dinnertime was over, and I watched as Cassandra put our wooden dishes into the empty stew pot and carried it away. It was obvious she didn't really think about herself. Happiness took many forms back in my old world, but the people in this one were too busy focusing on simply surviving to ponder what happiness meant beyond that. Being happy was just keeping yourself alive.

For Cassandra, I bet getting married to Ossandra would have been her own personal happiness. Or maybe not, since the village chief or her father might have stepped in to make sure that didn't happen. Maybe I just appeared at the right time, and they chose a stranger to be Cassandra's husband so she wouldn't get hitched to her cousin? Agh, I made myself more confused the more I thought about it.

Tomorrow I'd head into town to recruit both replacement hunters and new villagers to keep the village growing. Of course, if I really wanted to, I could make a break for it and try and start a new life in town...but then what would happen to Cassandra? Life was bad enough for her as the wife of a hunter, but I couldn't imagine what it would be like with a dead father and a runaway husband.

Damn it... No matter how much I thought about it, I couldn't come up with a good answer. If she told me she wasn't happy, I would've found a way to get her and Ossandra together. Or maybe they really intended to be together, and it would happen no matter what I did. The only part of Cassandra I'd touched so far was her fingertips, after all.

I was at a loss over what to do. I flopped back onto my bed as a whirlwind of thoughts swirled in my head.

"Um...Shooter?" Cassandra called out to me.

"Hm? What is it, dear?"

"I used the cloth Wak'wakgoro brought to knit you a pair of underwear. I wouldn't want you to be embarrassed in town."

"Oh, underwear! Yeah, I've heard good things about underwear!"

I got up to take the underwear from Cassandra. I was expecting it to be like another loincloth, but...

All right, you know g-strings? You know how guys generally do not wear g-strings? Well, my wife made me one. A g-string.

"Make sure to wear it so you don't get your fur loincloth dirty. It's the only good clothing you have, after all," she said with a tiny giggle.

God, though, she was so cute. Was that the first time I heard her laugh? I...I really liked it.

"Thank you. Thank you so much." I fought against the urge to just throw my arms around her and tried to put it into words. I wanted to hold her, kiss her, push her down on the spot as if she wasn't already taken, but Ossandra's face floated through the back of mind. That was just the way things were.

There was a single two-wheeled wagon waiting in front of the village chief's manor. It was the only vehicle in the village, and it had no canopy. The only ones riding in it would be me, Gimul, and the bones of our good ol' wyvern in the back. There wasn't anything like blue tarp in this world to cover it—just some kind of fur sheet to keep the bones dry. We had to get the remains into town to sell them, and we'd take any price we could get, no matter how small. It was kind of funny. We were selling the bones of the wyvern to recoup the huge cost of killing the damn thing.

The only ones gathered to see us off were the village chief, N'aniwa the woodcutter, and the girl who worked at the village chief's place.

"Then I will leave the negotiations in your hands, you two," the village chief said.

"You can count on us, ma'am," came Gimul's stiff reply.

The way Gimul and Alexandricia talked to each other made it hard to believe they were actually family, blood or no. Me, I was decked out in my usual hunter garb and ready to go, with my new, more luxurious fur loincloth. I even had *underwear*.

"I'm leaving the minute details to my son, but Shooter? You guard him well."

"Leave it to me. I have experience as a self-defense instructor, so I'll fend off any ruffians or ne'er-do-wells. It shall be nothing, milady," I said, giving the sword on my hip a pat.

"Good. You've already proven your bravery by slaying the wyvern, so I'm expecting great things. Your family, however...did you not want to say goodbye to them?"

"My wife is a bit shy. I think she stayed home."

"Then we'll be leaving now, mother," Gimul said.

"Yes, be well."

With that final short exchange, I hopped into the back of the wagon as Gimul whipped the horse into action and got the cart moving. I gave a short bow to the village chief, and wouldn't you know it, she waved me goodbye!

We trundled along at a leisurely pace on the road away from the village chief's home. Besides the Apegut Forest, I knew absolutely nothing about this world. This would be my first time seeing what it was like outside the village, and I would be lying if I said I wasn't looking forward to it.

"I can see your house from here," Gimul turned around to tell me. "And your wife, too."

I was shocked to hear him say that. Taking a look for myself, I saw Cassandra waving goodbye to me. It was a strange feeling, for sure—but not a bad one. You know what? I'd buy her a souvenir. Yeah. Something nice, something cute.

I waved back at her, feeling like I snatched a victory from Ossandra for some childish reason.

I'd get her something to make her happy. I'd make her *happy*.

Our Journey is Just Beginning

OUR CART JOSTLED as we traveled over the grassy plains to town, and a gentle breeze traveled with us.

My name is Yoshida Shuta, thirty-two years old, and these days I'm a hunter in this fantasy world. I was traveling alongside a man named Gimul as his escort on orders from the chief of our village.

"How much farther until we reach town?" I shouted to Gimul from the back of the wagon. It was a peaceful day, but our backs were turned and we had to speak up to hear each other.

"We should make it there in about three days at this pace. If we run at full gallop, we'll be there by evening, but there's no reason to rush."

"Gotcha. What are we going to do about sleeping arrangements? The village chief didn't mention anything about that."

"We'll be roughing it outside. It probably won't rain, so I'm not planning to sleep at some nearby village."

The Gimul I remembered was a man of few words. He would've told me to "put up with it" at any question, or maybe just shut every question down with a plain "no," but he seemed so much calmer now. There were plenty of reasons for that, I was sure, one of which being how I once kicked his ass after he got drunk and tried to murder me, another being how much the village chief praised me for my efforts fighting the wyvern.

The main reason, though, had to be how the village chief had taken an interest in me. If you can get yourself in good with the top brass of any kind of organization (say, for example, a medieval fantasy village), then suddenly everyone finds they can't talk smack about you anymore.

Way back when, I was working at a place that made crappy packaged convenience store meals. There was a younger guy supervising our production line, but the one I had my eye on was the old lady in charge of *all* the part-time workers. She'd been in the business for twenty-five years, and had been making mediocre C-store rice balls while the younger workers were pooting away in diapers.

A friend invited me to work there as a quick part-time job, but I stuck out like a sore thumb. I also colored my hair back then, so everyone treated me like some kind of stranger from another world. (Part-time jobs prepare you for all kinds of weird stuff, huh?) Anyway, I did everything the old lady in charge of the part-timers said, even if it contradicted the young guy supervising the line.

If you get in good with the higher-ups, no one can say anything against you. I made sure to do the same thing with the village chief, doing everything I could to get on her good side. Of course Gimul chilled out. Imagine if I tried to suck up to *Gimul,* of all people. Nah, I put my experience from before to work and made sure that if there was one person I was never going to disappoint, it would be the lady with power.

"Hey, Gimul?"

"What?" he shouted back at me from the driver's seat.

"It looks like someone's been following us for a while now."

"Someone's been *what*?"

He pulled hard on the reins, brought the wagon to a grinding halt, and whirled around to look in my direction.

"Right over there. See them? They've been following us ever since we hit the road."

"Yeah, I see them. Who is that?"

"Not a clue. Maybe a bandit?" I offered.

"No, it can't be. It would be a different story if we were taking the highway frequented by merchants, but this doesn't make sense."

Despite what he said, Gimul placed a hand on the sword he wore at his waist. He may have been born in the same village as Cassandra, but he definitely didn't have her sharp eyes. Gimul gave a frustrated snort—he couldn't make that hazy figure out— and turned to look at me.

"Want to use my sword?"

"No, I'll be fine using the one I got from Ossandra."

I had some experience from sword-fighting competitions, so I was well versed in the fine art of wielding inflatable plastic blow-up swords. My shortsword was just around the same length as them, so, you know, close enough. I don't know why, but karate guys are usually also sword guys, and I was no exception.

"You're not gonna use a bow?" asked Gimul.

"I'm still practicing with it. We're better off if I use a sword, unless you don't care whether I hit my target."

We tensed up, preparing for a fight. As the figure got closer, though, I saw that they were...waving?

"What, someone you know?"

"Seems like it," I said. "They're waving and everything."

"I can see that much, you idiot!"

While we were talking, we heard the figure shout something as they continued to run at us. "Hey, guys! You gonna give me a lift to town or what?"

Our mysterious pursuer was none other than Nishka, all dressed up in her best traveler's clothes. Okay, it was more like her usual clothes—a cloak over the blouse, vest, and hot pants that made up her usual outfit—but hey. She was panting slightly as she pulled herself up into the wagon, before she shouted an order to Gimul.

"C'mon, what are you waiting for? Let's get this show on the road!"

Gimul wasn't happy to hear that. But Nishka was an expert wyvern hunter, and she played a significant role in the battle taking out ol' dry bones in the back of the wagon. She earned the village chief's praise for her efforts just like I had, which was why Gimul was having such a hard time flat-out telling her to get lost.

I decided to feign ignorance to the whole affair as Nishka explained herself.

"I was getting jealous you were the only one going to town, Shooter, so I decided to tag along. I've never been, ya know?" she said. The wagon jostled. So did her massive chest.

"This isn't a vacation," I said. "Gimul and I are going on business."

"I'm coming along to watch you work, then. Besides, it's better to have two people on escort duty rather than one, right? All agreed? Great. Let the road trip begin!"

Yeah, it didn't matter what any of us said, did it? She wasn't listening to me at all. At first, Gimul was vehemently against the idea and kept telling her to go back. That was until Nishka came up to the driver's seat and leaned against him.

"C'mon, you're a man, right? Don't be such a killjoy," she cooed. "You're not gonna find a wife that way, ya know?"

That made Gimul shut up, most likely because she was pressing her absurdly huge assets against the back of his head and gently wrapping her arms around his shoulders. Lucky bastard.

With that settled, we set off again on our way to town. It was a pretty uneventful journey, all things considered. We were traveling in a wagon with two full-grown men, a girl, and a pile of wyvern bones all being pulled by a single horse, so we weren't exactly moving along at a breakneck pace.

I decided to ask my two other travel partners a question to kill the time.

"So, there's something I've been meaning to ask for a while now," I started.

"What, you want to know something about hunting?" Nishka nodded. "Ask away. Wyverns are my specialty."

"No, not that. Can we move past the wyvern stuff, please?"

"Then what? You wanna know what kinda guy I like? Sorry to say, but you aren't my type, Shooter."

Nishka was clearly not interested in listening to what I had to say. Gimul just stayed silent up in the driver's seat. He didn't really seem to know how to deal with Nishka.

"No, I'm not talking about that. I'm talking about breakfast! Nobody eats it in the village! I can't get used to that. Even if they only have enough to eat two meals a day, wouldn't a morning meal give you more energy to tackle the rest of the day?" Honestly it was one thing I was still completely unable to get used to since I got to this world.

"C'mon man, ain't it obvious? Skipping breakfast makes lunch taste even better, doofus," Nishka answered with absolutely no hesitation.

Gimul, on the other hand, did an audible spit-take and broke into a fit of coughs.

"She's lying," he said, whirling around. "We skip breakfast to strengthen ourselves against starvation, which makes our bodies store extra nutrition."

Nishka blinked. "Y-y-yeah, I mean, *obviously*. I-I was just messin' with you, Shooter! Ha, I can't believe you, uh. Fell for. That. Heh."

As one might expect from the son of the village chief, Gimul really knew his stuff. Nishka, on the other hand...didn't.

I remembered reading somewhere that even though tons of people skipped breakfast nowadays, it wasn't worth it. Going straight to work after waking up just caused nasty hunger pangs. People in this world went without breakfast on purpose, though, in order to train their bodies against that very phenomenon. The same problem tackled two different ways by different worlds with their own traditions...and now I was wondering which one was right.

Our meals for the road consisted mostly of preserved foods. I ate the meal Cassandra packed for me first, but now I was down to nasty biscuits and smoked wyvern jerky for dinner.

Gimul did his best to chew through the tough wyvern jerky, looking miserable all the while. Once he noticed I seemed to be choking mine down relatively easily, he spoke up.

"You seem like you're enjoying that wyvern meat."

"Ha, like hell. I've just had tanuki jerky before, and this tastes more or less the same as that."

Out of all the meat out there, nothing was more hit or miss (mostly miss) than tanuki. The taste changed depending on what it had been fed, but all the tanuki meat I ever tried was just awful. It was dry and tough as leather, which was just about the same as wyvern meat.

Nishka wasn't bothered in the slightest as she dug into her portion of wyvern. Made sense, given her specialties.

The next two days played out in about the same way, camping outside as we made our way toward town. When nighttime came around, we took turns crawling into the back of the wagon to sleep. On the third day, right when we were all reaching the point of exhaustion from our back-to-back nights roughing it outdoors, we finally made it.

We had arrived at the town of Bulka.

"This place is *huge!*" Those were the first words out of my mouth upon seeing Bulka. I was imagining something a few sizes bigger than the village, but the town blew it out of the water. "Wow, there're walls going around the whole city. How many people live here?"

Gimul shrugged. "What, you never seen a town before? That's just how they are. The population is over ten thousand, which is more than ten times the amount living in both the village and the nearby settlements combined."

"Dang, I guess that's the city for you."

Of course, back in my world Bulka would've been a dinky little town, but it was a virtual metropolis in this one. Watching all the people streaming in and out of the gates had an almost exotic feeling from my point of view. Japan isn't exactly brimming with roads and buildings of stone, after all.

Nishka, meanwhile, was practically picking her jaw up from the ground.

"There's more people here than that huge herd of deer we saw back in the forest!"

Well. We all have our unique ways of seeing the world, I guess?

● ● ●

I tried to get my personal appearance in order as we prepared for the border inspection outside Bulka. I was wearing a vest that once belonged to Cassandra's father (one of three), the beautiful g-string underwear she knitted me, and my fox-fur loincloth.

Aside from that, I wore a cloak as part of my traveling gear and a few bare necessities for any decent hunter—namely, a shortbow and shortsword. (I'd left my spear behind, since I decided I probably wouldn't need it in town.)

I may have seemed a bit lightly dressed for springtime, but at least I wasn't buck naked anymore. Yeah, I'd fit in just fine in town! Probably! Hopefully?

I spun around like a fashion model as I checked myself out, earning a wary peer from Gimul. "You got off the wagon just to twirl around like an idiot? The hell are you doing?"

"I was just wondering if my outfit looks weird or not."

"Funny coming from a man who used to be naked all the time."

"It's not like I *wanted* to be naked or anything. N'aniwa took all my clothes, so I didn't really have a choice."

"Don't be stupid. You've been naked ever since we found you wandering around the forest."

"Huh?"

Now *that* I didn't know. I could've sworn I arrived in this world wearing the same shirt and work pants I had in my old one... but nope, apparently the only suit I'd been wearing had been my birthday suit. So what, was I reborn here? Was God making me start over as a middle-aged dude? That didn't seem fair, come on—couldn't I just start over from the beginning?

"I thought you were part of some clan that took pride in being nude or something," said Gimul.

"As if. Back where I came from, being naked in public is a crime."

"Hm. Then you better be careful in town too. The only ones wandering around naked there are slaves and the crazy folks they call 'wise men.'"

Wise men? What the hell? At least being naked wouldn't be a crime here. Considering my (awful) luck with clothes, it was nice to know that.

"Wait, are we planning on going into town now?" Nishka whimpered. "Just like that? My heart's not ready for it yet!" She trembled and clung onto me.

Which squished her humongous melons into my innocent arm. There were no such things as bras in this world, either, so I could feel everything through her clothes. My little buddy downstairs raised his flag high, the patriotic little perv, so I tried to calm her down and get her boobs away from me.

"Don't worry, Nishka, just play it cool. You *are* cool. A badass, matter of fact, a *wyvern-slayer*. Be proud! Hey Gimul, what exactly happens during these inspections?"

"Usually they levy taxes on people coming through, but we're exempt from tariffs on authority from the village chief. They should just do a simple check to see what we've got."

I turned to look at the line ahead. There were about thirty people waiting to try and get through the town entrance. Some were travelers loaded with bags, others merchants using horse-drawn carts, and there were even some with fancy, properly covered wagons who were probably nobility.

I passed the time till our inspection trying to calm Nishka down, and it still seemed to take forever.

"Where are you coming from?" the guard asked Gimul finally.

"The village by Apegut Forest. We have business with the adventurer's guild, on orders from the village chief."

Nishka and I jumped out of the wagon and lined up beside Gimul. The guard went to pat us down for a body inspection. He was all business when he worked on Gimul, but was, shall we say, *very* thorough when it was Nishka's turn. There could be anything hidden in her cleavage, he said, or certain spots that only a girl could hide things in.

She shot him a glare befitting a wyvern-slayer, though, and the guard backed off. After a relatively quick pat down of the rest of her body, she was let go without any problems. There he went, from creeper to trying to get it over with as quickly as possible.

I understood the mentality behind the strictness, since people bringing weapons could be interpreted as trying to incite a revolution against the local authority. That said, carrying weapons for personal protection was fine. It was just having tons of magic amulets or cursed weapons that got the guards' hackles up.

Speaking of curses, even though I was cursed with being naked most of the time, they let me in with no problems—can you believe that? I didn't really like being touched by guys, so it was a real win-win if you ask me.

"Listen up, here's the plan," Gimul told us. "We're taking the bones to a trading company we've reached an agreement with and selling it to them. Once that's done, we'll find a place to park the wagon and find an inn for the night. I know a place that people from the village always use."

"All right, got it," I replied.

"We'll head to the adventurer's guild after that."

"Who cares about that stuff?" Nishka butted in, chronically shitty at reading the room. "Let's go look around town!"

Countless rows of stone buildings stood packed together like sardines along the main road. They reminded me of the rows of tchotchke shops at tourist destinations, and they were almost as crowded as one during the heavy midday traffic. It was like a bustling shopping district from back in my world.

While we only had a single wagon in our entire village, this place was so built-up that vehicles were an everyday sight.

Gimul brought the cart to a stop in front of a trading company. I jumped off the wagon and pulled away the sheet covering the bones. When Nishka followed, her two girls jumped around when she hit the ground. Nice.

As that was going on, a goblin had come out of the trading company and already started negotiations with Gimul.

"It's been a while."

"Good to see you, heir to Apegut." That was apparently what our village was called in Bulka, along with the Forest.

"It's still too early to call me that. My mother could always end up marrying someone else, which means the title would fall to them."

"Surely you jest. You're the legitimate child of the previous chief, aren't you? Not like you're going to have any competition, either—they say Alexandricia's barren."

"Keep your voice down, dolt!"

Gimul shot a glance my way, and I grabbed a few of the wyvern bones from the back of the wagon. The meat had been scraped away from the bones before cleaning them, and they'd been taken care of as well as you could expect. You were usually supposed to use these bones to make new weapons, armor, magical potions or whatever in your average fantasy world, but look. These are goddamn bones we're talking about. Hollow bones that have to be light enough to fly. What're you going to grind these up to fashion, a thimble?

Maybe they could be used for medicine, though? Dinosaur bones were an extremely valuable ingredient in herbal medicine, people told me, so why not?

However, wyvern scales surely had to have some use in armor-smithing. They were sturdy, lightweight, and I could guarantee how effective they were after fighting the thing they came from.

"Aside from its head, we've got all the bones here," said Gimul.

"And what happened to the head?"

"I left it with my mother as a testament to the strength of our village. We made sure to bring its scales though, so make sure to get a good look at them."

"I'm sure they'll make some fine armor once you finish getting them prepared, when you find some folks who can actually manage that," the goblin said with a laugh. Then he climbed into the back of the wagon and started looking over our wyvern bits, turning over the bones, squinting and *hmphing* and inspecting.

"How much can we get for them?" Gimul asked.

"Much more if you had the head, I can assure you."

"I see."

"With what we have here, I'm looking at twenty gold Bulka coins and five silver Church coins. Yeah, that seems about right."

"All right, we'll take it."

Wasn't there supposed to be bartering involved? I expected a little grumbling out of Gimul, maybe some hard-to-get for a few extra gold coins.

While I worried over Gimul's apparent lack of haggling talent, a bored Nishka opened the top of her blouse a bit and started to fan herself. She eventually caught on to me ogling and shot me a look of disgust.

"Eyes to yourself, man."

"Wait, you mean you weren't doing that on purpose? I thought you wanted me to see or something."

"Conceited much? Ugh, now I'm all self-conscious."

Wait, did having big boobs actually bother her? "Speaking of not-that-at-all, why do you think Gimul isn't trying to bargain with this guy? You'd think he'd try and haggle for a better deal or something."

"Are you kidding? Twenty gold coins is a ton of money! That's enough to eat fluffy bread and meat stew every day for the next decade!"

"Is it? And how much would that cost?"

"You could buy a whole twenty sets of full-wyvern armor with that much cash! That deal's ridiculous!"

"C'mon, really? I mean, the only thing you know about is hunting, so..."

"Wh-what, you making fun of me? Anybody can count money, ya jerk!" As Nishka got worked up, her chest got to jiggling, and naturally, Shuta Jr. started getting worked up as well.

Getting off the topic of jiggling, before long the goblin went back inside the shop and Gimul turned to face us. "I heard you wondering why I didn't barter. There's a reason for it. Listen to their demands now and you can leverage them later, use your knowledge to make better deals."

"Like a loss leader, sort of. Take a hit now, make a gain later."

"Right. The village gets all the supplies it needs from this company. What's more, even if they tend to undersell us, they listen if we really need something big taken care of. We can't get that with other shops."

Just like that goblin said, Gimul was really brushing up on his leadership skills for when his turn came up.

I had experience working to get a payment system in place for a startup company. Well, I wasn't working *on* the payment system—my role there was to clean up the place where the actual team worked. Still, I remembered something one of the bosses said:

"There's a reason we charge a higher handling fee than our competitors—so we can offer fuller support. We're the only ones working Saturdays to get their payments processed. *We're* there when our clients need us."

And that's why Gimul picked these traders—because they helped out the village when they truly needed it, even when other shops wouldn't comply.

"Expensive or cheap," I muttered, "there's always a deeper reason than you think. Today's losses are tomorrow's profits. I think I got a bit smarter today."

Gimul looked at me with a curious expression on his face as I said this to myself.

"Wh-what?" I started, flustered. "Does my hunter outfit make me look weird after all?"

"No, you dolt. I was just making sure you weren't about to do something stupid, that's all," Gimul snorted as he looked away.

We left the trading company behind and found a place to park the wagon. After paying a small fee to the attendant, we headed for the inn.

Gimul, being gigantic, was a great human bulwark to push our way through the crowds of people. The main roads were built wide enough to allow carts to pass through, but the alleys were cramped and packed full of street stalls.

"From what I can see," I said, "it looks like there's only humans and goblins here. Are there no other races around?"

"Yeah," Nishka piped up, "I thought there would be other long-ears like me around, but I'm not seeing any."

There were goblins everywhere in Bulka. Most of them looked like they worked as employees at shops, but some were decked out in fancy armor—they looked like warriors.

These must've been the goblins talented enough to make it into town that Wak'wakgoro told me about. The ones who'd chosen to leave their families. They might even be working as adventurers.

"Are people with long ears especially uncommon?"

"No," Gimul answered, "you can find elves in the settlements."

So long ears meant they were elves after all. Nishka didn't look too elf-y, though, especially with her head of violet hair.

"They are a bit rare to see around town, though," he continued. "Most elves live somewhere around the Apegut Forest."

"Do elves stick to the forests and mountains because they hate city life? And they don't get along with dwarves, either, right?"

Gimul snorted. "Slow down, brain-damage. There're tons of elves if you head toward the capital. Even the royal family has elf blood in it."

I turned to Nishka, a quizzical look on my face.

"Th-that's just because people like me are a bit special! Yeah, that's gotta be it," she said. Well, she didn't seem all that special compared to us humans, aside from that ludicrous rack.

"Bulka is a town way out on the frontier," Gimul continued, "so you won't find any elven nobility or city dwellers here."

"I see. So elves like Nishka are savages, then."

"Am not!" she shouted indignantly.

Soon enough, we arrived at the inn. That's what they called it, anyway. I hadn't expected anything as fancy as a hotel or travel lodge or something, but I thought we were headed toward something at least a little better. Maybe a place to kick back and relax. Like, tiny but roomier than a capsule hotel or something.

No such luck. The Sound of Joy Inn was as barebones as you could get. Gimul was the only one to get an actual room, while Nishka and I were shoved into a tiny twenty-square-foot room with two beds. Well, I say beds, but I mean hammocks.

Gimul got to take it easy, and we were stuck with the hammocks. Discrimination! Socioeconomic disparity, bourgeois oppression! With hammocks!

"We'll grab something to eat after we drop off our stuff," said Gimul. "Make sure to bring anything valuable with you.".

"Like what? I'm pretty much naked all the time back at the village, so it's not like I have anything more valuable than the fur loincloth I'm wearing."

"Can it. Just make sure to bring your sword."

Obviously. I was supposed to be guarding him, after all. No way was I letting go of that blade.

· · ·

We left the inn a little bit after noon to go find something to eat. I thought we were going to a restaurant or something, but we just grabbed cheap eats from a food cart. We sat down on empty barrels, drinking vegetable soup from a cup and scarfing sandwiches that were nothing more than meat packed between slices of hard bread.

Just a bit of trivia about this world, but you were never supposed to eat vegetables raw. They could contain parasites or viruses, so they always had to be cooked.

"I thought food in the city would be crazy delicious, but this isn't anything to write home about," Nishka grumbled.

"I bet we could find some better stuff if we went to a good restaurant," I said. "I'd love to try going to a bar or something."

"Hell yeah, a bar!" Nishka (chest and all) bounced up and down excitedly at the idea, but Gimul shot her down on the spot.

"Not happening. There's still daylight to burn, so we're heading to the adventurer's guild after this."

"C'mon, don't be such a buzzkill! I'm talking one drink, we've got time for that!"

"No. You came here without a coin to your name. I'm already paying for you to stay at the inn."

I sipped on my wine, watching the two of them go at it.

"How come Shooter gets to have wine?! Let me have some too, damn it!" she complained. So much for neutrality.

"I bought this with my own money," I said, "so that's a no."

Money earned from backbreaking work at the village, thank you very much, right from the village chief's coffers! Like hell I was spending my hard-earned paycheck on this barfly.

"Listen, buddy, this is, uh, that thing, with the, ah, profits that are tomorrow, and today we've got losses! But that's fine, because later we're gonna be at tomorrow. Yeah, that's it! So hey buddy, come onnnn, just buy me a driiiiiiiink."

I blinked. "What in the world are you talking about?"

"You might feel like you're taking a loss now, but you can ask me for something later, and right there? That's all it, baby. *That's* when you get happy."

"Uh huh. You're talking about what I said back at the trading company?"

"Yeah! So you make *me* happy first, and I'll owe ya."

Wow. All right, can't say I expected *that* from the supposed "Scalesplitter."

Slightly dazed, I picked up my wine bottle and offered it to her. "Fine, fine. I already had enough to drink. She's all yours."

"Really? Wait, really? You know that I'm gonna just drink this whole thing, right? Man, you can't take this one back. I will decimate this wine."

"I won't ask for it back. I *will* ask you for the 'profit' part of the deal soon enough, though."

Eyes twinkling, Nishka practically snatched the bottle from my hands and started guzzling down the wine. Oh, I was feeling downright diabolical now. What should I have her do for me? The possibilities!

"Ahhh, this hits the spot!" she cried.

"They don't just call her 'Scalesplitter,' you know," said Gimul. "A lot of us just call her 'Tipsy Nish.' She loves her booze, if that wasn't apparent."

"Yeah, I can see that. This right here does not look like a 'Scalesplitter.'"

"What's worse is she can't hold her liquor, so keep a close eye on her."

With that little misadventure out of the way, it was time for us to get back to work. Next step: find some capable hunters to bring back to the village with us.

"Hey, heyheyheyheyhey!" said Nishka. "I heard they've got a bar at the adventurer's guild, can you believe that? Let's grab a drink there, Gimul!"

Well, I thought, *here we go.*

The image I had in my head for the adventurer's guild was something like to a saloon from old Westerns, but that was only half right. It was closer to the inside of a bank, which made sense—I mean, apparently this place started out as an agency to help people find jobs. Sure, they called it an adventurer's guild, but it catered to shifty-looking mercenaries, adventurers, and even laborers and hunters. If you worked day-to-day, this was your place.

There were shades, too, of a brothel from an old Western movie, but a lot of it was a partitioned counter and bulletin boards posted along the walls. There weren't any receptionists waiting behind the counter like you might find in certain popular game franchises about being a monster-hunting guy—more like merchant and trader types. There were also a few people advising patrons from behind the counter.

I expected this to be a place full of adventurers who looked pretty much the same as those Vikings who helped take down the wyvern, but that wasn't the case. Just a healthy mix of men and women of all ages. Some of them were probably looking for adventure, but it looked like a lot of them only wanted to put food on the table and were willing to take whatever odd jobs needed doing.

"Where's the bar at?" Nishka groaned. "I'm not smelling any alcohol here."

Gimul and I ignored her.

"I'm going to talk with one of the consultants here about our request," said Gimul. "It's going to take some time. Keep Nishka occupied."

"You're talking our request for more hunters and stuff? I'd actually like to see how that works instead."

"Understandable, but I don't think we should leave her to her own devices right now."

"Heyyyyyyy, bar? We are going to the bar, right? We can drink if it's just a little bit! C'mon, pleeease?" Nishka said, tugging on my arms.

"I guess you're right," I said, sighing. "Let's go then, Nishka. It was just next door, right?"

Nishka practically dragged me out.

"Hey Shooter, did you know you can get beer in town? The village only has wine and the stuff made from potatoes, so I want to drink some of the good booze for once!" she said, and then unleashed her very best puppy dog eyes.

"Fine, whatever. But just one, got it? I've got my own expenses, you know," I said, jingling my wallet to emphasize the point.

"Y-yeah, I got it, I got it. Just one beer. And maybe something to eat, too. Then I'll be out of your hair."

"Yeah, yeah. But teach me how to use wind magic next time as payment. Which, by the way, doesn't count for the other favor you now owe me."

"Fine by me—if you can learn to use it, that is."

Not that I really needed to buy her this beer for her to teach me—Nishka replaced Wak'wakogoro as my hunting instructor after he became leader of the hunters. It was more of a personal favor.

Without further ado, we headed to the bar adjoining the guild. I paid for our beers and some beef jerky, and then we sat ourselves at a table carved from a log.

The beer was crap. The stuff was room temperature—I mean, come on—and there were all sorts of impurities floating in it. Totally undrinkable. If only it tasted like some kind of German beer. I lived on lagers, maybe even Belgian beer if I felt fancy. Whatever this frothy concoction was, it wasn't any beer I was used to. It even had a cherry on top for some inexplicable reason.

"Damn, this is great!" Nishka roared, slamming down her glass. "It doesn't taste like grapes or potatoes at all!"

"Happy to hear it, I guess. Ah, hell, take mine."

"Seriously? Hell yeah!"

Nishka didn't hesitate for even a second before she took my beer and started guzzling as I chewed on a strip of the beef jerky. Even that didn't taste right. It tasted like...dried squid? The hell? What a letdown.

I grabbed the water bottle Nishka left on the table and took a gulp to clear my palate, but ended up spraying everywhere as I spit it out instead.

"This is potato vodka!"

Nishka wasn't called "Tipsy" for nothing.

After a while, Gimul joined our table, his own mug in hand.

"You finish everything?" I asked.

"Yeah. They pinned up a notice with all the people we're looking to recruit."

"Well that's good to hear. Are we heading back to the village,
then?"

"I'd like to, but I was told that we'd need our own branch of the
adventurer's guild in the village if we wanted to get serious about
building the place up."

"A new branch location in the village?"

"Mm. They said it would be more convenient having people
there already rather than sending people from town every time,
like what happened with the wyvern attack."

Gimul took a few gulps of his beer, wiping the foam from the
drink on his sleeve. We ignored Nishka, who (as always) crowed
about how great her drink tasted.

"We could end up running into more wyverns as the village
continues to develop," I said. "It happened to Cassandra's father,
too." I thought of a considerably more sober Nishka telling me
how villages developed and displaced wildlife, even butting heads
with them from time to time.

"Exactly," said Gimul. "That's where you come in."

"Huh?"

"My mother and late father spent the last thirty years building the foundation for the village, expanding it, putting *everything* into it. If we want to keep pushing, we'll need to recruit more people to come live in the village, and we'll need capable adventurers to protect them. But not just anyone will do."

"You want me to become an adventurer?"

"That's an option if the village chief gives the okay. More specifically, a warrior of your skill should conduct interviews for potential candidates."

"I see."

"By fighting 'em."

"Wait, what?" I exclaimed. Niska munched her beef jerky obliviously "Fighting who?"

"Them. Whoever you think might do. Pick a fight with somebody, see how they do. Simple."

"Simple?! Easy for you to say! These guys are adventurers!" I shouted. (Gimul took a couple swigs of beer.) "Listen, man, I don't even have the guts to try getting to second base with my wife! My hands? Completely unboobed. And you think I can just swagger on up to an adventurer and pick a fight? I'd be dead in no time flat! Nishka, back me up here!"

"Uh, listen bud, no matter how much you ask, don't you even *try* to feel me up! Not happenin'! You are *not* gonna touch these sweet puppies!"

Cool. Thanks for the help, Tipsy Nish!

Gimul shook his head. "What are you getting all scared for?

You beat me with nothing but a laundry pole. Just do that again. The people you're interviewing are going to be coming at you with everything they got, so all you've gotta do is take them down."

"You're serious? A friggin' laundry pole? Can I not use another weapon?"

"Nah. And don't you worry about hurting them. We can just get them healed up by the guild's priest while their wounds are still fresh."

Ah, shit. This was revenge for beating him up earlier, wasn't it?

"You're strong," he said, "I know that much. As the number one warrior in our village, I'm expecting some good things from you." Gimul grinned. The hell was *that* supposed to mean? I-believe-in-Shuta grin? I-can't-believe-I-get-to-see-ass-kicked-Shuta grin? Aw, hell.

There I was, standing alone with only a laundry pole in my hands.

"C'mon, let's do this!" shouted a bearded middle-aged guy with one of those fake fantasy-Viking vibes to him. He was naked from the waist up, rippling with muscle. Think of a pro-wrestler with a Thor-vibe and you're on the right track.

We stood in an open area behind the guild, me with my laundry pole, my opponent with a goddamn broadax. Just a tiny difference!

Not like my laundry pole will snap in half because this is a broadax meant for choppin' oh wait that's exactly what axes do never mind!

"All right!" Gimul shouted. "Go get 'em, Shooter!" Acting all innocent, like he had nothing to do with this! Like he couldn't be the one holding the laundry pole. And Nishka just kept pounding down beer, not helping at all.

"If you're not comin' to me," Thorwrestler roared, "then I'm comin' to you! Hraaagh!" He hoisted his broadax over his head and at once this hulking giant was bearing down on me.

Way back when, I worked as a trainer and sparring partner for an athlete at this one karate organization. The guy was a beast—he even competed on a national level—but training with him from dusk-till-dawn was a real pain in the ass. Sometimes literally. Here I was, this nobody who won third place in a regional tournament once, and I specialized in form over combat to boot.

Still, the fact that I was so diligent in my form meant that I stayed faithful to the basics. Comparing my own movements to a guy at the national level helped keep his techniques on point. Maybe it *was* the right choice for me to "interview" adventurers for our village, see what they were made of.

Wasn't hyped about the constant, horrible pain, though. I was so bruised and sore from sparring with that guy back in the day that I constantly needed special ointments to take care of the pain. I'm talking zoo-animal-strength stuff, that's how bad it got.

That was what worried me about this guy too, but the whole mess ended up super anticlimactic.

The adventurer was a hulking monster of a man, that much was true. His broadax was real, too. Considering his body type, he probably chose the weapon because he had the power to put his all into it, just like my own physique made long-handled weapons right for me.

But you can't just rely on power. His movements were rough and unrefined, and he was slow bringing his hips down for a strike. Watching carefully, I dodged his first attack.

"You trying to kill me?" I shouted.

That strike could've taken my arm clean off, so I was getting desperate quick. If I got scared I'd freeze up, so I told myself it was going to be all right—just fine, just keep telling yourself it'll be fine—and took a step forward to fight back.

Broadaxes are large-headed axes, and their long wooden handles give them a decent reach. If I could just get in close, he wouldn't be able to use the weight of the weapon to its full potential, halving the power behind his hits. Then I could sweep his legs and send him sprawling.

As I thought through my plan, my body acted on it. All that practice really stuck with me. I swung the pole for a wide sweep, stepped back, took another step forward. Right when it looked like I'd make another sweep, I jabbed the end straight into his stomach instead.

The adventurer let out a grunt of pain as I leaned into him with the full weight of my body, pinning him to the ground.

"Nice one, Shooter!" Nishka shouted gleefully, and she raised her mug in the air. "Looks like you're strong enough to live up to that warrior name after all!"

Ignoring her, I went to help the adventurer up.

"Oof, that stings. Thanks for the help."

"You did good. Try working on your footwork a bit more, it'll make it easier for you to switch up your tactics when you fight."

"Footwork, eh? Got it."

"Yup. It's the basis for using any kind of weapon, after all."

After finishing our small post-battle chat, I shook the man's hand. Guys like him were a dime a dozen, so I'd hold off on deciding whether to take him. Huh. Being an interviewer was kinda fun.

"Something like that?" I said, shooting a quick look at Gimul.

"Yeah. Next up is a girl who uses a rapier. You want to keep going with the pole?"

"A girl? Seriously? No, I'll switch to my shortsword, thank you very much."

From a giant of a man to a girl, eh? I didn't think there'd be too many female adventurers, given what I'd seen of the Vikings back at the village, but I suppose that was just me.

Right, so I was wrong to think she was going to look like a Valkyrie or something. Nah, we were looking at an Amazon. A really, *really* butch Amazon.

She had short hair, and though her body was slender, she had the build (and face) of a guy. Could've sworn I even saw a beard. And her chest might as well have been padding for her massive pecs!

"I just need to beat you to pass?" she asked.

"Try and go easy on me, if you would."

"Hmph. You really think you can take me down? You must be dreaming."

The words hardly left her mouth before she delivered a lightning-fast rapier thrust. She was light on her feet, weaving effortlessly between offense and defense. I hurried to get into the right stance to deal with her barrage of thrusts and slices.

A circle...that was it, I could think of a circle around her. When she came close, I took a step to keep myself in front and just a little to her side. If I kept circling just a little, I could dodge—

And her rapier came whizzing towards my vest.

"What, you not going to fight back?"

"Eep! Is *everyone* trying to kill me?"

"Listen, you keep running away and I'll slice those cruddy clothes of yours to shreds!"

"Like hell you will!"

Her rapier went for my throat, but she changed direction—just a feint. She aimed the tip of her sword at my stomach. I deflected it...right down to my loincloth, which scattered to pieces, just like she promised. Another goddamn piece of clothing ruined! Again! *Again!* "Wait, hold it!" I cried. "Time out!"

"What, you giving up?" she cackled. "You surrendered easier than I thought."

"No, not giving up. Just need a quick time-out so I can strip down, then I can go all out against you!"

Quickly I slipped out of my vest and loincloth. My wife lovingly wove me this underwear, and I'd be damned if I lost her gorgeous, vaguely sleazy handiwork.

"All right," I said, balling up my clothes. "*Now* I'm ready." I handed them to Nishka. She was already red from the alcohol, and now she was even redder. "Hurry up and take these away, Nishka. My opponent's waiting."

"Okay, yeah—but I don't get why you're handing me your friggin' underwear! You just took those off, man, they're all fresh with, uh, dick energy! Dickergy?"

"Yeah, yeah, just hurry."

I went to face my opponent once more, now much lighter, wearing only a red scarf and my shortsword.

"Sorry to keep you waiting. Now, bring it on!"

But Nishka wasn't the only one turning red. "Eeek! You pervert!"

Huh. City girls were a lot more sensitive than I thought.

And just like that, I'd faced off against the adventurers—all two of them. As we made our way back to the inn, Gimul and I discussed whether we should pick one or keep looking.

"Let me get this straight, Shooter, you're asking what we're looking for in an adventurer?"

"Right. If we just want someone strong, then that butch girl with the rapier, what's-her-face...?"

"Electra."

"Yeah, Electra, she was hardcore. I think she'd be the best."

Personally, I wasn't so sure about how we were measuring these guys. Fighting one-on-one was one thing. Fighting monsters around the village was something else entirely.

"Well if we're going by specific criteria," said Gimul, "then we would want to hire someone who won't cause trouble."

Nishka cut in, "Aren't all adventurers pretty rowdy?"

"I suppose you're right," Gimul grumbled. "But beggars can't be choosers."

I shrugged. "Those two were fairly civilized after I finished interviewing them, so I guess they wouldn't be so bad."

"True, though Electra seemed a little...jumpy after your fight," Gimul added. We were just about back to the Sound of Joy Inn. "I'll let those two know they passed come tomorrow. All that's left is to find a few other people we might be able to use."

"Got it. How much longer are we planning on staying in town? I'd like to buy a present to take back home to Cassandra."

"Yeah! It's only been a day since we got here, and I haven't done enough sightseeing yet!" Nishka sighed and sulked and generally made it blatantly clear that she wasn't ready to leave.

"I'll head back with the two adventurers," said Gimul. "You two can stay here a bit longer."

"Huh?"

"Like I said, make sure to prioritize finding adventurers. You won't just magically stumble upon new hunters and new residents for the village, so stick to recruiting from the guild. Just don't invite anyone suspicious, you hear me? Really ask yourself who would do well in our village."

"Y-yeah, of course."

"If you make any progress, use a messenger bird to let me know. They've got a coop at the guild."

"All right, but shouldn't I be guarding you?" I asked.

"I'll have those adventurers with me. There shouldn't be any problems."

Gimul handed me a heavy hide pouch. It was full of those silver Church coins, along with some other silver coins I didn't recognize.

"There's some money for your stay. If it's not enough, I'm sure you'll find a way to make some more. And if you turn in good work, the village chief will likely give you some kind of reward."

"Are you sure I can take this?"

"Just don't run away. I'll send people after you if you do."

I shivered, remembering Ossandra's plan for me to escape the village. This...complicated things.

"I won't."

Gimul then turned his attention to Nishka, who lazed at the entrance with her hands folded casually atop her head.

"What are you planning to do, Tipsy?"

"Think I'll go ahead and soak in the sights a bit more before I head back."

"What about money?"

"Shooter has some, right?"

"But Gimul said this was *my* pay..." She was going to mooch off me even more, then? Really?

"Figure out a way to pay for yourself," Gimul told her.

"What, why? This is discrimination! It's because I'm an elf, yeah? How come only Shooter gets some?"

"Those are public funds, Tipsy."

Nishka looked devastated. She trudged back to the room we shared as if I'd killed and ate her puppy. Well, let her whine all she wanted. I wasn't going to sympathize, and I *definitely* wasn't going to buy her a drink!

• • •

We all headed back to our rooms at the inn. Gimul got the nice spacious room that had a bed, desk and chairs, the whole shebang. Meanwhile, Nishka and I were stuck in a room the size of a shoebox with double-decker hammocks for beds. We didn't have the luxury of furniture. We didn't even have our own light outside of the open window; it let in the waning city noises of the early evening and just enough streetlight to see the floor.

"How do you wanna handle these hammocks?" asked Nishka. "I think I'll top!"

"Whatever, man. I'll be bottom if I gotta."

You know, with the hammocks and such. It's not weird. It's *not* weird.

Once upon a time, I lived at one of the restaurants I worked at. The veteran chefs always took the lowest bunks, since climbing up and down the tiny ladders was always a huge pain in the ass after a long day's work. Not to mention, if they went out drinking and got smashed, they couldn't even climb the things properly by the time they got back.

So yeah, of course the other chefs immediately requested the lower bunks whenever it came time to change rooms. That, or they'd claim it the instant another veteran chef left and their bunk was up for grabs.

The beds at the inn didn't even come with a ladder, and you had to hoist yourself up to the top bunk. Definitely easier for me to drink if I was bottom.

"Then I claim my rightful spot on top! Live your life with the knowledge that I've won and that I'm always looking down on you, Shooter! Mwa ha ha ha ha!"

"We had a saying back where I came from. 'Two things like high places: smoke and the stupid.'"

"Hold on, whaddya mean 'stupid'?"

"Oops, sorry. Maybe it was 'idiots'? Fools? Morons?"

"Making fun of *me*? The greatest wyvern-slayer Apegut's ever known? You *know* what they call me."

"Tipsy?"

"Mrrraaaaaaaghhhh!" Nishka bopped her fists against me in frustration. I just stood up, headed out to the hallway, grabbed the barrel of lukewarm water, and brought it inside.

"What the hell? Why are you taking off your clothes?"

"Because I'm gonna wash up."

Earlier, I paid the goblin at the front desk for a bathing set that included a clean cloth, a sponge, and water to wash myself with. I wasn't about to let the bathwater I paid for go to waste. I was always naked in the village, so there was no way it bothered her *that* much. Plus, I wanted to mess with Nishka a little.

"You're right," said Nishka. "We're gonna get sick if we don't use that water before it goes cold."

"Yeah...I mean, uh, what? Wh-what are you—?"

Because now Nishka was stripping along with me. She threw her vest onto the top hammock before sliding off her hot pants, then undid her blouse button—and by button I mean a small monster fang, whittled down to function as a button.

After undoing her blouse not-button, her hands suddenly stopped. Instead of continuing to take it off, she started on her panties. She just tossed 'em on top of her other clothes. Another thong. So that was just what everyone wore here, huh? How...interesting.

Finally, the blouse came off. *Boing.*

Now here we were, naked in the same room together.

"Sit down," said Nishka. "And I'll wash your back."

"B-but I have a wife."

"Mmhm. And now you'll get home all clean for her. Oh yeah, we should get you some new clothes in town before we leave."

"Yeah, some new clothes for me and a present for Cassandra. But um, right now...I mean, is this really okay? This isn't exactly chaste, ya know?"

"Just sit your ass down already! The water's gonna go cold."

There weren't any chairs in our tiny room, so I sat on the edge of the barrel, gritting my teeth and bearing it as the hard wood dug into my butt. When Nishka lifted up her arms to fasten her hair with a pin, I got an eyeful of her armpits—and the forest of hair there. Looks like people in this world didn't shave their underarm hair...and, well, damn, I guess I was developing a new fetish.

"You're on your own washing your front," she said.

"Yeah, uh, I got it."

I wrung the water out of the sponge and handed it over to Nishka. She started scrubbing.

"Um." I swallowed. "You're going awful gentle on me. If you keep that up, I'll, like...feel *good*, you know?"

"Well, duh. Everyone feels good after getting clean. You're just gonna have to put up with it if it tickles."

"And why are you just focusing on the same spot?"

"To get all the dirt off, doofus. Your back is stupid huge though, Shooter."

"Well, yeah. That's just a guy thing, right?"

Thank goodness the room was dark. Would've gotten way too excited if it was brighter...but then again, things were already getting pretty wild down there, and maybe that was *because* it was dark.

I wondered if this was the norm in this world. I'll admit it—I never spent time messing around with girls I didn't know too well back in my world. You shouldn't play around with women, honestly, and entertaining "friends" seemed expensive to boot. Part-timers like me didn't have that kind of money.

"All right," she said—and I heard a quick splish—"time to switch. I scrub your back, you scrub mine."

"You sure? I mean, I'll do my best and all, but—"

"'Course I'm sure. After all I did for you, you're not gonna scrub my back? C'mon, man."

I turned around, and there they were: Nishka's hulking knockers in the dimness of the room. The accursed darkness—I raged against it, raged I say! Even if I wasn't quite sure...

"Nishka, what is this, even? I've never even touched my wife, and yet here I am washing your back." Up and down, up and...down...

"Nah, this stuff's normal. It's not like we're doing anything lewd, and anyway, you're the one who walks around naked all the time."

"Y-you've got me all wrong! I don't wanna be naked, I just wanna see naked! Women, that is!"

When I finished washing Nishka's back, we dipped our feet into the water and started to scrub them clean.

Then came the knock. I could hardly prepare before it flew open and whoever it was saw the both of us, completely naked! Which, I mean, was fine for me, but—but Nishka!

I panicked and turned to see the intruder—what kind of ass would be so lacking in any semblance of privacy?

"G-Gimul?!"

"Hey. I need a word with you, Shooter."

"Yo, Gimul. We're in the middle of a bath right now, so if you'll just give us a minute...?"

"Sure. Come to my room when you're finished."

The door creaked shut, and Gimul left the room as if nothing at all had happened.

"Y-you don't think he's got the wrong idea about us, do you?" I stammered. "I have a wife, after all."

"I don't get it. Is there some kind of problem?"

"Of course there is! How could there not be?!"

Overwhelmed, just thoroughly done, I jumped out of the barrel and hurried to get my clothes back on.

● ● ●

With my surreal bath extravaganza behind me, I went to visit Gimul's room. I couldn't say what time it was, exactly, since there were no clocks I knew of in this world, but my gut told me that since the sun had set about an hour or two ago, it was probably around eight in the evening. I knocked.

"Enter," came a reply from the other side, so inside I went.

"Hey there."

"I've been waiting for you."

"Erm. I'm sorry you had to see that earlier."

"You walk around in the nude all the time. I didn't think you could get embarrassed."

"I just felt a little, uh, guilty about the whole thing, I suppose," I said, and awkwardly shut the door behind me.

Gimul hunched over a small desk, on top of which was a candle and some paper.

"I was writing something to give to the guild."

"Up writing this late? How exhausting. Is it about those two adventurers we're accepting?"

"No, we can just tell them in person. Take a seat," said Gimul, gesturing at the bed. I sat myself down and listened.

"This is a recommendation letter for you to give to the guild."

"Huh? Don't we need the village chief's permission first?"

"If you're staying here, you need a way to make money. If you're going to be recruiting adventurers, I figured it would be better for you to experience what it's like to be one. I'll be sure to tell the village chief as well, so no need to worry about that."

"Yeah, that makes sense. Thanks for doing all this."

"Letters are how small communities like our village stay in contact with the guild. I'm used to it."

Gimul handed me the sheet. Considering this was a fantasy world, I kind of expected it to be written on sheepskin or whatever, but it was more like some crappy recycled paper made out of hemp. In fact, I think it was somehow even worse quality than recycled paper.

I remembered reading somewhere that the process to make papyrus back in Egypt was too complicated for it to be mass-produced, so I wondered what this could even be.

There was something else I noticed as I looked at the words on the paper.

"I can't read this. What does it say?"

"It says that I'm leaving a hunter named Shooter and a girl named Nishka in the guild's care, and that they're both away on work. As such, they'll need a way to earn money for themselves while they're here in Bulka. I'm really putting my reputation on the line here for you, you realize, so make sure you don't do anything stupid."

"Y-yeah, of course. We'll be sure not to cause any trouble for you," I said with a nervous smile. "Actually, since you're headed back and all, I was hoping you would pass on a message to my wife for me."

"Hm? Let's hear it, then."

"But, erm...can she read?" I asked, fidgeting uncomfortably.

"You don't even know that about your own wife? Of course she can't read."

"We *are* just newlyweds, after all..."

"Tch. Illiterate hicks, the both of you."

204

Despite the vitriol in his words, Gimul took out a new piece of paper and dipped his pen in the inkwell on his desk before turning back to me.

"Tell me what you want to say. I'll write it for you."

"B-but she can't read, right?"

Gimul sighed. "I'll read it for her. Just talk already."

Back and forth between being supportive and snarky. If Gimul were a girl, the hot-and-cold routine would be a little cute, but come on.

"All right." I cleared my throat. "'Dear Cassandra, I hope all is well with you. Bulka is a regular metropolis, dotted with faint midnight streetlamps, and though the city can overwhelm the senses and leave one flailing in uncertainty, at times I recall the comfort that your magnificent cooking brings me after a hard day's work. Upon Gimul's orders, I have agreed to stay longer here, so—'"

"Too long. Paper is precious. Shorter."

"O-okay..."

"Now."

To my beloved wife: My stay here is going to be longer than I expected. I want to see you again, but this is part of my duty to the village.

"How's that? Ha. Ha?"

"'S'all right."

"Good. I'm going to buy her a present tomorrow, so could you give it to her when you read it out? What do you think would make a good souvenir?"

"Ask Nishka."

Gimul set the letter aside for the ink to dry, then pulled out a bottle of booze.

"Now, then. I said I needed a word with you."

"Y-yeah? What is it?"

Gimul looked so profoundly serious. Freaked me out. I was half expecting him to tell me how he'd always hated me or something. I mean, sometimes it felt like he had it out for me ever since I arrived, and that he might not have been happy about me catching the village chief's eye. Now would be the perfect time for him to make that clear.

"Drink?"

"Sure."

"I took your wine back then. I'm sure you recall. Well, this is my apology. Drink as much as you want."

"Yeah, I remember. I just figured we were even after you got hit in the face."

"We both know that wasn't enough."

He offered the bottle of wine to me. It would be rude not to take him up on the offer. I wasn't used to this world's beer yet, so crappy wine with stuff floating in it suited me just fine.

As Gimul watched me drink, he began to speak. "Our village has grown over the course of thirty backbreaking years thanks to my father, and then due to the efforts of my mother after his passing."

"Yeah, I remember hearing something about that."

"As long as things stay the course, it'll either be me or one of my siblings who take the reins and continue that work."

"Yeah, that seems about right. You have siblings, Gimul?"

"I don't...for now. It may not always be that way."

"Huh? I'm sorry if this comes off as rude, but isn't the village chief..." I swallowed, made myself finish the sentence, "infertile?"

"Did my mother tell you that?"

I shrunk back from Gimul's withering glare. The goblin from the trading company said it earlier, and Wak'wakgoro knew about it, too, so I thought it was fairly common knowledge. Gimul's face hardened when I looked away from him.

"That damn apeman couldn't keep his mouth shut, could he?"

I examined my hands.

"Doesn't matter," said Gimul finally. "What does matter is that it isn't the truth. My mother probably spread that rumor herself to keep potential suitors away."

"So you're saying that she can actually have children?"

Gimul snorted. "Of course she can. If she couldn't, she could've just gone to the church to be healed." He paused. Took a drink, let out a long sigh.

"Let me be frank with you. I hate outsiders."

What could I say?

He continued. "The village was where I was raised, and the villagers there were my family. Outsiders have only ever sought to steal that away from us." He spoke with a quiet fury. I could only imagine what could have happened to him to fuel that rage.

"My mother is still young," he said, "and so there were other governors. Other village chiefs, all trying to court her. There was even an idiot that called himself a 'knight' who tried to get in close. I disposed of that vulture."

Gimul may have been an amateur at sword-fighting, but he was still absolutely ripped. Some fake knight would've been nothing.

"So," I said, swallowing dryly. "That's why you were so wary of me?"

"I do feel sorry for that. You were just, what, some naked man wandering around back then?"

"Yeah, and just wandering aimlessly around the forest..."

"Shooter, I won't tell you to help me. I don't know if you would. What I want is for you to help my mother. There's no one I love or respect more than my parents. *We* have to be the ones to build up the village, and I have no intention of letting anyone else have it."

And there we go, there's that Oedipus complex. But hey, I could hardly blame him—she was a quick-witted and gorgeous woman, and still probably more like his older stepsister than mother.

He wanted me to help her, huh? What was I even good at? Hunting, maybe. Teaching karate? I squirmed under Gimul's intense gaze, when all of a sudden—

"Hey, doofshit, really? If you really wanna help out your mom, then get yerself a wife! Make a grandkid or two or nine or whatever, ah hell!"

There she was, flinging the door open, waltzing in—Tipsy Nish, flushed to hell and back and back again to hell a few more times. She was in full-on casual mode, wearing nothing but her yellowed blouse and panties.

"Wh-what are you saying?" Gimul roared. "And why are you here? This is a man-to-man conversation!"

"Maybe you'd do better with the wifin' if you got that stick outta your ass! Yo, Shooter! This is a guinea pig dumpling I got from the restaurant downstairs. And beer, too!"

Paid for by who? Was that all on her tab, with me footing the bill?!

Nishka brought her spoils from the restaurant over to the bed and plonked herself down on it.

"Y'all," she groaned, "are being unfair. Leaving me out of all the fun? You gotta invite me if you're drinking!"

Gimul shook his head. "Tipsy Nish, eh?"

"Shut it! Do you wanna apologize to Shooter, or do you want him to help you? Stop pussyfooting around and make up your mind, damn it!"

Nishka winked at me and flashed a smile. A...wink. Hold up, what about that eye patch? Didn't she have an eye patch?

"What happened to your eye patch, Nishka? Are you, uh. Cleaning...it?"

"Heh. I guess so, eh. I washed it when cleaning my face, then left it out to dry. Who cares about that, though?"

"I do, a little."

"Never mind that, look at this muscley doofus!" Nishka curled into herself, screaming with laughter. "Aww no! I sure hope nobody bangs my hot mom! Better turn that into my entire motivation forever! Holy shit, what a drooling hyperdweeb, how can he even take himself seriously? What a loser, goddamn!"

It was hard to describe just how unhappy Gimul looked as Nishka mocked him. Every time she laughed, her bountiful bosom bounced along with her, and she tried to wrap her arms around me, too...

And just like that, the three of us spent our first night in town drinking together in the candlelight until the break of dawn.

• • •

It had been a while since I pulled an all-nighter, and in a fantasy world no less. Candles, firewood, and lanterns were all valuable commodities here, so usually I'd just eat dinner and get ready for bed as soon as the sun went down back in the village.

I had been hitting the booze hard last night, but I somehow managed to wake up when the sun came up...though I think I was the only one who managed that.

I rose to the smell of burning dried herbs coming from a corner of the room. Incense wasn't anything too fancy in this world, since it was just a way to keep bugs away. The ingredients to make them were pretty much the same as what you would find in one of those mosquito-repellant coils.

As I stretched out and yawned in my cramped hammock bed, I heard my body pillow mumble something next to me. Wait, my... my what?

Sure, the thing was soft and comfortable enough for me to fall right back asleep—but the problem was, the Sound of Joy Inn didn't provide a body pillow.

That soft sensation? It was Nishka. Or, to be more specific, one of her boobs.

I tumbled out of the hammock, crying out without thinking. "Why are we sleeping in the same bed?" Not a bed, just a hammock, but my brain was all over the place and, *Oh god how was this why were we what did I gahhhh...*

I mean yeah, okay, I helped Nishka back to our room because she was drunk out of her mind, and somehow even managed to get her into the top bunk. I even remembered throwing a raggedy blanket over her. But hey, Nishka, why the hell was *Nishka* in the bottom bunk?

"Hey, Shooter! Gimme one more shot, will ya? Just...one...more...mh..."

Even in her dreams, Nishka was still drowning herself in booze. She flipped over, taking up all that space I left after getting up out of bed, her leg dangling off the side.

Taking another look around the room, I saw that our bathroom pot was nearly overflowing. Nishka had most likely gotten up to use the toilet in the middle of the night, then crawled into bed with me after she finished.

Hmm. Here I was with a pretty girl, maybe with a *chance* with that pretty girl, and...I hadn't taken that chance, had I? I mean, I was a newlywed and hadn't even shared a bed with Cassandra. I hadn't let my libido get the better of me...right?

Nope. Underwear still on. I was in the clear.

I sighed, grabbed my vest and loincloth off the bed, and got dressed.

"Jeez," I muttered, mostly to myself, "you sure know how to scare me first thing in the morning. You keep playing with me like that and I actually will make a move on you sometime. Can't keep holding myself back forever."

"Pssh. Sure you will, ya coward...blugh..."

Oh no, had she heard me? My heart skipped a beat, but the next moment her mouth was hanging open and she was snoring away.

I was only half-joking there, but it was true that for a wyvern-slayer, Nishka looked more like a hard-partying slob. She had a few of the eye patches she washed yesterday hanging off the top bunk, as well as her panties.

Speaking of her eye patch, I remembered seeing both her eyes practically sparkling last night as we drank together. Maybe she only wore it for fashion's sake, or maybe she really was an over-grown junior high edgelord. Who knew?

At that moment, there was a knock on the door and Gimul pushed his way inside.

"You're up? Good. We're going to the adventurer's guild."

He wore the same tunic as always. He had a knapsack slung over his shoulder packed with all the things he needed for his trip back home and his sword hung from his waist.

"Nishka's still asleep, though."

"And how useful she'd be. No, she can stay here. We're going to the guild to find those adventurers, then we're going to do some shopping."

"Gotcha. I'll leave my stuff here, then."

"Make sure to tell the counter you're going to be staying longer before we leave. You need to pay up front."

Gimul and I made our way to the front of the inn to pay up, then set off for the adventurer's guild.

It had only been about an hour since sunrise, but the townspeople were already becoming a crowd. People set up vegetable stalls, meat and fish stalls, even a few chicken cages. We dodged between carts and wagons, cutting through the throngs before reaching the guild.

"I'd like to hire the two adventurers who the guild introduced me to yesterday," Gimul told the person at the counter, "can you put me in touch with them? One of them is a woman named Electra, and the other's a man called Dyson."

I was hoping to take the letter he wrote me and get my adventurer registration done while he talked on and on, but I remembered that Nishka wasn't there with me. Might as well wait till later, I supposed.

"Dyson and Electra? Those two always show up sometime in the morning. I'm sure they'll be in soon, so I'll tell them to wait here if I see them."

"Please do. We'll be running a few errands, but we'll be back in a few."

"Understood. Then I'll be sure to pass on your message."

"Thanks."

With that done, Gimul called me over.

"Do you think we can find a good souvenir this early in the morning? I want to get something Cassandra will really like."

"The craftsmen start pretty early, so it shouldn't be a problem."

After we left the guild, we took a different road that led away from all the food stalls. This street was lined with all sorts of odd stalls selling bits and baubles, including makeup.

"You seem to know where all the good stuff is, Gimul."

"My mother asked me to get her souvenirs before."

"Ever the loving son, I see. I think the best gift you could get her would be finding a wife and grandkids."

"Shut it," he barked at me, and blushed as he gazed at the ground.

Heh. I'd feel the same way if my parents didn't already have grandkids, but I wasn't gonna say that out loud. See, the older of my two younger sisters had already married. She wasn't planning on having children for a while, so that did worry me just a bit. She and her husband were both going to save up a little first. I didn't even have a plan, and here she was saving for her future. Good for her!

Wow, that bummed me the hell out. I decided to take a look down the rows of shops to get it off my mind.

"A hand mirror, maybe?"

There were some covered in decorations, others simpler but far more polished, and all manner in between. Our house didn't have any kind of mirror in it, since we didn't really need one. But hey, Cassandra was a girl, so maybe it'd be nice for her?

How long had it even been since I picked out a present for a girl? I reached into my coin pouch and told the girl at the stall which one I wanted. At two silver Church coins, it wasn't exactly cheap, but I was willing to splurge a little for Cassandra.

"Decided on something?" Gimul asked me when I came back.

"Yeah, I bought this hand mirror for her."

"Pricey. You gonna be all right, money-wise?"

"I should have about two silver coins left from what the village chief gave me. I'll have to find a way to earn enough money to buy my own clothes, though, especially when I have inn fees to consider."

I handed the mirror to Gimul as I counted out my cash. The mirror had a tortoiseshell design to it, and while it may have seemed a bit plain to me, I wasn't from this world. Cassandra didn't wear the fanciest or most stylish clothes, and we didn't have much, but what she wore looked great on her all the same. Plain didn't matter so much.

Yeah, we were forced together by the village chief. But I wanted it to work. I wanted to trust one another, to care for one another, to build something worth having.

But what I really wanted was to get Ossandra out of the back of my mind.

After meeting up with the two adventurers at the guild, the four of us swung by the village wagon before heading to the gates of the city.

"I'm counting on you to recruit more adventurers," said Gimul. "If anything happens, send a message by carrier pigeon."

"You got it. Electra, Dyson, I'm leaving Gimul in your capable hands."

Electra beamed. "Of course, honey. I might not be as strong as you, but I'm pretty confident I can handle myself in a fight."

"Yeah," Dyson added. "The only things we might have to worry about are kobolds on the way there, but we can handle them."

I took a deep breath. "Gimul, please pass on my best wishes to my wife. It's important to me."

"Will do."

"And give her the souvenir I bought her ASAP, okay?"

"Ah, can it, ya corny old sap," Gimul grinned as he cut me off.

After saying my goodbyes to them all, we finally parted ways. On my own, I decided to head back to the inn for now.

It was probably somewhere around nine in the morning, and there were even more people in the streets than before. In an effort to avoid the crowds, I went down a back alley Gimul and I had taken earlier.

This place had a "red light district" kind of vibe to it, and there were barely any people around so early in the morning. Empty, filthy wine casks were littered here and there, as well as boxes piled full with rotting vegetable scraps. The only people I saw were guys who looked like they'd been out drinking until morning, and girls of a certain "profession" hanging around. It didn't exactly feel like the safest place in the world, but at least I had my sword at my side.

Once upon a time, I used to work as an assistant manager for a strip club at a sketchy red light district not too different from this one. The manager usually took two days off a week, and I'd cover for him.

There were a couple reasons I was hired. One was because of my customer service background, and another was because of my experience with karate. I was pretty sure they picked me because they thought I could handle any customers who got violent.

My first night on the job, there was this young guy who was kind enough to pick up another customer's dropped wallet and try to give it back. The older man he tried to return it to shouted that the nice guy stole it from him and sent the poor dude flying with a punch, then had the gall to demand his punching bag pay *him* for the trouble he caused. This all happened five minutes into my very first shift. Someone called the cops, I got questioned about the whole thing—it was a big mess. It was a crazy experience, no doubt about it, but all that had happened back in my old world, not here.

While I was lost in thought reminiscing, I bumped shoulders with a group of guys I could have easily taken to be a bunch of street thugs. The impact caused one of them to drop some kind of vase onto the ground. Ugh, looked like a bunch of drunks out early in the morning.

Despite what I thought of them, I immediately started bowing out of reflex.

"I'm sorry about that. I'll be more careful next time."

"The hell you think you're doing, asshole?" one snarled. "You're dead, you hear me?"

Though I kept bowing, I made sure not to take my eyes off him and his other goon friends. There were five of them total, all adventurers wearing chainmail armor. The one I bumped into dropped the vase he held, which now lay shattered on the ground. Anything could've been inside that...

Stopping to look at the vase was a huge mistake. The yelling man swung his fist faster than I could see, catching me square on the chin.

Out cold.

Even in Town,
the Shunning Continues

As I woke—gradually, achingly—I found myself inside a jail cell. Which was becoming a little too common, if you ask me. I was in a stone room, iron bars blocking my view of the hallway. At least I wasn't in shackles like back in the stone tower in the village. The only problem was, I was completely naked. They'd taken all of my stuff. Once again, I was back to being treated like livestock in a cage. At least I picked up a nice present for my wife before being beaten senseless. Little blessings.

I sat myself cross-legged on the ground, gingerly touching my swollen chin.

First off, where was I? Nothing I could see gave me the barest hint. The most I could make out were a few rows of cells across from me, all exactly like mine. I could also hear the whimpering and groans of what sounded like...elderly people?

This was bad. Really, really bad.

I pulled myself toward the bars to take another look around

219

and saw a goblin in the cell directly across from me. He wore dirty rags and was sprawled out on the ground, asleep. He barely lifted his head when he noticed me staring, going right back down. Were these guys slaves or something?

I released my grip on the bars. Light streamed through the small window behind me, so at least I knew the sun was still up. It couldn't have been more than a few hours since I got beat up by the street thug, unless a whole day had passed already.

No use thinking about it now. I took a page out of my goblin cellmate's book and laid down to conserve energy. I didn't want to waste my strength and end up paying for it the next day. I didn't even know if they were going to give me food or water!

All of this because I'd been too hungover to watch where I was going. What a valuable lesson in moderation.

A rusty metal door creaked open somewhere out in the stone hallway. Someone was here.

I stayed still, listening. From what I could tell, there were about four someones total. The way a few of them walked...I knew that sound. Toe to heel, toe to heel. A telltale sign of experience with martial arts. There were probably adventurers among them, too.

"Get up. ...Boss, this one's still sleepin'."

"Throw some water and wake him up."

"Yes, sir."

I didn't have time to speak up before a bucketful of water splashed over me. I wanted to scream, curse somebody out, do *something*, but I managed to restrain myself. God, though, I was starting to get pissed off about this godawful morning.

If I continued to lay still, someone was bound to unlock the door and try to force me to get up.

"What should I do with him? He ain't movin'."

"Pull him out!"

There was a rattling sound as someone fumbled with the lock on the door before it finally creaked open. Someone came toward me. Judging by their footsteps, it was an adventurer. They grabbed me by the arm. "Wake the hell up!" the guy shouted.

They delivered a hefty kick to my ass, but I latched onto his arm and dug in with my hand. A hit to the ass is rough, but I'd manage. I used my assailant's arm as leverage, pulled myself up, and slammed my head straight into his chin.

"Gah! Bastard!"

"Payback's a bitch, ain't it?"

My head was pounding from the headbutt, but revenge pulled me through. I sent the guy flying out of my cell with one good sideswipe kick. Three other men waited outside the cell, probably comrades of Chinsmash McJerkass. One of them wore an expensive-looking red vest, while the other two were adventurers wearing chainmail armor.

One of the adventurers caught up with the guy I sent flying out, a guy who looked pretty familiar.

"Hey, I remember you," I said. "You're the one who knocked me out."

"Y-you asshole! I'm gonna cut your ass up!" he shrieked, drawing his blade.

"Aww, you giving up on fists now?"

Then I realized this adventurer was completely bald, with the lanky build of a Chinese movie star and the fighting style of a lightweight boxer. Ah, shit.

"Nupchakan, sir, I'm afraid I'm gonna have to kill him."

"Wait. I wish to speak with him, first. Don't forget, this man's valuable property."

"Heh fine. I'll only beat him *half* to death. You ready for this, asshole?"

I ignored his caustic words and thought over how I'd deal with him. I was a self-defense instructor at one point, so I still remembered the basics when it came to disarming a guy with a knife, at least.

"All right, bring it on. I'm buck naked, so why don't you get on my level? Get out of those clothes and let's go." No idea why I said that, but. He...did?

"Fine, you're on!" The guy actually took the time to remove his armor before trying to come punch me. If he wasn't pissed before, he sure was now. But he was slow. There was no point trying to drag this out, so I aimed straight for the guy's heart. He came at me with another hook, just like the first time. I prepared myself to take the hit as I launched a punch of my own right into his sternum. That'd definitely be enough to throw his pulse out of whack and slow him down.

I drove my fist home, and his punch barely grazed my head. I was just a step closer than him, so I got my hit in without having to take one in kind. Baldy went down. His two friends jumped into the cell and...

It was over for me in an instant. Karate practitioners fight one-on-one, but adventurers just gang up on people. They beat me up for a bit before making me prostrate myself before the guy in the expensive red vest.

"Kneel before Mister Nupchakan, asshole." Another kick, with a spit to go with it.

"Seems like we have ourselves quite the lively one," said the guy in red. "Good work."

"Thank you, sir. I never expected him to start swinging while still in the cell, though."

"Is he some kind of adventurer?"

"From what we could see from his belongings, he's a hunter from a remote village who came here to make a living. There's supposed to be a girl with him as well, so, hey. Fresh meat, ya know?" He grinned wolfishly.

"I see, I see. If he stays this lively, he's going to make us a quite a bit. That pretty girl will make us even more. We have to ensure we do it in accordance with the law, however."

Oh, the *law*. How nice. These scumbags were hunting for people to make into slaves according to the *law*. Bunch of assholes throwing people into cells.

"What's your name?" the man in the red vest asked me.

"It's Shooter." I was used to giving a quick bow whenever someone asked me that question, so I ended up blurting out my name on accident. The man stooped down to my level, lifting my chin.

"My name," he said, "is Lutbayasky Nupchsay Nupchakan. Do you understand that? Hm?"

Oh no. No, that was…there was no way I had to remember *that*, right? "Lutbayasky…?"

The bald man picked himself up off the floor, sputtering and coughing, and dealt a vicious a kick to my stomach.

"That's *Mister* Lutbayasky Nupchsay Nupchakan!" Oh, that one was nasty. I started tallying people to pay back for all this, with baldy racing to the top of the list.

"It seems," said Lutbavasky, "you were the one who broke my precious vase, were you not?"

"Who knows?" I answered.

I remembered the bald guy dropping a small vase when I accidentally bumped into him, but it hadn't looked fancy. Then again, I had no experience with how much things cost in this world, so really, who knew? What I did know was that these guys were pulling the same scam you'd find in my old world, where people purposefully bumped into you, dropped something that was supposed to be "priceless," and made you pay for it.

"I was quite fond of that vase, I'll have you know. I practically had to beg the merchant to part with it; it was as dear to him as it was to me. That particular vase was worth a whole ten gold coins, but to me…why, it was worth even more."

"Oh, certainly." Like hell. That thing was probably only a few bronze coins at best. You could find crap like it at the dollar store! That was just the way this scam worked, though. I had no idea how much things were worth in this world, so couldn't even figure out the actual value.

"I shall ask you once more: You were the one who broke my vase, were you not?"

I was at a loss for words. It was kind of true that I was the one who broke it, but it wasn't my fault. I hadn't tried to break it on purpose. These guys, though...they almost seemed happy to have lost the "priceless" piece of trash.

If I said yes here, Lutbayasky would hold it over my head and make me pay through the nose to compensate him.

"Say it. If you don't, it could spell trouble for that lovely young girl you came with. Oh, what was her name? Perhaps we should ask her. So talkative. So...loud."

There we were, then. I was trapped on all sides, and there was no wriggling out. On top of that, they were threatening to drag Nishka into this.

"I suppose it's true."

"Then I'd like to ask you to compensate me for my loss. Ten coins would fill the hole in my heart."

"W-well, unfortunately, I don't happen to have that kind of money. Not that I can't get it! I was just about to become an adventurer, so if you can wait a bit I'll just pay you back."

"Ah, I would love to believe you, but there are so many dreadful people out there who have used that exact same excuse to run away from their debts," Lutbayasky said with a thin smile. "You possess no form of identification, and only a few silver coins to your name. Judging by your entry papers, I would say you aren't even a citizen of Bulka."

"That's true, I'm not."

"Your other belongings were a sword and a letter of recommendation to the guild, which stated you were a hunter. Am I incorrect?"

"No, that's right. I'm only a fledgling hunter, but before that I was a, uh...a warrior."

That was what everyone else called me, at least.

"You are *not* an adventurer, then?"

"I'm not, no. This all happened before I could register as one." I offered a feeble laugh. If I'd actually registered, the guild might have been able to help me out of this jam.

Lutbayasky took out my money pouch and played with it, listening to the jingle of silver.

"Th-those are public funds from the village. You can't take them. The village chief will kill you."

"Are they really, now? It's so easy to come up with excuses. I hear them all day. Sometimes I write them in a little book. I'm afraid you have no way to prove your claims, so I'll just have to assume that these are fantasies of yours and take these coins as a down payment. With that said and done, how exactly do you plan on compensating me for my vase now, hmm? This silver will, unfortunately, be insufficient."

I glowered at him. That "vase" was probably as precious as a pickle jar back in my world. Probably cheap as a damn chamber pot. I needed to think up an excuse. Something, anything that could get me out of this situation. They were talking about slaves earlier, so I knew where it would go if I didn't—

"Well, lucky for you, I just so happen to have a proposition."

Of course he did. Hmm, I wonder what *that* might be.

"Yes?"

"What do you say to paying off your debt with your own body? Buyers adore a lively, punchy lad like you."

"Th-that can't be legal."

"It can. It *is*. If you lack the funds to pay, you sell your body to acquire funds. Did your little village not have slave labor?"

"No, we had actual human decency. I don't think you'd get it."

"What a cute, happy little village."

Yeah, so happy when wyverns slaughtered our people. There wasn't enough help to go around, either, so if we really got into this Class-A awful messed-up institution, I guess we'd be more in the business of buying slaves than selling them.

Lutbayasky sneered at me. "If you gallantly refuse to become a slave, then I suppose the debt must fall on the girl that came with you, yes?"

Like hell. "Unfortunately for you, we ended up separated once we arrived in town. I was looking for her when I happened to run into your pack of oafs—I mean, adventurers."

"Oh? Is that so?"

"Oh yeah. A-and she isn't even a big fan of me, even though we're from the same village. She's a cold one, so! Sorry! Wouldn't do a thing to help me, ha ha."

Lutbayasky scrutinized me, and I yammered on. I didn't want to drag Nishka into any of this, but I was more afraid of news getting back to the village and causing trouble for Cassandra.

This was probably all part of Lutbayasky's plan to make me give in—just keep me freaked out, talking and justifying and lying till I wore down.

And it worked.

"All right, fine. Make me into a slave. I'll pay back what I owe with my body."

I had no choice. These guys had to be pros at hunting down people from the countryside to turn into slaves. Nishka didn't even know any other places outside of Apegut, so I could easily see her getting forced into slavery as well, or even ending up captured by the authorities if she made a scene.

"Then the deal is struck. I shall provide a slave contract as proof you agreed to compensate me for my vase. Sign right here, if you would."

"Sorry, never learned how to goddamn read."

"No need for that. All I require is your thumb."

One of the other adventurers dug his hands into my wrist, dragged my right hand up and cut my thumb open before pressing it against the parchment. A deal sealed in blood. I forced a smile at Lutbayasky as he waved the contract in my face. And then he was done with me.

"He's all yours."

"You damn country hick!" The adventurer smashed his foot into my face with a kick, and once again, I was out like a light.

"Lucky you, we already found a customer willing to buy you."

They woke me with another bucketful of water. Groggily I

remembered Cassandra's mirror—I could only imagine just how handsome I looked after my latest beating.

I was in chains, thanks to the ruckus I caused. They dragged me out of my cell now, forcing me down the hall and outside. I could feel the stares from my fellow slaves as my captors led me. Weird that I was selling so quickly, what with me showing up so recently. All the others, who'd been imprisoned so much longer than me, stared back with looks of heartbreaking pity.

When I made it outside to an open yard, the guards dumped yet another huge bucket of water over me. They kicked me to the ground and cleaned me off with mops. Then they tied me to a pillar and had someone forcibly shave off my beard. My body wasn't even dry before they dragged me to a room to meet my lucky buyer.

Back when I was registered at a temp agency, I used to work a job where I lugged packages around all day at different distribution centers. They held onto packages briefly before sending them to their final destination, and I ended up working a lot of yearly holiday rushes.

No one got paid well, but you couldn't complain about it. Try, and the company would file their own complaint with the temp agency and get you fired.

One time on the way back from that center, I stopped at a nearby bar to grab a drink. There I saw someone from the temp agency and a manager from the distribution company drinking together. I'll never forget what that guy from the temp agency said then:

"That's where the real cash is—selling people. Human trafficking. Not those idiots who break the law, there's a perfectly legal form. Just start a damn temp agency."

The sentiment sent chills down my spine. It was true. And here in this world Lutbayasky must've been making a killing with his own legalized slavery. He'd take people like me—without papers, easily lost, unable to compensate him for his trash-vase, and turn us into money.

The amount I owed him wasn't actually that high, if you looked at the big picture. It was like taxes or rent or anything with interest in my old world—never that bad when you step back. But since I couldn't pay him even the relatively small sum of ten gold, here I was. A slave, auctioned and sold.

"So this is the slave warrior you told me about?" a high-pitched voice said from behind me. "He seems pretty strong, I'll give you that. I'm a bit concerned about those injuries, though I suppose Ganjamary should be able to fix him up."

A girl? Or maybe a kid? I couldn't see them, but maybe they were a different species altogether. Whatever they were, I was pretty sure that voice belonged to my potential buyer.

Since one of Lutbayasky's lackeys was forcing my head down, the customer was the one to come to me. They leaned over and peeked down at my face.

"What's your name, Mr. Slave?" A girl *and* a kid.

● ● ●

Yeah, the buyer was a tiny little kid gazing curiously at me. Her eyes were blue sapphires, and wavy blonde hair fell down her back. Her ears were pointed ever so slightly, just like Alexandricia's. She wore a dress that was held up by a knot tied right at her chest.

If she was here to buy a slave worth at least ten gold coins, she must belong to the higher echelons of society.

"M-my name is Shooter." I was bowing and scraping again before I knew it. "Pleased to meet you, master."

"I like this one! I'm Yoi'hady Jumei."

I'm sure you love those unpronounceable goblin names just as much as I do. She was about the size of a human child, but that was probably the goblin blood in her. In that regard, she looked like the polar opposite of the village chief.

"A pleasure to make your acquaintance, um…Miss Yoi? Please purchase me, if it pleases you."

"That's Miss Yoi'hady Jumei, dirtbag!" the bald adventurer screamed at me. "Can't you get that into your thick skull?"

Look, any name with a random apostrophe is going to make your life just a little harder. God, these fantasy names were going to be the death of me. I blamed Frank Herbert.

"It's fine," said Yoi, "I don't really mind. Where are you from, Mr. Slave?"

"From, um…the countryside…"

I couldn't just blurt out that I came from another world, she would think I was nuts. You've got to make a good impression with an interview, and I'd much rather be owned by a well-off goblin over Lutbayasky. Not only that, but I was dealing with a little girl. I might even find a way to escape if the opportunity presented itself. I had a wife waiting for me back home, after all.

"I'm looking for the kind of slave who can delve into a dungeon and hold their own. Can you fight?"

"Y-yes, I can. I can use spears and swords, though I'm still training to use a bow."

Smiling, Yoi turned to Lutbayasky.

"It's true he's a warrior then, right? How much for him?"

"What exquisite taste you have, Miss Yoi'hady Jumei," Lutbayasky purred. Unctuous little shit. "He can be yours for the exceedingly low price of twenty gold coins and eighteen silver pieces."

Twice the price of my vase. Temp agencies, am I right?

"Not bad, I suppose. But it's a bit expensive."

Yoi wasn't exactly jumping at the price he gave her. You've got to sell yourself in any good interview. All the more when you really, really need to sell yourself to get out of a hellish alternate universe slave market. Yeah, all right, she mentioned dungeons! Fine! I could panic about that part later.

"Miss Yoi, please buy me so I may be a faithful, humble servant to you. I will do anything you ask of me."

"Hmm! Anything, you say?"

"Anything!"

"As stated, I'm planning on going into dungeons. You would have your work cut out for you, and lots of it."

"That won't be a problem at all. I've done plenty of jobs that required physical labor," I said, stretching my smile wide as I could manage without bleeding (much). My face screamed in pain from all my injuries, but I had no choice but to put up with it.

She batted her eyelashes. "Aww. Are you sure you can't cut me a better deal on him, Mr. Slave Trader?"

"Well, let's see. He's damaged, I'll admit. I suppose I could let him go for nineteen gold and eighteen silver pieces."

"Aww. I want a good warrior, but do you have anyone else?"

"I have plenty of young goblin males in stock. You could buy two of them instead, and at half the price I'm asking for this one."

"No," she snapped suddenly, "goblins won't cut it. They're cheap, and they're *goblins*. Come now." She cleared her throat. Smiled girlishly. Not fond of goblins then. And not just because they oh so disappointingly didn't even fetch a high price at the goddamn slave market.

"If goblins aren't to your liking," said Lutbayasky, "I have a thirty-year-old man who used to work as an adventurer. There's that three-decade discount, you know. Twelve gold coins and five silver pieces?"

"Guys that age are so sickly. I'll pass."

The retired adventurer wasn't her type either. Poor guy, already...thirty? Wait, come *on*, thirty wasn't that bad. Right?

I pretended not to hear any of this, obviously. I think Wak'wakgoro brought it up before, but apparently I looked much younger than I really was in this world. Being clean-shaven must've helped.

Yoi frowned. "Hmm."

233

"Very well—eighteen gold coins and two silver pieces. How does that sound?"

"Ah, how reasonable! I'll take it. Give me his slave contract, please."

"A pleasure doing business with you."

With a wide grin, Lutbayasky snapped his fingers and sent one of his lackeys to fetch my contract. I had been sold for a grand total of eighteen gold and two silver pieces.

"Looks like you're coming home with me, Mr. Slave!"

"Thank you so much, Miss Yoi."

Still fully in the nude, I prostrated myself before the young girl. (Listen, context is extremely important here.)

There I was, Shuta-age-thirty-two-you-know-the-drill, walking around the town of Bulka buck naked. Or I guess, wearing only a collar around my neck, with a young girl who legally owned me holding the end of the chain attached to it.

I was a dog. I was an honest-to-god dog being taken for a walk around town.

I had a knapsack slung over my back with my shortsword and cloak in it, but Lutbayasky's goons shredded my vest to pieces. As for my wife's lovingly knitted underwear? Missing. Damn it.

I thought that the slave contract stuff would've been more complicated but Lutbayasky handed the contract to Yoi, I was once again forced to use my blood to press my thumbprint on the paper, and that was that. There was no magic to it. There didn't *need* to be magic.

If a slave killed their owner, they'd be charged with murder. If they tried to run away, people would come after them and kill them on sight. Even so, I was sure there had to be ways to make an escape where they wouldn't be able to catch me.

There was this piercing on my belly button too, unfortunately, irremovable proof that I was a slave. Here I was at the ripe old age of thirty-two, and now I had my first belly-button piercing. Extremely punk.

"Guess what?" said Yoi. "I'm actually an adventurer!"

"Oh? An adventurer, Miss Yoi?"

"That's right! I'm gonna be trying to tackle a dungeon, so I need an adventurer-slave who can protect me, carry my stuff, and even be my shield if the situation calls for it."

"I'd be more than happy to carry your belongings, and I've had experience acting as an armed escort before. As for being a shield...I haven't experienced anything like that yet, but I'll do my best to fulfill the role."

I wasn't exactly sure what Yoi meant by "dungeon," but the first things I imagined were old ruins or labyrinthine natural cave systems or something. You know, fantasy stuff. I was probably close enough.

"Before all that, we're going to the adventurer's guild to get you registered as an adventurer."

"Oh! My adventurer registration!"

"We'll go buy your weapons and gear after we get that done. Then I can go introduce you to my partner-in-crime."

"Thank you so much, Miss Yoi."

Weird. Here I was, ending up exactly where I intended to go anyway with Nishka. But where was she?

I paid our room ten days in advance, but she didn't have a coin to her name. Once she ran out of her food, she'd be in trouble. Selling off eye patches and thongs wouldn't be enough. The thought of a penniless Nishka wandering around the back alleys of the shopping district gnawed at me.

But I couldn't do anything about that just yet, and there was something else I noticed while wandering around town. Every once in a while, I'd see goblins just as naked as I was. The slaves Gimul was telling me about, I guessed.

While most of them were goblins, I spotted some naked men and women as well, all either carrying sacks packed to the brim with goods and produce or following after fancy nobility types. I may have been naked too, but I was also armed to the teeth. It was a little surreal.

Though I hadn't really noticed it when I first arrived in Bulka, it was hard to overlook the fact that there were so many fabulously well-to-do people around here—and in this one particular neighborhood. Compared to the chaos and squalor in the parts of Bulka I'd already seen, this place seemed fairly orderly and clean, though it was just as busy. Rows of stone buildings there might be, but they all rose much higher than three stories.

"I'm terribly sorry if this comes off as rude, Miss Yoi, but I was hoping to ask you a question."

"What is it, Mr. Slave?"

"Would you happen to be part of the nobility? You paid quite a lot for me, after all. Do you really make that much from being an adventurer?"

"Oh dear, no, I'm actually a spellcaster."

"A spellcaster?"

"Yup. Spellcasters are pretty rare, so they never have trouble finding work. If they can make it as adventurers, then they can make tons of money from it, too."

Would that make Nishka a spellcaster as well? She could use that wind magic, after all. But then, that was all she could cast. Maybe you needed to be able to use a ton of different spells if you wanted to be called a "spellcaster" or whatever.

"Does that mean you can use all sorts of magic, Miss Yoi?"

"Mmhm! My specialty is earth magic, but I can use fire and water magic as well."

"What about wind magic, if I may ask?" If Nishka could use it, maybe it was commonplace in this world...and maybe I could learn it.

"I'm not as good with it as earth magic, but I can use it."

"Oh, I see! That's wonderful!"

"Sure is! And so I'm always the main firepower of any adventurer party. He he!" She stopped walking and put her hands on her hips, puffing out her (practically nonexistent) chest.

"Err. I'd expect nothing less from someone as great as you, Miss Yoi. I would be grateful to have you teach me wind magic too, if you would so...deign at me with all that stuff."

"Hm. We'll see," she said curtly.

I was her slave, so what was I expecting? What time would there be for me to learn anything at all?

Oh. I really *was* a slave, wasn't I? Huh.

I wondered how horrible life was for slaves in this world. From what I read, slavery took many forms throughout history. Slaves in ancient Rome were supposed to have had a decent amount of freedom despite their status, sort of like temp-workers. On the other hand, there had also been chattel slavery, when they worked all those people to death back in the Age of Discovery and Industrial Revolution.

There was a simple reason for the difference: In the Roman Empire, prisoners of war or people who went broke were relatively common and could easily be forced into servitude. But during the Age of Discovery, slaves were brought to North and South America from faraway places like Africa and Asia, and had been treated more like things than unfortunate people. They had been made to perform backbreaking labor, like being put to work in mines or making their owner's property profitable, with no chance of ever winning back their freedom.

I wasn't going to be put to work in the coal mines or anything, so perhaps I had a chance at a decent life as a slave in this world... or as decent a life as one could get as a slave. All I had to do was carry stuff, after all. Or maybe get used as a sacrifice so Yoi and her friend could escape. How nice.

"Usually it's just me and my partner who go into dungeons, but that limits what kinds of dungeons we can go to, and how far we can go into them. But with you here, we're sure to get better results!"

"Of course! Whether it's carrying luggage or taking up my sword, I'll put my all into it!"

This girl bought me for eighteen gold coins. It had been twenty gold coins for the wyvern bones and skin, which Nishka said would be enough to eat like a king for a whole year. If that was really true, then they probably wouldn't just toss me to the nearest monster if things broke bad.

I felt oddly sad for Yoi, sure, but I had to think of a way to make my escape from here. And as those thoughts swirled around my head, we finally arrived at the adventurer's guild.

● ● ●

Or rather, *an* adventurer's guild. "Huh? This isn't the right place. I mean, it looks the same, but the location's wrong."

"Oh yeah? There are a few different guild locations all around town, so maybe you went to one of those?" Yoi offered, pulling me along with her chain.

Despite the fact it looked like a grown man was being taken for a naked walk by a little girl, no one so much as batted an eye at us. Was this just a thing? Did accomplished adventurers just take slaves for naked walks around the city?

When we approached the counter, a salesperson-like young man offered me an actual piece of parchment to sign rather than the crappy recycled paper Gimul used.

"I'm sorry, Miss Yoi, but I can't read."

"Then I'll fill it out for you, and you just stamp your thumb-print on it!"

I lifted my small master so she could reach the counter and fill out the paperwork for me. I pressed my thumb into a red inkpad before affixing it against the form to seal the deal.

"Then that wraps up your adventurer registration," said the young man working the counter. "I'll go and make your adventurer tag for you, so hold on while I get that done for you."

"Adventurer tag?"

"That's right. It's a tiny metal plate you wear around your neck that has your registration information written on it. And it comes in a set of two. Here, like this."

The receptionist pulled out a sample to show me. Looked a lot like those dog tag-looking things you'd find at those America-centric military shops in Osaka and Tokyo. All the Gen-Z types seemed into that stuff.

One of the tags was supposed to stay with the guild you first registered with, while the other was for the adventurer to keep. If they ever decided to travel and make a different guild their main base of operations, then they'd take the guild's tag and bring it to their new primary location.

Right now, I was in the West Gate Bulka guild. The guild I visited before was near the East Gate. No magic here, either—just a little tag. A fairly primitive system, all said and done.

"Then I'll get started on those tags for you," the receptionist told us before disappearing into a back room with my form.

We went and sat ourselves down on one of the benches to wait.

"You can't read or write, Mr. Slave?"

"I can't, unfortunately. I come from the countryside, so I never really learned."

"I think you should practice until you can write your own name, at least."

"I'll do just that, then."

It really was a good idea, if I was going to keep living in this world. According to Gimul, Cassandra didn't know how to read or write either. If this world was somewhere around the Middle Ages in terms of culture, then the literacy rate probably wasn't all that high.

It might take more time for a thirty-something-year-old like me to learn new things, but I at least wanted to get to the point where I could write my own name, and maybe read some simple sentences. If I was going to be an adventurer, I needed to at least read bulletin boards—otherwise somebody might try to pull a fast one on me. Every world's got its own horde of Lutbayaskies.

That said, there was one thing I *could* read now: "adventurer's guild." This was the third time I'd come to one of the guilds, so I'd come to recognize the sign. *Maybe you* can *teach an old dog new tricks*, I thought, taking a seat on the bench. Right when I did, though—

"Hey! What do you think you're doing, huh?"

A girl's voice shouted that before sending me sprawling with a swift, nasty kick. Didn't lay me out completely—I rolled a little and reached into my knapsack for my sword. More adventurers trying to pick a fight with me. Cool. I kept my guard up as I looked to see who that kick had come from, and I saw...a girl.

"Hell's your problem, lady?"

"That should be *my* line. What's a slave like you trying to sit down without permission from his master, hm?"

The girl placed a hand on her hip as she glared at me. She had long, straight black hair, eyes that reminded me of acorns, and glasses too—the first I'd seen in this world. She wore leather armor over her sleeveless dress, a cloak, and a longsword hung at her waist.

"Th-that was my mistake, then. I'm sorry, Miss Yoi."

Yoi smiled. "It's okay, I don't mind!"

But what was up with the glasses chick? She kicked me before I even said my name. Girls in this world were really all over the place.

She folded her arms. "If Yoi says it's fine, then I guess it's fine. Be more careful next time."

"Yes, of course. Thank you for your kind consideration."

"Ganjamary, when did you get here?" Yoi asked the girl.

"We promised to meet at the guild in the afternoon, remember? It looks like you managed to get your slave just fine."

"Uh-huh! He's a hunter from the countryside who used to be a warrior. It sounds like he can use all sorts of close-range weapons, and even bows!"

"I'm still learning with the bow, actually," I cut in.

This other girl looked surprisingly Japanese to me. She had a button-nose, and round eyes, too.

"Mr. Slave," said Yoi, "this is my partner-in-crime. She's part of the Templars here, and an adventurer, too!"

"Yes. I'm Ganjamary, slave. I suppose I should say it's nice to meet you."

"Pleased to make your acquaintance as well. I'm Shooter," I said, bowing.

Ganja...mary? Top-tier stoner name. Might as well give her the last name Jane, or perhaps Jawanna?

"Shooter, huh." Her lips twitched. "Give me a break. Just looking at your dumb face makes me think you're Japanese. I bet your real name is something lame like 'Shuta.' You're not close to my type, either. And what's that down there? Is that phimosis? Nasty, dude."

I wasn't sure if she meant to say all that under her breath or not, but it was definitely loud enough for me to pick up on.

"Wait, did you just say 'Japanese'?!"

I definitely heard it, clear as day.

Ganjamary took her hand off her hip.

Then she put the full weight of her body behind her fist and smashed it into my face with an audible crunch.

I couldn't fight back, and it made me furious. My experience with karate helped me minimize the damage I took, but I pretended that I was reeling after her punch. Which, great, cool, but hold on, Japanese, what?

"You don't seem to know how to talk to your superiors despite the fact you're a slave," she spat.

"Wait, just hear me out! You said I looked 'Japanese,' right?

Then I bet your name isn't Ganjamary—maybe something more like... 'Gangi Mari,' right?"

"So what, slave? Yours is probably something stupid like 'Shuta.' What's your last name then, huh?"

"Ow! Stop with the punching! And the kicking, just the whole scene *oww*. It's Yoshida, my family name is Yoshida! I'm Yoshida Shuta!"

"See? You're Japanese too, aren't you!" She snorted haughtily, adjusting her glasses as all of her blows—the punches and kicks— sunk into me.

I glared back, wiping the blood from my cheek with my arm. This violent glasses-wearing wench...

Yoi cleared her throat lightly. "Mr. Slave, do you and Ganjamary know each other?"

"Well, erm." I started. "How should I explain this?"

"No," Ganjamary interrupted, "we don't know each other. It just looks like we're both from the same place."

"Oh, you mean that other world you were born in?" Yoi responded, completely unfazed.

Oh, that other *what*? I was at a loss. And just like that, for the first time I met another Japanese person in this new world.

"How did you end up here, anyway?" Mari asked me.

"I was on my way back from work and was going to grab a drink at a nearby bar. Everything after that gets a bit hazy. Before I knew it, I was wandering around a forest in this world before being caught by a woodcutter from the village I've been staying in."

"Hm. Interesting."

"What about you?"

"I was going home from school, and then poof! I was in some church here. Everyone had been praying super hard when I suddenly showed up. They all freaked out, called me some kind of 'holy maiden,' all kinds of stuff."

"Were you naked?"

"*Buck* naked. I did still have my glasses, at least. No idea why."

While Yoi went to pick up my finished adventurer tags, Mari and I traded stories of how we arrived. We sat on the bench, the chain to my collar firmly in her grasp.

"Aha, so your glasses are just another part of your body, then?"

Mari's eye twitched. "How *dare* you?"

She didn't like that one at all, balling up her fist to punch me in the face. No thanks—I cleanly dodged the hit.

"I grew up in Saitama," she said, moving on. "I was fifteen years old and in my first year of high school when I got sent here. I'm nineteen now."

"You've already been here four years? Dang, I guess that makes you the expert on this place. I'm thirty-two, and I was hopping between part-time jobs back in Kyoto before this all happened. I grew up way out in the sticks."

"Hopping between jobs? Funny. Trash back home, and trash in this world, too," she remarked, eyes full of scorn.

"Oh, give it a rest," I snapped.

"Am I wrong? How did you end up as a slave? Did that village sell you off after they caught you?"

"Nah, I was actually here in town on business for the village. I ended up caught in a scam involving a stupidly 'expensive' vase and some adventurers who were working for a slave trader. One thing led to another, and, well, here I am."

"Hmph. Bad luck, I suppose."

"There's someone else that came with me here, a girl. I was the one with the money, so she's probably wandering the streets alone right about now. I also have a wife waiting for me back at the village. I don't know if you could..." I didn't know what I was going to even ask, and it didn't matter. She couldn't. She was barely listening, after all.

Mari yawned. "I don't really care, to be honest. You're Yoi's slave right now, so don't even think about running away. They'll catch you, you'll die, and we'll move on."

"C'mon, don't be like that! We're both kindred souls from the same homeland, right?"

"Aw no, what a tragedy! What a terrible injustice. You gonna take it up with the police? *What* police? Gonna talk to the guards? They'll probably claim it's none of their business."

My heart sank like a rock as Mari said exactly everything I didn't want to hear.

"Hey, Mr. Slave! I got your adventurer tags!"

Yoi came trotting back from the counter and looped my tags around my neck for me. The future seemed...gone. "Let's go buy your weapons and go home!"

It was early in the afternoon when we left the guild and made our way to the weapon shop. I felt everyone's eyes on me and my chains as we walked. This was normal for slaves, right? Right?

Well, I wasn't about to let myself die a horrible death in some dungeon. No, I'd give Yoi my best puppy dog eyes and get myself some decent equipment, and then I'd hope it'd be enough for whatever lay ahead.

Weapon Shopping

YOI WAS ALL SMILES as she pulled me along the road by the collar around my neck, wagons and carts passing us by. Suddenly, though, we changed course and turned down an alleyway.

A cramped shopping district awaited us, located in the shadows of the other tall, imposing buildings lining the main road. Although the entrances to the shops were all tiny and narrow, they led to long, snaking passages that stretched back deep into the stores. There were all sorts of weapons and armor on display, and the stores were cramped enough that some of the products jutted out into the road.

"All these weapons and junk in a narrow side street...weird," I mumbled. "I thought for sure we would've hit up a shop on the main road."

Yoi turned around at that. "This is where all new adventurers get what they need to get started!"

"Oh, I see!" I turned to Mari. "So these shops are all geared to novice adventurers, then?"

Mari seemed annoyed that I asked her, but she still answered. "They have some new equipment here, but most of it is second-hand. It's not a problem—polish it up and it works well enough, so it's perfect for newbie adventurers. I went here too when I started out," she added, folding her arms.

With such a flat chest, folding her arms did nothing to emphasize what little Mari had to work with. Mari glared back at me as I marveled at her sheer boobless cliff-face.

"Where the hell do you think you're looking?" she snapped.

"Sorry, I was, uh. Just dumbfounded by all the new sights."

"You're not some country yokel on vacation, so stop looking like one! It's embarrassing!" Mari landed an open-handed slap on my bare ass with all her might, and I tried very hard not to let out a little shriek. (Unsuccessfully.)

Yoi turned to me with a smile. "Now that we're here, let's go get all the stuff you'll need to be an adventurer, Mr. Slave!"

"Yes, that sounds great, Miss Yoi!"

It was hard not to smile back when she was so damn chipper.

Wasting no time, we scoured the first shop to find a good weapon for me. While we searched, Mari told me that I needed something fairly general purpose if I was going to tackle a dungeon with it.

"Swords are always useful, sure, but there are times you'll be up against something with skin too tough to pierce with a blade."

Yoi nodded. "That's when you'll need a blunt weapon to get the job done, Mr. Slave!"

"A blunt weapon, huh?" And wouldn't you know it, here was a corner of the store filled with just that type. They had everything, from sticks with hunks of metal fastened to the end of the handles, to more traditional armaments like morning stars.

I picked one out and hoisted it up. Yeah, a mace had to be the most basic of your basic blunt weapons.

Maces were an evolution of crude clubs and cudgels, and you could use them without worrying about upkeep—also, any lack of sharpness was more than balanced out by their ability to deal impact damage through even the toughest armor.

"You ever use one of those?" Mari asked.

"No, but I did get used to swinging a bat around back when I was playing a two-bit thug for this TV show I worked on."

I hadn't been given a gun since I was just an extra, so they handed me and the other "gang members" a metal bat for our scene. Together we trashed an office belonging to a rival gang. That particular role ended with me getting shot by the rival gang leader.

Swinging the bat to deal damage was different from swinging it to play baseball. You needed both hands and you needed to really put your everything into it. I think maces were one-handed, though.

"What's a 'tee-vee show'?" Yoi asked.

"It's a type of play. He was an actor," Mari explained.

"Oh, I getcha!"

A perfect explanation. It had been beyond me to explain. Mari pushed up her glasses with her finger and turned to me. "Right, you said you hopped between part-time jobs back on Earth."

"I guess that's one way to put it. Think of me more as a 'part-time warrior,' wandering from job to job."

"Because you couldn't hold a job."

Mari's barbed words almost knocked me flat onto the ground. Just talking to her was throwing me off my game, so I decided to Not Do That as much as possible.

"Which weapon do you think would be a good fit for you, Mr. Slave?"

"It's hard to choose with so many options, but I think for me, simple works best. I would be honored if I could have this one, Miss Yoi." I picked one that felt good to hold and bowed over and over to my little master as I made my request.

"'Kay! Go and get this paid for, partner-in-crime!" she said to Mari.

The mace I picked out cost a whopping three silver pieces, but Yoi paid for it like it was nothing at all. Well, if she was willing to pay that much for me, I'd be sure to put in the sort of work she deserved!

"Then we're done here," said Mari. "Yoi and I have everything we need for camping outdoors, so we're good on that front."

"Um, aren't we still forgetting something?"

Mari sighed. "What?"

We'd just gone back out into the narrow alleyway after purchasing my mace, and Yoi had already run on ahead of us. "If we're going to be camping outdoors, shouldn't I have something to wear?"

"No. You're a slave. What do you expect? Slaves are *supposed* to be naked, idiot. We'll take your chains off, though. Can't have you work as an adventurer for us while you're all tied up."

With another haughty snort, she gave my chain a suffocating yank.

If this was where I ended up, I had to make the best of it. The harder I worked, the better I'd be rewarded, right? Well, I was gonna become the kind of slave to earn his own shiny pair of underwear!

BUCK
NAKED
in ANOTHER WORLD

CH. Dungeon and Slave
-Part 1-

HEY, EVERYONE. So I guess I've washed a little girl's underwear now. That sure is a thing, scrubbing the front part of a tiny thong, but I swear it's not like, a sex-crime thing? I currently worked as a slave for Yoi, the young girl I called master, and did all the chores that needed doing in her day-to-day life.

My name is Yoshida Shuta, but these days people mostly called me 'Shooter' or 'Mr. Slave.' I've worked all sorts of part-time jobs starting from back in high school, but I've never worked at a cleaner's, unfortunately. It wasn't like this was the first time I was stuck on laundry duty, though.

Back when I lived with my old karate instructor in Okinawa, I ended up doing laundry for him and his family quite a bit. One of those family members happened to be his high-schooler granddaughter, who was pretty fussy when it came to her things. It was always, "Put that in a net!" or, "You have to wash that by hand!" with her, but her underwear obsession took the cake.

She eventually got so tired of nitpicking that she told me she'd just do it herself. Her face got weirdly red when she yelled at me, but I think that's just a puberty thing. Extra...face-blood? Look, I've never worked as a biologist either.

One more person lived at Yoi's mansion, a girl by the name of Gangi Mari (or Ganjamary, depending on who you asked.) She didn't even lift a finger to wash her own underwear, despite the fact she used to be a high school girl back in our old world as well! Not only that, but it didn't seem to bother her that a guy like me was the one doing it. I always thought girls her age were finicky when it came to this stuff, but it looked like I was wrong. I just don't understand girls, I swear.

Anyway, it was a slave's job to take care of their master.

Taking a look around the town of Bulka, it was plain to see that slavery was a part of daily life here. You'd see slaves following their masters around wherever you looked, carrying belongings and just generally doing whatever they were commanded to do.

I didn't know what Mari had seen since coming here, but she didn't seem to even blink at slavery, so I suppose she accepted it as just a reality of this world. She was also a part of the Templars, an armed religious group working under the Church, which probably made her close to the bigwigs running the town.

There'd been warrior-monks in Japan too, back in the day, and they held considerable power in medieval and feudal Japan. The difference between me and Mari was like the difference between heaven and earth. Though we'd both been sent to this world and gotten a fresh start on a new life, *how* we started was completely different, a fact made painfully evident just by looking at our lives now.

"Doing slave labor really does suit you," Mari commented nonchalantly as she watched me wash.

"I've been meaning to ask—you're not bothered having me wash your undies, even though I'm a dude?"

She shrugged. "Why should I be? You're a slave, and it's normal for slaves to handle all the little stuff like that."

"Listen, Mari—"

"You don't get to call me that. That's *Miss* Gangi Mari to you, understand?" She aimed a ferocious kick at me as I scrubbed away at a camisole, but I was used to it these days. I just jumped out of the way.

"Why are you dodging?" Mari huffed. "Just sit still and let me kick you!"

"Yeah, weird that I wouldn't want to be kicked, huh? Look, get off my back. I'm very busy. Slave stuff, you know?"

"Hmph. So, what were you going to ask?"

"You were born and raised in Japan, so shouldn't you be a little more, I dunno..." What was the right word? "Bashful? Shy? Like, traditional Japanese lady stuff."

"You're just breathtakingly stupid, aren't you? How about *you* get bashful and shy in this world and see how far it gets you," she snapped, venom dripping from her words.

Those words shook me. What had Mari endured, to make it this far? Spending puberty, the most tumultuous years of her life, in another world, and as a girl on top of all that. I could hardly imagine it.

• • •

Anything you brought into a dungeon needed to have a certain amount of varied utility and, of course, you had to make sure it was well maintained.

"Maces," I muttered to myself, polishing my new secondhand mace with an old rag, "are pretty interesting weapons when you think about it." I'd been talking to myself a lot recently.

I didn't really have experience with a blunt weapon. Poles and tonfa back at karate, sure, but the only real similarity in this case was ease of use. All you had to do was swing them around at your opponent and, unlike with bladed weapons, you didn't have to worry about what angle you got 'em at. It took time to learn how to use a bladed weapon properly, so it had been a good idea to pick the mace instead. Made me thankful to Miss Yoi for allowing it. "Y'know, I can't help but think of Saki'cho when it comes to maces."

Though I'd lived in the village for around two weeks by the time he passed, I hadn't spoken a word to Saki'cho, that previous leader of the hunters. He dual-wielded maces—or he had against the wyvern—but I knew nothing else about the poor goblin. Maybe he could've given me a few pointers on maces if he were still alive... except no, if he were still alive, I wouldn't have been sent to town looking for replacement hunters in the first place. I'd still do well enough with my mace. "But still," I mused, "there's a bigger problem."

Or rather, a scantier problem. I had nothing practical in the way of armor. Yoi didn't need anything too heavy because she was a spellcaster, and Mari was decked out with her own set of armor to hold the frontline. Me? I was just the pack mule of the group. I had to get by with a pair of shoes and a cloak.

From the adventurers I'd seen back in the village, I thought they all wore chainmail and cosplayed Vikings, but at the very least Yoi and Mari were exceptions to that rule.

In order to keep myself from breaking out in blisters, I started wearing boots. Naked with nothing but boots on gave me enough bad vibes, but it really crystallized when I pulled on my cloak: I was dressed like a flasher. A real top-tier, balls-out kinda flasher too—a dark-cloaked sausage-unveiling alley-lurking hellpervert.

"They look great on you, Mr. Slave!" Yoi cooed.

"Th-thank you..." Hooray. Well, whatever. Shoes and a cloak, count your blessings. Besides, it was the norm for slaves to be naked. Even a sweet little girl like Yoi wouldn't think to give me clothes. Even so, our party felt a wee bit light compared to other adventurers. Hmm! Wonder why?

I may have been naked pretty much the whole time since I got to this world, but this was the first time I was worried about a lack of protection.

The worries swirled in my head but time marched forward. With Yoi and Mari's things in hand, the three of us headed off to the dungeon together.

As we walked along a country road after leaving Bulka, Yoi began to explain dungeons to me.

"There are two types of dungeons: ruins that our ancestors left behind, and big webs of connected cave systems."

Yoi was much wiser and more learned than her youthful appearance suggested. She had mountains of books back at her luxurious mansion, and it was a good bet that they were magical grimoires, given her occupation.

It was all fine and dandy for her to stay up studying, but it felt like a waste of lantern oil for anyone to stay up that late, so I hoped she'd learn to go to bed earlier here on the road. Even just the previous night, she drifted off and fell asleep into her open book. Not only that, but while she slept, she had a slight "accident."

Which, by the way, is why I was taking extra care to scrub that underwear of hers. Comes with the territory, all right? "Dungeons come in all different sizes, too. The one we're going to, for instance, is a little base of ruins just out of town. People say the whole thing's pretty small, though!"

I adjusted the baggage on my back. "Would that be classified as a naturally formed dungeon, or would it fall under the ruins archetype?"

Yoi put a finger to her lips as she pondered. "A little bit of both, I guess?"

"Really, now?"

"Mmhm! Most of the dungeons Ganjamary and I have visited lately have been smaller ruins. The one we're going to this time used to be a cave, but people long ago built stuff on top of it, and now they're ruins. So if you think about it, they're kinda like 'naturally formed ruins.' They don't go that deep either, but then again, we haven't gone that far inside."

I nodded. "So it's a combination of both. It doesn't seem like there would be many you could clearly say fall into one category or the other, if you put it like that."

"That's right."

"Then may I ask one more question?"

"What is it, Mr. Slave?"

Gah! What a cute kid! "What, exactly, is the definition of a 'dungeon'?"

"Definition?" she asked, cocking her head to the side. Too cute, it was ridiculous!

Mari answered. "It depends on whether or not it has a master."

Hm. I was expecting it to be all about treasure or magic or something. Also—ugh—I wasn't asking *Mari*.

Ah well, it was an answer. "A master? You mean the only difference between ancient ruins, caves and such, or a dungeon is a boss monster?"

"Yeah, basically. Huge monsters might make a deserted ruins its new home, or some weird monsters might just naturally migrate there. For caves, we're usually looking at ogres."

"Would it be *ogrely* presumptuous to assume that these are big, butt-ugly monsters?"

"No," she said, ignoring my brilliant comedy. "They're pretty much the same as the folklore versions in our world."

"Got it."

"You're so smart, Mr. Slave!" Yoi gleefully exclaimed.

"You think?"

"Yeah!" She hopped to her tiptoes and reached up with her hands. Oh! Head pats? I crouched down and bowed my head.

"Good boy!"

"Thank you so much, Miss Yoi."

Aww! Wait. Aww? Aww, no, nope. I was being trained like a dog by a goddamn kid. *No* to Stockholm Syndrome, *yes* to my waiting wife.

Mari looked down on me with a gaze that was half-scorn, half-eye roll. "He went to school, so he should at least know that much. You graduate college?"

"No, I dropped out."

"You really are the scum of society, aren't you?"

Cold. Murderous. Rage. I don't think I'd ever been that angry at her before, but I had no choice but to grin and bear it for now. Here I was thinking that we were starting to understand each other a little more, but it always ended like this. Oh, I'd wipe that smug look off her face sooner or later, let her goddamn wait. I guess we'd both have to wait, come to think of it, because we were heading into dangerous territory. Couldn't lose focus, not now.

"Now then, everyone!" Yoi cried. "Let's get off the road and head to the base by the dungeon!"

Our destination was already in sight.

• • •

We arrived at the remains of a small abandoned settlement after about a half-day's trek from Bulka. There were only about twelve houses here total, and an ancient building bigger than anything else in the area. The roof was caved in, but its sturdy stone walls still stood. Small as the rest of the settlement was, this old building was far more impressive than any of the clay and dirt houses back home. I mean, back at Apegut.

The surrounding area was coated in thick shrubbery and dotted with enormous, overgrown trees. As humans vanished, nature came to reclaim...all of her shit, just the whole scene, with big trees and stuff.

"This village has been here since long before the governor of Bulka came to rule over these lands," Yoi explained as we entered the dilapidated stone building. "There couldn't have been more than a hundred people living here, though, judging by the number of houses. Anyway, the dungeon is further inside."

It looked like Mari and Yoi had been using this area as a base of operations. We were close to the dungeon now, so they were getting cautious. As a spellcaster, the only melee weapon Yoi had was a knife for self-defense. Her true weapon was a rather extravagant grimoire that looked a little ridiculous in her tiny hands, which I assumed was a medium for her magic.

Aside from that, she held a small, odd lantern as we prepared to delve into the dungeon.

"What would that be?"

"A magic lantern! It uses mana to keep the flame burning. There's an incantation engraved inside it that ignites once you add a teensy bit of blood. It draws on your mana to activate, so even people who can't wield magic can use it!"

"Yeah, it seems pretty handy to—hold on, hey, can we focus on that blood bit?"

"Hold out your hand please, Mr. Slave. I'm going to prick your finger with this little needle."

"Agh, wait, I'm not good with pain!" I said, squirming and shuddering.

I offered up my finger to her all the same, which she promptly pricked. A small droplet of blood formed from the tiny wound, which Yoi put inside the lantern.

"If you turn the knob here, then it lights the flame," she explained.

"Yeah, I can see. Huh."

"People like me need to really conserve our mana, so I don't usually use it."

"Is that right?"

"Mmhm! Everyone has mana inside them, so we usually use front-line fighters or pack mules to activate these magic tools. Got it?"

"Yes, I understand, Miss Yoi!"

As Yoi and I talked, Mari prepared to head into the dungeon. She wore iron-reinforced leather armor over her normal sleeveless outfit now, something that looked like it was made by pressing tan leather between some kind of iron plate.

There was almost nothing better than metal armor in terms of protection, but it was also heavy and cumbersome, and left the wearer susceptible to both heat and cold. It's a conductor, you see—if it was cold, it stole your heat, and if it was hot, you were damn well gonna get hot too. Combining leather and metal sacrificed some defense, but also prevented the slow, environmental exhaustion of full-metal armor. Mari's particular armor sure as hell didn't come cheap.

Then there was her longsword. For some reason, people in this world seemed to have a particular fondness for broader, thicker blades. These were made to emphasize endurance over sharpness, and if they dulled you could still use centrifugal force to absolutely wreck somebody's day.

Mari pulled her sword from its scabbard and inspected it; the way she looked over the blade and the hilt gave me the impression she had some practical experience. You always gotta check the hilt, just as I told young actors back when I taught part-time sword lessons in a theater group.

"Have you ever killed someone with that?" I blurted.

"That's a stupid question. I'm a Templar working for the Church. If they order me to kill a bunch of bandits, I do so without a second thought."

"O-oh..."

Utter nonchalance as she slid her longsword back into its sheath. Afterward, she pulled a few small glass capsules off her belt and inspected them.

"What are those?"

"Potions, all with different uses. They boost stamina, physical strength, perception, recovery, and even adrenaline. You need some, too?"

"What, so they're like 'roids? I think I'll pass on that."

"Hmph. Suit yourself."

An RPG is one thing, but real-life health potions or stamina-enhancing medicine gave me hardcore junkie vibes. Nah. I'd pass.

Mari, on the other hand, casually poured the contents into a strange container and injected it into her arm, just like a syringe. "You pour one into this special tool and stick it into your arm like this. Guhh—!"

"Which one was that?"

"Strength enhancer. The effects last about half a day, so it's perfect for pushing through to the deeper parts of the dungeon."

"Are there any side effects from using a bunch at once?"

"Yeah, if you're not cautious. I can use magic, so that gives me a certain amount of control over my body. You're a newbie, so you better not take on too many at once. Ha." Mari looked ecstatic after her hit of potion. She turned to Yoi, who was poring over a map of the area. "I'm ready to go."

"Roger that! You take the front like always, and I want you in the back, Mr. Slave. We've already taken out anything that could get in our way, so let's head straight for the deeper parts."

"Got it," said Mari.

I nodded as well, adjusting the baggage on my back. With a mace in my right hand and the magic lantern in my left, I was ready to enter the dungeon.

"All right, then," Mari said, smirking. "Let's do this."

Just like you'd expect from a cave, the entrance to the dungeon proper was fairly wide. Imagine the entrance hall of a fancy apartment building and you're on the right track. The walls were meticulously carved from stone to be *proper* walls, and the people who once lived here probably intended it to be a residence, or a warehouse, or maybe even some kind of shrine.

"We're gonna lose sunlight the moment we go deeper inside," said Mari. "I'll be making my own light using my mana. You make sure to hold that lantern carefully so Yoi can see using yours."

"Will do. You can use magic even though you're not from this world?"

"I trained my ass off to do it. It took four long years of blood, sweat, and tears to get to where I am now."

Sounded rough, but at least I'd be able to use magic too if I just trained hard enough. I was already powering the lantern with my own mana, so maybe I just had to learn the theory. The four years of blood, sweat, and tears part was a bit concerning, admittedly.

Although I'd been tossed buck naked into a forest just outside of Apegut, Mari had descended on a town church like an angel. Whatever her horrible, *horrible* personality, people saw her as some kind of holy woman. She probably worked her butt off to meet the expectations that came with that.

I held my mace and lantern in my left hand, pressing my other hand against the wall as we headed further inside.

"From what I've heard, there should be a shrine in the deepest part of the cave. It's been fifteen years since anyone's been here, and there haven't been any adventurers to clean up any monsters either," said Yoi.

"The, uh, 'dungeon master' showed up because no one lived here?" I asked.

"That's right. Right now it's just the master of the dungeon and some kobolds camping out inside."

Ah, those jackal-headed guys again.

"Kobolds always seem to nest in caverns and abandoned mines," said Mari. "Places like that are easier for them to live together, I've heard. They especially like to get their paws on weapons or tools some shmuck left behind."

"I see. That's pretty useful to know."

"There's also the giant snakes. Forgot to mention the giant snakes. It's humid in these kinds of places, which means it stays warm even in winter. There's a chance we might run into one. We eliminated most of the kobolds last time, though."

I didn't get the feeling Mari would use kobolds like a hunter. Killing them would be enough for her.

"The problem is going to be the deepest part of the cave. This used to be a shrine of some sort, yeah, but even deeper inside I hear there's an underground lake. If there's a boss, that's their hideout."

"Who are we up against? A wyvern or something?"

"No. Not altogether different, though."

"What do you mean by that, Mari?" The clacking sound of our boots echoed throughout the cave as we marched.

"You know what a basilisk is?"

"No, I don't. Sounds like a manga."

"Tch. This is what you get for being illiterate."

"Come on, cut me some slack. I haven't had a day to myself ever since I got here."

"Mr. Slave," Yoi piped in, "a basilisk is a giant lizard monster with a crest on its head, like a rooster. You can think of it like a dragon that crawls along the ground."

"Oh, a dragon! Thank you, Miss Yoi." I was so happy to get an answer that I found myself giving Yoi head pats right back as I thanked her. She let out the most ridiculously adorable giggle I'd ever heard and I was just gonna die, it was too much, my life was over, too cute, end me now.

"Back in our world," said Mari, "a basilisk was supposedly a venomous monster that could turn people to stone with its gaze. You really never heard of such a thing?"

"Can it do the same thing in this world?"

"Nope. Though it won't turn you to stone or anything, it can paralyze anyone it encounters with fear."

"Using its roar?"

"Hrm. So you do know about it."

"Back when I was at my village, I took down a wyvern with another hunter," I said with a smirk.

"Oh?"

Mari looked completely uninterested.

"You did, Mr. Slave?" There we go. Some appreciation!

"That I did. When I was working as a hunter back in this village way out on the frontier, a wyvern came out of the forest and started causing all sorts of trouble. Me and another hunter named Nishka the Scalesplitter, one of the strongest hunters near the village, teamed up to take it down together."

"That's amazing!"

"Really, now. It hasn't even been a year since you got here, right? There's no way you could've pulled that off."

"I did, though."

Mari suddenly stopped and placed a hand on her sword. "Then how about you prove it to me."

"Huh?"

"There's a wide-open area coming up with some kobolds we haven't taken care of yet. We're not even looking at ten. Think you can take them on with me?"

"Yeah, I'll give it a shot."

"Hm. I'll take the right, you're left."

I set the baggage I was carrying on the ground, then double-checked that the sword at my waist was ready to be used just in case, and tightened my grip on my mace.

"And as for you, Yoi..."

"What is it, Ganjamary?"

"We could end up drawing the basilisk to us if we make too much noise, so no combat spells, okay?"

"Okay!"

"Do you think you could light up the ceiling with some magic, though?"

"Leave it to me!"

The three of us nodded to each other, our roles decided. I crouched down and trailed after Mari as we followed along the wall, eventually coming upon the wide-open area she described. The kobolds were there, plain as day.

One, two, three...you know, hearing ten was a little different from *seeing* ten.

I understood Mari not believing I'd taken down a wyvern, but there wasn't much I could do about that. What I could do was show how useful I could be. The better I proved myself, the sooner I might get freed for outstanding service.

"Ready for this?" Mari asked.

"You know it!"

Pumped as hell now, we broke into a sprint toward our targets.

Mari and I kept our posture low to the ground as we ran. She drew her longsword and kept it ready at the right of her waist, just as I'd seen in my time practicing swordsmanship.

I wondered, had she used swords before entering this world? Wasn't a bad stance, after all. But the way she kept her grip on the handle told a different story. She held it with both hands pressed against each other, no space in between like you were supposed to in Japanese swordsmanship. She was planning to let centrifugal force do the work for her and really do some damage, but that was risky stuff.

Her technique, if you wanna call it that, was actually a blind, murderous charge at the enemy where she had to get the first hit in—no other choice. Not with the way the move left her wide open. She was probably relying on strength to get the job done after that potion. Not a bad tactic, all things considered.

Yoi fired off her light magic, illuminating the inside of the cave. In the newfound brightness, I saw Mari rush off into the group of kobolds on the right side.

It was a bloodbath.

Right as she sliced off one head, she was already bringing her blade down in a broad sweeping motion to slash through more flesh in one clean line.

I wasn't about to let her show me up, though. I checked out my left flank and went for it, swinging my mace into the kobolds there. While I had zero experience using anything like a mace before, I couldn't have been more thankful that it was easy as hell to kill with.

The tip of my mace connected with a kobold's skull with a sickening crunch. I wondered why anyone would bother with bows at all as I kicked away my first hapless victim and set my gaze on more targets. The kobolds were armed with weapons carved from what must've been bone, but their movements were clumsy. I nimbly dodged them, bringing my mace down to crush another kobold's head as their group descended into chaos.

"*Metai!*"

"*Metai metai!*"

The kobolds were screaming something in what I assumed was their language as they worked on surrounding me. Which wasn't as bad as you'd think—if I could get them to drop their guard, then they were easy enough to take care of.

For some reason, the kobolds kept attacking me instead of running away, which flew in the face of what Wak'wakgoro said about them being cowards. Though they were still clearly afraid of *something*. If I had to guess, I'd blame the basilisk deeper in the cave.

I aimed every blow squarely at their heads. The shock of impact rang through the handle into my fingers as their heads caved in one by one, and yet my hands never went numb no matter how many I crushed dead.

Five swings total and it was over. But the sensations from my new weapon had my muscles trembling in shock.

"How's it looking over there?" Mari shouted.

"Mission accomplished. They're done."

"Good. I'm done over here, too. Yoi! Which one of us was faster?!"

Mari was barely breathing harder than normal as she flicked blood off her blade. Had to admit, the way she slowly slid her sword back into its sheath was pretty badass.

"Mr. Slave was just a little bit faster."

"What? You can't be serious!"

"I was taking on five over here. What about you?"

"Four..." She shook her head. "What kind of monster *are* you?"

"Hey, man. I do karate, okay?"

"Cheater," Mari said, glaring and pouting.

I just smiled. "I've never killed anyone before, though. Anything I did was usually at a dojo."

"Wh-what, you trying to say it wasn't even a challenge?"

I wiped the smile from my face. "No, I'm not. You may come off as a bit wild, but your technique was sound. Your movements were nothing short of impressive."

"H-hmph..." Mari turned away from me and snorted. Oho, but what was that? Was somebody's face getting a little red? Was somebody a little embarrassed?

"Then let's hurry up and take our spoils from them," said Yoi. "Mr. Slave, you take the ones over there, and you can get the ones here, Ganjamary."

I didn't get it. "Spoils?"

"Their sharp teeth! We can take them back to the guild, and they'll give us a reward. Kobolds are usually causing trouble outside of town, so there's always a bounty for this work."

I nodded. "Gotcha."

I pushed on a smashed kobold face with my foot to check on its teeth. Not pretty. This was going to be one nasty job.

"Here, use this." Mari handed me a thick carving knife, holding onto the sheath while offering me the handle.

"Thanks."

"First you bash their gums with the handle," she said, "then you dig out the tooth with the blade."

"Looks like you're already a pro."

"Taking care of pests is another part of a Templar's job. When it gets really bad, they send a whole squad of us to deal with it."

I followed her example and started collecting the kobolds' canine teeth. Yoi used some water from the canteen to prepare a damp cloth for me, which I used to wipe the blood from my face and hands.

"You have my humblest gratitude, Miss Yoi."

"Of course! It's a master's job to take care of their slave!" she said, proudly puffing out her chest.

I patted her on the head again, and in a millisecond her proud demeanor crumbled into contentment.

Mari sighed. "What do you two think you're doing? C'mon, we have to keep moving. There was something strange about these kobolds."

"Yes, ma'am."

Mari, meanwhile, still had some blood splattered on her face. Aside from that, she barely had any blood on her elsewhere—just went to show how skilled she was at doing this. I could learn a thing or two from her.

I hoisted our baggage onto my back once more, holding hands with Yoi as we followed Mari into the depths of the dungeon.

"It's starting to smell pretty rank down here," I noted.

Mari nodded. "We made it about this far the last time we came. The mark I left on the wall is still here, too. I think I'll go ahead and carve it again to make it clearer." She took out the same knife she used to dig out kobold teeth and dug it into an X-shaped mark on the wall.

"How much farther do we have left?"

"According to the old building plans I saw," Yoi offered, "I'm guessing around a thousand steps to the deepest part. It's not that far if we make a beeline for it, but there's always the chance we'll run into some scary monster."

"This is supposed to be one of the smaller-scale dungeons, right? Does that mean the bigger ones take days to get through?"

"Yeah, something like that," Mari said slowly, thinking it over. "There are some ancient ruins with complex layouts that take more time, and the abandoned mines definitely take a few days to get through. For a place like this, you're usually in-and-out in two or three days if nothing happens. The problem for us is going to be the basilisk."

"But monsters as huge as basilisks need to eat tons of prey in order to survive, right? How do they survive if they stay holed up in a dungeon?"

"There are two ways to explain that, Mr. Slave."

"Oh? Please enlighten me, Miss Yoi."

The two of us still held hands as we followed behind Mari, the latter keeping her attention on the forward search and spilling magic light from her hands.

"First, it could be there's another entrance to this dungeon, and it uses that to head out into the rest of its territory. That, or it could just be asleep."

"Asleep, huh? That makes sense. Back when I took care of the wyvern, we waited for it to go back and rest at its cave before finishing it off."

"Wow! You're so clever, Mr. Slave!"

"Well, I *was* a hunter, after all. That, and I had a skilled partner with me."

"Partner?" Yoi asked, laying a finger on her cheek.

"That's right. Her name was Nishka the Scalesplitter, and she was famous to the point that everyone near our village and the neighboring settlements knew her name. She was a fierce warrior who had hunted as many wyverns as she'd spent winters being a hunter. She did happen to have one more, not-so-impressive name..."

"Not so impressive?"

"Mmhm. They also called her 'Tipsy Nish,' cause she drank like a fish. Even in town, she kept bugging me to take her to the bar."

"Ha ha! Tipsy Nish the drinking fish!"

"It's true that she's a skilled hunter, though. Even back when I used a longbow—badly, I might add—she made it so I hit the wyvern's weak spot in just one shot. She's the strongest hunter in all of Apegut, no doubt about it."

Yoi had a big smile on her face as she listened to me talk. But Mari, she stopped moving forward and turned around to face me.

"Hmph. She's a girl?"

"Wh-what, is there a problem with that?"

"Look at you. You've barely done anything since you got here and you already found yourself a wife and some side-bitch hussy. What a lucky creep you are."

"Okay, one, you've got it all wrong. Two, I'm a *slave* right now, remember?" I fired back.

'Doing well,' my ass. Nishka was a girl, sure, but there wasn't anything weird going on between us.

Mari's eyes narrowed as she glared. "I worked for myself, you understand? I worked myself half to *death,* and..."

Her words trailed off, almost as if she didn't want to finish that sentence. Maybe something had happened to her in the past that she thought I wouldn't be able to understand. Maybe something kept her from telling me.

Mari stopped. Turned her attention to the ground—it looked like she'd found something.

"Now, then," she said slowly, "I'll tell you a third possible reason."

"A third what?" Yoi asked.

"A third reason why the basilisk is holed up here."

Mari crouched down, keeping a wary eye in front of us. There was some kind of bone at her feet, something that looked like a primate skull. Next to that was a completely different, serpentine bone. "This first skull belongs to a kobold. *This* one belongs to a spotted pike. Look at that, there—we've even got some dungeon-worm droppings."

I blinked. "A pike and a what-worm?"

"Spotted pikes are like pythons, while dungeon-worms are more like giant caterpillars. They feed off corpses and grow to enormous size. This place looks small, but you have to remember that it's really a massive ecosystem. Big enough that the things living here don't even have to go outside to find prey." She adjusted her glasses. "There's also something else here, something that kobolds and spotted pikes both eat. Take a look." Mari pulled out her sword and stabbed it into the wall.

Taking that look she asked me to, I saw some kind of huge winged insect pinned to the wall. "The hell is that?"

"Moth flies. We had them back in our world, too. I said there was an underground lake here, didn't I? Well, these moth flies must be coming up from around there, and by the ton. Hate these super-sized bugs." With a grunt, a disgusted Mari wrested her sword free from the mammoth-sized moth fly and slid it back into its sheath.

She continued. "Droppings from things like kobolds, spotted pikes, and moth flies all mix together and run into the underground lake, which is where moth fly larvae are born. That's what the kobolds and spotted pikes end up eating, and the cycle continues. I'm sure there must be other bugs there as well, though."

"What do growing moth flies eat, then?"

"Use a little imagination. There must be something here that feeds off moss and algae as well, since the walls are so clean," she said, once again moving forward.

Suddenly, a thunderous roar from the depths of the dungeon shook the walls of the cave. It wasn't the first time I'd heard something like it. It was nearly the same roar as the wyvern who'd terrorized the village, which meant it had to have come from something similar.

A basilisk.

Trembling, I reached for Yoi's hand again—but she slapped me away. Giant horrible lizard time wasn't also hand-holding time. Okay. Fair enough!

●●●

Walking over uneven terrain puts a surprising amount of strain on you.

Back in the Edo period, people going on journeys supposedly traveled around twenty to thirty miles every day. That may not seem like much, considering people running a marathon can cover that kind of distance in just a few hours or so, but you've got to keep in mind that people back then had to take days to make it over bumpy roads and mountain passes. You can't compare it to the smooth, paved roads in modern times, and it wasn't like these guys could just travel in a straight line, either.

So people back then would mostly cut their progress short to save energy in case of any unforeseen inconveniences. It was the same idea as we journeyed toward the heart of the dungeon. We'd head straight for a while, have a quick bite to eat, check our equipment, then continue on.

After "cleaning up" the remaining kobolds, we found a nice hollow area off the beaten path where we could keep ourselves hidden. That was going to be our base-camp for the day.

"Usually you have several parties moving forward together when tackling the bigger dungeons," Mari explained as she turned the lamp into a makeshift stove by removing the outer case, grabbing some cooking utensils for us too. "For ruins, you search every nook and cranny and eliminate any monster nests you find. Once you secure a safe path, the stronger parties have a straight shot at the center of the dungeon."

Her explanation reminded me of what mountain climbers did when trying to reach the summit of Everest. Similar principles, I guess, but you climb down and kill stuff.

"Why try to explore dungeons in the first place, though?" I mused as we cooked the night's meal. "We're making our way through a place other people have already been through before, right? Treasure isn't going to respawn or something. Or are you going to tell me money just pops in out of nowhere?"

"Well, Mr. Slave, our ultimate goal is to beat the masters of these dungeons."

"Beating the master of the dungeon, huh? Understood, Miss Yoi."

"There's also the earl's commitment to protecting the territory," Mari added. "In exchange for collecting taxes, the earl of Bulka has a duty to protect their subjects."

"Fat lot of help they did for me," I snapped. "I got forced into slavery, so what's this guy doing? Something's messed up if he's letting slave traders and their idiot adventurers do whatever they want. I'm not being protected at all!"

"There's nothing strange about that. You're not a citizen of Bulka, after all."

"What...?" I could barely muster words. Wasn't the village chief supposed to work under him or something?

"You said you came from some remote village called Apegut, right?" asked Mari. "There would be a completely different governor over there."

"I mean, you're not wrong." I rubbed my temples. "Hold on, I need you to explain this to me. The village chief may be the governor of our area, but she only holds the rank of a knight. That's a lot lower than an earl, right? How is she not working for whoever's in charge of Bulka?"

"That's where it gets a bit tricky. There's actually multiple governors who all work together to control a single, larger territory. The one in charge of all *those* governors would be the earl."

"Then what does that make the village chief at Apegut?"

"An assistant to the earl, more or less," said Mari. "Don't think of it like an employer-employee relationship, it's more like a fresh-man-senior thing. Or, no—" she frowned "—maybe it's closer to a captain of a sports team and the rest of the players on that team."

"Not a sports guy, but I got the gist. This earl guy is the leader, then."

Yoi added ground wheat to the portable cookware as we talked, along with some dried vegetables and bacon. Beside her I peeled potatoes, cutting them into smaller pieces and throwing them in the pot as well.

"Then wouldn't that lead to a confrontation between the different leaders? The number of people under your control shows the kind of power you have, so shouldn't the village chief be trying to get me back as one of her subjects?"

Mari shook her head. "Interfering in territories outside of your own is a crime. As long as the leader of that particular area doesn't give the go-ahead, there's nothing another leader can do, not to mention the power difference between the leader of some remote village and the earl. We're talking the difference between the captain of a sports team and some no-name player who just got *on* the team."

Mari stirred the contents of our portable cooking pot as she gave me another weird sporty explanation. I understood it well enough.

After the pot come to a boil, I turned down the heat and put a lid on it. "So even though they're both governors, it's more like a peerage system than anything."

"Yeah, that's about right. I bet the whole reason you became a slave in the first place was because you didn't have anything to prove who you were. Fresh meat to those types."

"Would it have been any different if I'd been registered at the adventurer's guild?"

"Nah, probably not," Mari said as she stretched out. "Adventurers are pretty loose with their money, and plenty of them end up selling themselves as slaves anyway to pay off loans they took out to get started." She cracked her neck. "This world isn't a kind one. You've got your ferocious beasts lurking outside of civilization, and your greedy rulers lording over you if you *do* stay. It may seem like only the powerful rule here, but really it's even worse than that. If you don't have authority, you don't get to be human. You became a slave before you realized what was going on, that's all. You won't get any sympathy from me."

I nodded. "I see..."

"But it's not all bad, Mr. Slave!" Yoi chimed in.

"What do you mean?"

"You're a *contractual* slave, not a criminal or war prisoner-turned-slave. As long as you work hard enough to pay off how much you were bought for, you'll eventually be set free."

"Seriously? So if I can put my spear to good use and save up, I can buy my freedom?" I asked Yoi, keeping my expectations tempered. I didn't want to hold it against her if I'd misunderstood, but I did shoot a glance at Mari to check if Yoi was telling the truth.

"Yeah, that's true and all, but your master needs to approve it as well," said Mari. "If Yoi doesn't let you go, then you'll just have to live with being a slave forever. Too bad."

"I'd never do something that mean!" Yoi protested. "As long as he works hard, I'll be sure he gets rewarded!" Guhhhh she was so *cute* as she frantically tried to assuage my fears! Mari, on the other hand, just stuck her tongue out at me.

What a dick. Just about everything she did pissed me off, so I made a promise to myself that I'd get her back somehow. I wasn't going with the "revenge is a dish best served cold" route either—I wanted to get payback as soon and nastily as possible.

With palpable tension in the air, we took turns eating the soup from the pot and taking swigs from the bottle of wine we passed around.

All the while I waited for the right time to strike. I'd make sure to teach Mari a lesson as soon as I saw my chance.

It was probably about six in the evening, in a world where time got measured by hours. The sun would be moving behind the mountains on the horizon. It was a bit too early to go to sleep, but my body was exhausted from all my work.

"I think it's about sleepy-time for me, Mr. Slave."

"Understood, Miss Yoi. You're still young, so it's important that you rest up. You brushed your teeth? You went pee?"

"You're treating me like a kid! Hmph! Fine, I didn't pee yet, but I'll do it now, 'kay?"

Yoi acted like she was mad to hear me nagging her, but she still got up to take care of her business. She left our little alcove to head to the main road.

I'm thoroughly against monsters murdering pissing kids, so I hastily grabbed my mace and stood guard until she finished up. I arranged some of our baggage as a makeshift cushion for Yoi before tucking her in with a cloak.

With Yoi asleep, Mari was first on lookout duty, followed by me, then Yoi once she woke up.

This was a golden opportunity for me, though, and I wasn't about to let it pass me by. I got up, calling out to Mari as she played with her hair.

"Hey, Gangi Mari."

"Don't call me by my full name."

"Then how about you start using mine? It's 'Shooter,' in case you forgot."

"Pass."

"I get not making an effort to be cute for some stranger, I guess, but do you have to be downright nasty?"

"I don't need for you to think I'm cute..." she paused. "Shooter."

Look at that, she actually bothered with my name. Did she actually feel like being considerate now?

"Right, uh. Thanks, though."

"Hmph."

"I've got one more request," I added, "if you don't mind."

"What now?"

"Do some sword sparring with me. We're about to turn in for the night, right? I've got a little too much energy left over to sleep, so I want you to help me burn some off with some... training."

I didn't mean that in a dirty way, of course, but the expression on Mari's faced changed in an instant. There'd been a glimmer of shyness when she finally called me by my name, but now her face was ashen pale. The muscles in her face twitched, and the snobby look she usually had disappeared. Bizarre.

"*Training*, huh?"

"Right, just a bit of light sparring. Any weapon will do, but how about swords? That's something you can use, right?"

"What's your aim here?"

Mari spoke in a hushed whisper, and it wasn't just because she didn't want to wake up Yoi. My karate instincts told me one thing for sure: she was ready to kill me depending on what I said next.

She slowly reached for her sword as I spoke.

"It's simple, really. I'm human, and I've got a little something called 'pride.' And you've treated me like trash the whole time we've been together."

"Ha. What, you want revenge? I'm a Templar, and you're a slave. We're worlds apart."

"Nasty thing to say."

Mari glared, her hand now firmly on her sword. A spark of something indescribable flared in her expression.

"I think it's about time for a venting session," I said. "We're both party members in the middle of making our way through this dungeon, and we've got to help one another, don't we? As it stands, I'm never going to feel like doing a damn thing for you. And you feel the same."

Silence from her.

"I've taken down a wyvern before, but what about you?"

"I haven't."

"I didn't do it alone. In the air or on the ground, a lizard like that's not something you can take on half-heartedly or by yourself. Even in a group, it took all we had to put a scratch on it. If we had squabbled with each other, it would've been a whole lot worse than a few injured, a few dead. Much, *much* worse."

"Tch!" But no words.

"That's why I want us to put all this hate and ill will toward each other to bed. Tonight. Easier said than done, right? So let's make a bet: If I lose, I'll do anything you say from now on, and I won't ask to be treated as your equal. I'll be your slave along with Miss Yoi's."

I didn't know about the legalities behind that, but I would admit defeat if I lost. Which I was *not* going to let happen. Someone as bloodthirsty as Mari...I knew exactly how to handle that sort.

"And if I win—" I started.

"Fine, you're on. I don't need to think about what will happen if I lose. Because I won't."

"You say that, but you're talking to third-place in a regional karate tournament. Maybe think twice, buddy."

"So cocky. I'll crush that arrogance from your body, pipsqueak. You're dead."

She stood up and unsheathed her sword. I think she really meant to kill me. I reached over for my own shortsword, pulled it close. Stood.

Mari dragged the tip of her blade along the ground as we went to the main road. She didn't say a word, just pointed with her chin that I should follow. Though her back was turned to me, I could tell she hadn't let her guard down.

I held my sword in my right hand as I trailed behind her until she eventually turned around...with a potion capsule already loaded into her syringe device. The machine hissed, and the potion disappeared into her arm. There was no needle in the applicator. It used some kind of magic.

Damn. I hadn't thought about doping up. Each of the potion capsules were different shades, so you could tell what you were shooting up if you knew the colors. The problem was, I *didn't* know what each color meant, though I was willing to bet she'd just shot up some kind of adrenaline booster. For all her talk of having enough control not to get addicted to potions, she sure seemed to jump at any opportunity to use them.

After her eyes briefly rolled back in ecstasy, they opened. They were a shade darker, now. Even if these potions weren't having some effect on her mind, they were doing *something* to her body. Even just overworking your body normally makes your muscles sore beyond the next day, after all.

I guess it was my fault for not going over some ground rules before challenging her.

"No magic, all right?" I said.

"Of course. I'll let you have that as a handicap."

"Not much of a handicap after you shoot up with potions first!"

I dashed at her as soon as those words left my mouth. She threw out any semblance of fair play the second she used her potion, so to hell with it.

Shortswords were surprisingly easy for me to use. Think of it as having a blade for a hand. You thrust forward, almost like you're trying to punch your opponent, and as for defense? You just have to think of the blade as the hardest part of the body, something to block any attacks aimed your way.

Mari, on the other hand, wielded a longsword. Her particular style relied on centrifugal force, which meant there had to be openings between each swing.

Just as I predicted, she crouched down low with her sword when she saw me rushing. She probably planned on doing the same thing she'd done with the kobolds, just one straight slash right across my torso.

Too slow, Mari. I closed the distance, got up close.

Despite the fact that we were using real swords, I wasn't about to kill one of my party members. Mari didn't seem to share the sentiment. Her shoulders were tense with rage, and her movements even more wild than when we faced the kobolds. I didn't want this to be over before it really got started, so I thrust my sword with the intent to graze her neck.

My blade sliced clean through part of Mari's hair. The expression on her face changed in an instant as she backed off, raising her sword. Instead of pushing her blade with my sword, I pressed it with my left hand.

"Aww. Just one step too slow."

"Just *die* already!"

Mari moved quick, fueled by potion, and aimed a slash that could slice me in half like a paper doll. I retreated, but Mari followed up with a flurry of strikes. Might've been brute forced, but she knew how to handle a sword.

It was time to finish this. If the fight lasted too long, it might affect us tomorrow. I took an open, lazy stance to lure her in, tempt her into using all that raw strength. She happily obliged.

Sword raised high above her head, she rushed at me. At the last second I dodged to the side, tripping her up, and sent her crashing to the ground. My sword clattered to the ground a few feet away, but now wasn't the time to care about that.

We grappled one another on the dungeon floor, each trying to get into a mount position, battling for scraps of dominance. Finally I pinned her arms and legs with my own. Victory for me, and an overwhelming one to boot.

"Too bad, Mari."

"L-Let go of me!"

"Nah. You'll just start flailing around again."

"What are you planning to do with me?" she spat.

She was frantically trying to fight me off, practically trying to bite me.

"Do you give up, Mari?"

"No! Kill me!"

Wow, that was...intense.

"I'm not gonna kill you. Now stop struggling, it's over."

"Wh-what, are you planning to do, ravish me? Like a big ape-man or something?"

"No! What? I—oh man, of course not!"

"Then what are you planning to do?"

"I want to be *done*! I just wanted us to work off our stress and get rid of the bad blood between us. I wanted a fellow Japanese person to see me as an ally! I'm so sick of this!"

Silence.

"Can't we just stop this already? You really do treat me like some giant apeman, so can you just...stop? Please?"

"Hmph." Mari stopped struggling beneath me. Once I was sure she wasn't going to start thrashing me the moment I let go, I loosened my hold.

"We're equals from now on," I said. "Two members of the same party. Sound good?"

"Yeah, party members."

I stood up and offered Mari a hand.

"*Equal* party members."

"Tch. Don't get carried away," she spat back.

"Right, then that's all I wanted as my reward for winning."

"You serious?"

"Yup, that's it. I'm satisfied with having you see me as a proper ally..." I shrugged. "For now, at least."

"What do you mean? You planning on asking me for something later?"

"Maybe, we'll see. But that aside, Mari..."

I watched as she kept her gaze on the ground.

"What?"

"This thing about a giant apeman. What's that about?"

The murderous glare Mari shot back told me everything I needed to know. It looked like I was right on the money.

"There's nothing to talk about."

"Yeah. Of course there isn't."

Of course there was. Some high school girl stuck in another world with no way to defend herself, young and weak and desperate to find strength. Horrible things happened first. Then came the endless potions, the constant rage, the reliance on strength above all things.

"Forget what you heard," said Mari quietly. "All of it."

"Don't know what you're talking about. We were just training, that's all."

The awkwardness in the air was palpable. Mari picked up her sword before heading back to the alcove where Yoi was sleeping. After watching her go, I went to collect my own shortsword as well.

What an awful world this was. If Mari didn't rely on potions to protect herself, to become stronger, then she'd live and die as a high school girl. She could wait for death or pick it on her terms, with the slow creep of potions through her veins. Those were the thoughts going through my head as I crushed her empty potion capsule under my foot.

What Happened with Nishka

WHEN I WOKE UP, I found out I didn't have a coin to my name.

"Urgh, I feel awful..." I batted at the air. "Be a pal and grab me some water, Shooter."

Guess what? Shooter wasn't there. I was the only one left in the empty room, still hanging around in my hammock, sunlight blazing right into my eyes. The only thing left was the smell of the bug repellant that had been burning all night long.

Water. I was dyin' of thirst. Need...water...I crawled out of the hammock and buttoned up my blouse. Come to think of it, where *was* Shooter? I struggled to stay on my feet as I grabbed one of my kickass eye patches from the top hammock. It was a different one than I'd worn yesterday, but no one really seemed to notice or care. Looked pretty good on my right eye as well, but I was hoping for some guy to come up and be like, "Dang, your right eye looks as beautiful as your left!" or something like that. Nobody notices these things! New shoes, new eye patches. Clueless.

Hold up, wasn't I supposed to be sleeping in the top bunk? Wait. *Wait*, why was I in Shooter's bed? Panicking, I checked my clothes to make sure I still had 'em all on. Thankfully, my underwear was still present and accounted for. Safe again from the antics of Tipsy Nish. And yeah, before you ask, of *course* I don't put my underwear on after sex. What kinda weirdo would do that?

Whatever. Water. Needed...water. I grabbed the canteen I saw on the hammock and took a swig.

And it was booze. Great. I thought it was Shooter's canteen, but it was just mine. Was there really no water nearby? I grabbed my knife and belt from the side of the bunk bed and hooked it back around my waist. First thing's first: water. That good shit we organisms crave. Next step, find out where those two went off to. I got hold of the goblin running the counter downstairs and asked him if he'd seen the boys anywhere.

"Gimul and that loincloth guy? Yeah, they left earlier this morning."

"Where to?!"

"Hell if I know. I know they paid for ten days in advance, but that's about it."

Which meant someone would be coming back soon, at least. Gimul said he was going back to the village today, so I guessed he'd be going to the guild to pick up those adventurers, which meant Shooter would come back later. Maybe soon, if it was almost lunch.

"Hey, man, I'm dyin' of thirst. Give a girl some water, would ya?" The goblin stuck out his hand.

I blinked. "What? You wanna shake on it?"

"Water's gonna cost ya. Need to cover costs for firewood, so pay up."

"No, you moron! I'm talking about water to *drink*!"

"Only seeing one moron around here, missy. You really gonna drink water without boiling it and vomit all over my inn? Nah. One bronze coin."

Friggin' cheapskate. I reached inside my pockets and started to rummage around, but then, uh. Right, I was still in my blouse and a pair of underwear. Bad enough, that, but also? Broke.

I didn't have much of a choice, so I cut some vodka with well water and drank it down. The booze rushed down my throat, finding a home in my empty stomach.

No matter how long I waited, Shooter didn't come back. It was right around sunset that I got a bit nervous. I dug into some of the nasty biscuits and wyvern jerky we brought as portable rations, just to get something in my stomach. What I really wanted was to put it in a stew or something, but that was out of the question since I didn't have the cash for firewood.

I was dead broke, after all. If Shooter wasn't around, I wasn't going to get any kind of decent meal. Not that I regularly have money problems, thank you very much. I'm just a good big sister. Left the cash back home. *Plenty* of cash, which we always have, because I'm great at money when I need to be.

Still, I probably should've brought some cash just in case something like this happened. The only thing on me that was worth anything was the wyvern scale I wore around my neck. I used it as proof of my skill as a hunter, but I also heard certain moneybags with too much money bought 'em up. Something about crushing them up and using them for medicine, if I remembered correctly.

My plan was to go to one of the trading counters they had at every guild and see how much I could get for it, unless I found Shooter first. I retraced our steps from yesterday and followed the road to the adventurer's guild. I may be from the sticks, but we hunters gotta memorize any routes we take the first time around.

Eventually, I moseyed on down to the guild counter. "If you're talking about that lightly armored warrior," said the girl at the desk, "he hasn't come back here since this morning."

Well, shit. No luck here either. "Got a question for you."

"Please, go ahead."

"Whaddya think of *this,* huh? Fancy stuff, don't you think?" I said, wiggling my necklace at her.

"Um...it looks nice? Did it come from a dragon?"

"A wyvern, actually. I've hunted as many wyverns as I've seen winters since becoming a hunter."

"Okay! That's! Very cool?"

Uh. How was this not impressive? "W-well, you can sell stuff here, right? How much do you think I'd get for it?"

"Probably about twenty copper coins, I'd imagine."

"Not even one silver coin?"

"Not from the guild, no."

"But I won't be able to even feed myself with that! I'm starving here, tell me you know a place that would buy it for a bit more!"

After drinks and a teensy bit of food, twenty copper coins would be gone in no time. Everything cost an arm and a leg in this place. What was I going to do if I ran out of money before I found Shooter?

"C'mon, you gotta help me out here! Please!"

"I'm sorry, Miss, but there's nothing much I can do for you. If you're strong enough to handle a wyvern, I would think registering here at the guild would be the best way to secure your future."

"Hrm..." She had a point. I was a hunter, so killing monsters would be a snap. I didn't have much in the way of hunting gear, but I wouldn't need much to handle kobolds or some wild bears. From what I heard, it wasn't like all adventurers did was hunt monsters, either.

"Then fill me in on what I need to do for registering. You don't charge a fee for that or something, do you?"

"I would be happy to help. And not to worry, we don't charge a registration fee," the receptionist said, smiling.

Ugh. Well, whatever. She led me over to an adjacent counter to get me squared away.

"It just so happens that we're accepting applicants for an ogre-hunting quest! Anyone who's already joined, please wait there. We're also looking for people for a temporary farming quest!"

I stood outside the guild, working to sell passersby on the quests available inside. Look, I needed cash and food fast. The sun was already low in the sky, but the guild was livelier than ever since the appearance of a group of ogres in a village on the outskirts of town. Advertising opportunities were through the roof, apparently.

I kinda wanted to do the ogre quest—would've made bank on that one—but the receptionist said she would treat me to food after this marketing job was done, so I went with it instead. Shooter hadn't come back, so I didn't have much of a choice.

"Ogre-hunting quest, right here, folks! Step right up, don't be shy! Ogre come, make danger, taste adventure, smell heroism! Anyone who wants in, just ask at the counter. Everyone who's already signed up, gather up over here, please!"

Stupid Gimul, stupid job, Shooter, you asshole!

Shooter's Perspective

"**A**H-CHOO!"

I let out a huge sneeze as I scrubbed away at Yoi's underwear. Huh. I guess being naked makes you sneeze more? Mysteries upon mysteries.

CH. Dungeon and Slave
-Part 2-
6

I'M UPDOG! What's updog, you ask? Penis joke. I was gonna do a penis joke here, but I just remembered that I already did the damn thing earlier. Pretend to be surprised. Anyway. Boner. Had one.

I was wrapped up in my cloak as I slept, which was only long enough to cover my top half. My bottom half, on the other hand, was exposed for all the world to see...and morning wood was, here as anywhere else, inescapable.

Yoi was just a kid, so I tried to nope out of there quick as I could...but still found myself on the receiving end of a swift kick from a very unhappy Mari.

"Wh-why the hell is your thing like that first thing in the morning?"

I hurried to cover Shuta Jr.—one kick was bad enough, and I really didn't want a second kick to hit somewhere else. "Ow! Quit it, Mari! We're supposed to be allies, right?"

"Ganjamary, what did Mr. Slave do?"

"Even though we're *right* here, his d-di...his *privates* swelled up! Pervert!"

"Hold up, I'm naked, sure, but this here's just a natural reaction! All it means is that I'm a healthy, uh, slave man!"

"You make me sick!" Mari yammered on. "You can't use magic, you can't read, but what you *can* do is show off your gross dangly bits in front of two innocent ladies! What the hell is wrong with you?"

The day was off to a good start. It really was an honest, perfectly natural reaction, so there wasn't anything I could do about it. Unless, that is, Mari wanted to help me get it under control.

She must've been a mind reader or something, because she seemed to know exactly what was on my mind. "Just die! Then die again and go straight to hell!"

I think I might've worried Yoi, since she took Mari aside and started speaking to her in hushed tones while I had my back turned away. Not quite hushed enough, though.

"Mari, did something happen between you two when I was sleeping?"

"N-no, nothing happened! Don't worry about it!"

"That's the truth?"

"Nothing happened, really," and she sighed. "But, see, that's the problem. I was ready for him to do something to me, but *nothing* happened."

"Huh?"

Whoa, the hell? Just what kind of guy did Mari take me for?

Me a married man, Mari the friend of the girl who owned me. Did she really think I'd...?

"I thought he was the just the worst kind of guy, and I was going to treat him that way...but then he has the nerve to be nice! Ugh, now I don't know what to think!"

"Tell me—do you like him or hate him?"

"Don't be ridiculous. He's a slave! You can't like a slave and you can't hate a slave, so...neither! I'll admit he's a bit more of a gentleman than I thought, but he put the bar so low already. I mean, he's buck naked!"

That hit me like a ton of bricks; I almost fell over on the spot. I finally managed to get Shuta Jr. calmed down and turned around to face the girls once more, looking as innocent as I could, but Mari didn't continue that line of thought.

We started getting ready to trek further into the dungeon. Mari took me aside and whispered, "W-was that really supposed to be a natural reaction?"

"Yeah. They say us guys get like that in life-threatening situations."

"You're not messing with me, right?"

"I mean, I'm no scientist, so I can't say for sure. But if we're going to go up against a basilisk, then yeah, I think I'd consider that a threat to my life."

"I guess you've got a point there," she admitted. "But please keep that thing out of Yoi's sight."

"Yeah, I didn't mean for it to turn out like this. You're still a young woman, too, so you seeing it wasn't exactly proper either."

"I-I'm fine, really."

Her face now a nice bright scarlet and getting redder, Mari quickly shoved her face into the map.

With our hardest problem out of the way, it was time to get back to the dangerous one—tackling the rest of this dungeon. We were past the point Yoi and Mari got to last time, and were somewhere toward the middle of the whole thing.

Just as Yoi explained, this dungeon was small enough to clear out in just a few days. That was how it looked on the map, at least, but our map was a copy made by explorers who last visited fifteen years ago. Yoi was creating a whole new one as we made our way deeper inside.

When I asked why, Mari answered, "Sometimes, we run across dungeons that have some kind of magic-powered mechanism that changes the layout of the place each time you go there. Ancient technology built by forgotten civilizations."

I wish she'd given me a second to digest that. Absolutely insane.

"They're few and far between, though. But if you don't take that kind of risk into account, you can lose your whole party to a monster attack. I know from experience."

"That actually happened to you?"

"Mm. It was back when we were clearing this dungeon in the south, swarming with giant apemen. That's where I first met Yoi."

That would explain why they were so diligent about making the map, then. And...wait. Was that dungeon where Mari...? Oh. Shit. No, best not to think about it.

"We don't have to worry about this dungeon, though, Mr. Slave. It's not the kind of place with those devices. The fact a basilisk is here proves it."

"Good to hear," I said, beaming. "You're so clever, Miss Yoi. You're always on top of these things."

"Eh he he!" She broke out into a dreamy smile as I gave her a couple of head pats.

"But for the naturally formed dungeons," she continued, "you have to worry about cave-ins. That's why it's important to keep maps as up-to-date as you can!"

"It's a wonderful sentiment, Miss Yoi. Let's make sure to turn ours in to the guild once we finish up here."

"Okie dokie, Mr. Slave!"

Just stupidly, ridiculously cute. Gahh! Back in college, I took care of an older karate compatriot's son every once in a while. I wasn't babysitting him or anything, I think the kid was already three or so years old at the time. I would just give him piggyback rides and take naps with him, stuff like that.

It was kinda nice! I got all the fun parts of having a kid without all the work, kind of like what was happening with Yoi right now. She really was a smart girl, so it brought me no small joy to be with her.

And by the way—just in case you're a certain kind of reader—I don't have a lolicon thing. That doesn't mean I have a little boy thing, either. Kids are just goddamn cute, and that's all there is to it. Mari, on the other hand, looked absolutely disgusted with the mushy faces I was making at Yoi. "Let's get going, you two," she called back as she started to walk away, the pool of light magic shining around her.

I hurried to gather up all our belongings, then, holding hands with tiny Yoi, followed.

We ran into some spotted pikes as we made our way further inside, and even crushed some moth flies we came across. We checked out a few side roads along the way too, but most of them were swarming with monsters. We marked those places on our map, then took 'em out before we delved deeper.

Though we talked about cave-ins earlier, I hadn't been too worried about them—until we came across a huge pile of rubble.

"The road's out..." Mari sighed, placing a hand on the pile of stone and ruin blocking our path. "Looks like it happened recently, too. Going by the architecture, the surroundings, everything...I'm thinking this was a year, maybe six months ago."

Mari lit up the ceiling with her magic, so I lifted my lantern to cast more light as well. She pulled out her longsword and stood on her tiptoes as she poked at the crumbling parts of the ceiling. Yoi, meanwhile, had crouched down and was inspecting the bits of earth on the ground, shining her own light magic on the pieces. Magic really was a wonder. Maybe someday I'd be able to use it too.

"It doesn't look like this happened naturally, Mr. Slave. Since it's a bit more cramped in this area, it seems like something scraped along the ceiling and walls to force its way through," Yoi mused. "There's traces that show it has a tail, too."

"Yeah," Mari added, "those definitely look like tail tracks to me. It's completely different from a spotted pike's, too."

So a basilisk dragged its giant body through here, and that caused the cave-in. Got it. "Do we have any alternate routes?"

Yoi shook her head. "There's only one road that leads to the underground lake."

"So this is our only route," said Mari. "The ground isn't too hard—we might be able to force our way through."

"You're right. I'll try and open a way with my magic, then. Here, hold this, Mr. Slave!"

Yoi stood and handed me the dungeon map she'd been working on, along with the older version. She opened her grimoire and flipped through the pages until she stopped on a bookmark.

"If Yoi's going to open a hole for us to get through, I'd back up if I were you," said Mari.

"Whoa, hold on, won't trying to force through just cause another cave-in?"

"Maybe. Got any other ideas? Besides, it's not like we're just blasting our way in. Watch."

I decided to take Mari's advice and copy her. As we turned our backs to the cave-in, something shivered through the air. Yoi had only used light magic up until this point, but I was about to get a taste of the real deal. Well, as much as I could with my back turned.

In the enchanted, electrified air...things were getting a bit breezy downstairs, so I covered my important bits with one hand while we waited for the wondrous enchantment. Mari saw this. She did not like it.

"You have *got* to be kidding me."

"It's cold going commando, okay? I'll be frozen stiff!"

There was a loud rumbling, then, and a hail of dirt and rocks pelting my back. And my backside. C'mon, I just had a cloak on here, my bountiful buttcheeks were just hanging out. I did *not* need that shit today. The barrage of debris died down, and I heard a short gasp from Yoi.

Now for the cheerful, "I did it!" Any second. Now. Now?

But she didn't say a word.

Mari was the first to turn around. I followed suit, and I barely believed what I saw. "Um, what the hell is that?"

"H-how should I know?" Mari stammered.

"It's like some kind of dragon, almost!"

"Well, yeah, I guess, but—!"

"Kind of like if a T-rex got down on all fours and sprouted a big ol' crest on its head, right? Right, Mari?"

"Please, please, *please* shut up—Yoi, get back!"

Yoi's magic had blown away all the debris blocking our path—but in the place of the cave-in was now a lizard the size of a minivan—specifically, a 2008 Fnord Excavator.

Well, Mr. Basilisk, meet Mr. Slave. I threw down the stuff I was carrying and readied myself for a fight.

● ● ●

There it was before us, the end of our dungeon: the basilisk. In no way did it feel like I had enough time to prepare.

I didn't feel great about taking it on with only a mace, but it was the only weapon I could rely on now. My shortsword couldn't pierce through those thick scales.

If Nishka were here, I bet we could've put an arrow in the basilisk's eyes and taken it out with one good shot. But good ol' Nishka *wasn't* here, and I didn't exactly have a bow. Man, I found myself wishing that I'd taken it from the inn, but without Nishka I'd just be flailing it menacingly till the big lizard murdered me.

Okay. Enough freaking out. What was this thing's weak point?

Let's start from humans. Focusing on our noses, mouths, ears, and lungs is usually a safe bet. What kinda organs do dinosaurs have? Must be mostly the same stuff, yeah? Didn't dinosaurs have three brains? I feel like I read some book as a kid that said dinosaurs had three or four brains, so a whack on the head wouldn't do much. Too much brain. Or maybe—did that mean there'd be more brains to mess with? Argh.

Maybe Mr. Basilisk would take it easy on me?

As I steeled myself for an arduous fight, Yoi was flipping through her grimoire, turning it to one specific page before sticking her bookmark inside.

I turned to her. "Please get back, Miss Yoi!"

"It's all right, Mr. Slave. I'll take the first shot!"

I wanted to pull her away, but I hesitated. Did she really know what she was doing? We're talking a lizard the size of a comfortable but surprisingly economic and fuel-efficient van, here!

The basilisk let out a low growl. I think it was just as flat-footed as we were. Now would be the time to strike if we were going to make the first move, but…did I really want to take the time to attack when my little master was in danger?

"Come on, we're charging in after she gets her spell off," Mari hissed.

"She's gonna be okay, right?"

"Just watch. Yoi is stronger than you know."

So I backed off. I would rush in as soon as Yoi was finished with her attack, but only then. I didn't know how much damage Yoi would do, but I'd take a chance on pummeling the softest basilisk bits I could get, preferably on its big, ugly snout.

"We don't have to kill it. All we have to do is keep it busy until Yoi can—"

Yoi launched her attack before Mari even finished speaking. An electrifying aura surrounded her, filling the air with indescribable and overwhelming power. She drew a symbol in the air with her hand before shouting an incantation: "Physical, magical, kaboom!"

Countless tentacles burst forth from the walls. Before the bewildered basilisk could react, the attack began. Not only that, but Yoi's magic summoned hundreds of sharp spikes, driving into the monster's underbelly as the tentacles lashed.

"Now's our chance!" Yoi cried. "Let's attack it from both sides!"

With no plan beyond whatever *that* was, I prepared myself to fulfill my role in the attack with Mari. I didn't know if she trusted me now or what, but she sure didn't hesitate as she sprang into action.

A good number of the spikes pierced the basilisk's stomach. It tried to rear up and escape, but there was no room for it to move in the cramped cavern. Several of the tentacles wrapped around the monster's legs and tore it down to the earth.

"Let's do this!"

Beside me, the tennis ball-sized orb of light Mari used to light her way burst into flames and she hurled it right into the basilisk's face. Didn't know how powerful it was, but the basilisk roared in pain, so it clearly did *something*.

The fear-inducing roar—the thing that all species of dragon shared—reverberated throughout the small cavern. I did all I could to resist, but I still ended up screeching to a halt right in front of the basilisk.

Mari, however, was unaffected. Right after loosing her fireball, she popped some kind of potion capsule to nullify the basilisk's roar. She kicked me out of the way of danger before switching to an underhand grip with her sword and shoving it into the monster's cheek.

"Take that!" she roared, and the beast roared right back.

And ah. Ah, shit. As soon as I was freed from my temporary paralysis, I started sprinting toward the basilisk. I said T-rex before, I know, and I'm sorry for making you rethink the whole visual layout here, but we were looking at more of a bear. Taking a blow from one of its not-remotely-vestigial front legs would be instant death for Mari.

With a running tackle, I shoved her away from a swipe that would've taken her head. We tumbled to the floor together, rolled, pulled ourselves up. I unsheathed my shortsword and stabbed it into the ground.

"Here," I cried, "use this!"

Mari's sword was still lodged into the basilisk's cheek. She was only alive right now because she let go of it, but I wasn't about to leave her without a weapon.

As for me, I still had my mace, and the only option left to me was to find a place to whack the basilisk with it. It was tied down thanks to Yoi's magic, sure, but its struggles were violent, and the spell looked like it wasn't going to hold much longer.

Yoi shot me a desperate look. "Can you buy us some more time, Mr. Slave?"

"I'll try!"

It wasn't going to be easy, though. The eyes were too difficult to hit, so it had to be something else. Ears? Yeah, the ears!

Just before the tentacles loosened their hold on the basilisk, I rushed forward to land one solid blow right on its earhole. It let out an enraged howl of pain that sent shockwaves of magic flying.

But I couldn't run away, I *couldn't*. Nope. I'd stand up. Yeah. Stand. *Up*!

I could see Mari sprinting behind the monster out of the corner of my eye. Maybe it was because of her experience in battle, but she could fight through the roar with the best of them. No minor setbacks would break her spirit.

At the monster's back, she slashed the tip of its tail lightly, just enough to get its attention. It whirled around. Now that it was free of the writhing magic tentacles that once bound it, the basilisk seemed torn: me or Mari?

Turning around was a fatal mistake. This wasn't a dungeon built by people, but a naturally formed cave. The size of the passageways weren't uniform, which was perfect for humans like us. We can navigate uneven terrain. We can turn it to our advantage.

Yoi stood in a narrower part of the cavern, and while my area had a bit more room, it was still small enough that the huge basilisk had some problems turning. The area Mari was standing in was just as narrow as Yoi's.

One last mistake for a big, dumb lizard.

"I'll get its legs!" I cried.

"And I'll slice open its neck!" Mari shouted back.

The basilisk wiggled its front left leg in the air, frantically trying to twist its body to face Mari. I threw everything I had behind my mace and smashed the raised limb. Painful, and right in the goddamn pinky toe.

Big or small, tough or weak, cramped spaces made it hard for any monster to be on the defensive. Which was cool, but I had no idea what do after landing the hit. I'd have to dodge. But there was no room to do it.

Mari was supposed to be a Templar. Maybe she prayed to the same goddess that let the priests in Apegut heal me up. I was going to need it after this.

I completely shattered the bones in the basilisk's pinky toe with my mace, and shit that must have hurt. The monster shot straight up in agony despite the low ceiling. Mari popped another potion and went into full-on berserker mode. Swish—one decisive slash across the monster's neck.

The basilisk thrashed in pain, sending Mari flying with one swipe of its front legs. I couldn't get over to protect her, either, unless I wanted to die as well.

"Run, Mr. Slave!"

Yoi came to our rescue. A burning spear of earth burst from her grimoire, and she sent it hurtling at the basilisk. It pierced the monster in the left side of its chest, and as the arcane weapon ruptured its heart, it collapsed instantly. I desperately crawled away to avoid the basilisk's crumpling corpse.

Holy crap. To think such a cute little goblin master could be so strong...wild. If Yoi had pulled off this kind of attack at the very beginning, Mari and I would've just been standing over the sizzling corpse twiddling our thumbs.

I was a little worried when I saw Mari wasn't moving, but it turned out she was still alive.

"Whoa. You okay?"

"Potion..." she said hoarsely. "Light blue potion..."

She barely got the words out of her mouth as she lay spread-eagle. I did as she told me and picked out a light blue potion from the stock she kept in her belt, then searched around for wherever her syringe device had ended up in the heat of battle. Once I found it, it was simple enough to load the capsule that even someone like me could do it. I don't know *how* it worked, but at least I could get it working; once I pressed the applicator against Mari's upper arm and pushed, the contents of the capsule disappeared inside her.

"Ahhh." Mari beamed. "That's the stuff." I never bought her excuse that she wasn't a druggie, but with a look like that on her face? Yeah. Come on.

Once upon a time, I worked a part-time job as a waiter at a cross-dressing bar, just one part of a mini-mall sort of building. The owner of that particular bar wore his beard nearly as well as his skimpy outfits—now *that's* power. Anyway, I remembered we were cleaning up after the place closed, and he suddenly let out a low-pitched scream.

He'd found a syringe in the public bathroom right outside our shop, and we were pretty damn sure it wasn't from a diabetic. Sure enough, some poor shmuck had collapsed on the stairwell outside, and the look on their face was pretty much the same as Mari's.

"I'll be fine after a bit," she said with a dreamy sigh. "That was a health potion."

That was enough for me, at least. Yoi looked decidedly more worried, and cradled Mari's head in her lap.

"No going overboard like that, Ganjamary."

"Heh. Nah, that's what I'm here for. I keep the bad guys at bay so you can line up the shot. It would've been different if we had more space to fight the thing, but we didn't really have a choice."

True, we hadn't had much choice, since the thing came at us out of nowhere. Mari might've been able to keep the basilisk pinned down with fireballs from a distance, but the smoke from the explosions would have obscured our line of sight. Knowing when and how to use spells was a lot more complicated than I initially thought.

"Aside from that, you look like you're all right, Mr. Slave, but... are you?"

"I'm pretty much fine, Miss Yoi. Somehow." I'd earned a few bumps and scrapes, sure, but nothing serious.

"Then we'll wait for Ganjamary to recover and just head straight for the underground lake. We'll update the rest of the map some other time."

"Makes sense. We can't force Mari to push herself, so let's just wrap it up." I glanced back at the collapsed basilisk—there couldn't be much to worry about after taking out the dungeon master.

Everyone's at their most vulnerable after a battle. Not that I'd really experienced anything like that in my old world, but it happened all the time in those monster-hunting games. In fact, it happened more times than I could count when I was freeloading at my karate teacher's house in Okinawa.

There was no greater joy than taking out a monster within the time limit, me and his granddaughter plugging away at the thing, sitting in front of the TV without a care in the world. But of course, just when I landed a clean hit on the monster and broke part of it with my hammer, one of his huge buddies would wander onto the map and wreck us.

This was real life, though, and I couldn't afford to let my guard down. It was like those movies where if you die in the game, you die in real life...except this was no game. So, err, it was like...if you died in real life, you'd *die* in *real life*.

I've lost control of this metaphor.

"Is something wrong, Mr. Slave?" Yoi asked. We were walking hand-in-hand, but I think she could tell I was feeling high-strung.

"I don't think so, nah. I'm just trying not to let my guard down till we're out of here, even with that thing dead. Never assume it's over till you're home; that's what you learn as a hunter and a warrior."

"You're amazing! I really got lucky when I bought you!"

Trust me, those words are really cute when it's a little girl saying them.

"But if you keep doing this much work," Yoi continued, "we'll have to say goodbye to each other a lot faster than I thought. Don't go away yet, Mr. Slave!"

"Of course not. I'll be around to watch you grow into a fine young woman, Miss Yoi." Except I wanted to get back to the village, right? But who could say no to that cute little kid? I put on my brightest smile to hide my conflicted feelings, but the look on Mari's face said she wasn't buying any of it.

We were on our way to the deepest part of the dungeon, a place that housed an entire underground lake. Yoi compared the terrain to the old copy of the map as we moved along, updating her own version but ignoring the smaller branching paths.

We hadn't carved the basilisk before we left. I would have considered that a failure on my part if I were still a hunter—but right now, we were a party of adventurers. That was why we took only a part of the basilisk while leaving the rest behind.

"I wonder if other monsters will come pick the corpse clean if we just leave it there?" I said.

"Maybe," said Mari. "It's possible something else could come along, eat what's left of the basilisk, and become the new master of the dungeon. I've heard spotted pikes can grow to be pretty huge if left alone for too long."

"Seriously?"

"Still better than a basilisk, though."

As we kept talking, we finally arrived at the underground lake. The ground around the lake was slick, and it was easy to slip if you weren't paying attention. Things could've been a lot worse if I hadn't been wearing those boots. Whatever covered the ground was slimy, and I was willing to bet it would be miserable walking on it with bare feet.

"It's a lot bigger than I thought, Mr. Slave."

"So it is, Miss Yoi."

We were awestruck. The place was the size of a gymnasium! Although they called it a "dungeon," it was actually a naturally formed cavern. Still, you could see evidence of human intervention from when it'd been turned into a shrine. Pillars had been sculpted straight out of the walls, with elaborate reliefs of angels and ancient tales hewn beside them. Some carvings had been weathered away by the passage of time into plain rock. Rays of sunshine spilled from the ceiling of the cave, illuminating an enormous statue of a goddess on the opposite side of the lake.

Mari knelt on one knee and offered a prayer to the goddess. "O Goddess from which the earth was born, we thank you for your daily blessings..." Even though she was from Japan, she was a Templar for the Church now, so I guess she was a convert. I remembered the priest presiding over the funerals at the village saying something similar.

Oh yeah, I meant to ask the priests about whether people who died here went to other worlds. Might be a good idea to try and grab hold of one after we make it back to Bulka safe and sound. I somehow doubted Mari wanted to talk theology with me.

Once Yoi and Mari finished admiring the view, we needed to explore the underground lake and the dome that contained it. We were all dead tired, so I was kind of hoping to hurry along. I was sure there couldn't be anything worse than a basilisk lurking nearby, but spotted pike snakes were still large enough to strangle Yoi and swallow her whole. I wasn't about to get careless.

"Let's get to exploring, then," said Yoi. "Somewhere down here we'll find the basilisk's nest."

"Right, let's split up and get this over with as fast as possible. Shooter, you head over there with Yoi. I'll go check out the other side."

Hey, she'd actually called me by my name! Ah, little victories. "What should we do about the other side of the lake?"

"We'll have to have someone swim over there and look. And would you look at that, you're already naked. Go ahead, slave."

And tiny defeats. Bossing me around and once more, not calling me by my name, just great. I glumly took Yoi's hand and walked away from Mari. I always used *her* name when I talked to her, so why couldn't she do the same? Maybe calling her "Mari-chan" would be better...

"Well, this doesn't look good."

I wasn't thrilled to find a giant egg. In fact, I can't think of many situations where *anyone* would be thrilled to find a giant egg. It was about the size of a half-deflated basketball, but molded into a vague oval. It wasn't similar to regular chicken eggs either, those being more elongated than this was.

Eerily, it reminded me of something from a book I read back in elementary school—a book about dinosaurs, no less. In fact, it looked exactly like the book's picture of a fossilized dinosaur egg.

"M-Mr. Slave! What's that?!"

"A basilisk egg, I'd wager. That, or a spotted pike egg."

Yoi nodded. "That was the first time I've even seen a basilisk, so I don't know, either."

There were three (what I assumed to be) basilisk eggs here, with the third one being nothing more than an empty shell. Had it already hatched? And if that was the case, where had the hatchling gone?

Yoi crouched and began inspecting the empty eggshell, and all I could do was hope she'd figure something out. There was already one problem even someone like me could see: if there were eggs here, then there had been parents to lay them.

The basilisk had a mate.

"What's wrong?" Mari called out from behind me.

"Uh. So, hate to say it, but we've got a problem here. A really serious problem."

She snorted dismissively...and then she saw the basilisk eggs. And froze.

"One of them is already broken," she said, her voice trembling. "If it hatched, then that means the others could hatch at any second."

"As long as they're fertilized," I added.

"And if that one *did* hatch...then where did it go?" It seemed like fear was keeping Mari from saying any more than that.

"There's a chance the other parent is around," I said.

She nodded. "Yeah. Do you think the one we fought before was the mother, or the father?"

That was the million dollar question. If basilisks were anything similar to wyverns, and the size difference between males and females was night and day, we could have a big problem on our hands—literally. If the basilisk from before was a female, it wouldn't be a stretch to assume the male would dwarf it in size.

"Either way," said Mari finally, "we can't just leave these eggs like this."

"Agreed."

If we left them alone, we'd be responsible for unleashing dungeon-bred basilisks upon the world. They could easily reach villages near Bulka and cause all sorts of chaos and destruction.

Mari and I nodded to each other, then I picked up my mace.

"Please back away, Miss Yoi. I'm going to smash these eggs."

"Okay!"

Right as I was about to bring my mace down with extreme prejudice—

Crack.

"Uh oh."

Something was starting to break through the egg from the inside. The tip of a beak wriggled through the hole it made in the shell. Next it managed to get its hands through, then finally pushed all the way out, tail swishing back and forth.

"*Kwee?*"

I found myself face-to-face with a newborn basilisk hatchling.

I was speechless. I couldn't bring my mace down on it now. If I'd only done it a few moments earlier, I probably wouldn't be feeling these pangs of guilt. Yeah, pretty much anything looks cuter as a baby, but even worse, I looked it right in the eyes. If I maced it now, I was gonna have nightmares.

"Wh-what are we gonna do about this?" Mari hissed.

I gulped. "I...have no idea."

"If we don't hurry and think of something, the other parent could come back," Yoi interjected. "Let's just get away from it for now."

"Where to? Could you show me the map?"

"There's a stone room in the shrine on the other side of the lake. We could hide there."

"We'd have to swim for it, then," I said. "I can manage, but what about you two?"

"I can make do if I get rid of my armor," said Mari.

Yoi swallowed. "I...can't swim."

"*Kwee!*"

The three of us hunched over the dungeon map, considering our options. Every few seconds, Mari looked up to scan our surroundings for potential danger.

If it came down to it, I could bring Yoi along with me and make it across the lake together, but I was worried about Mari casting aside her armor. If we ran into trouble, she was going to need it. Not to mention that we'd have to abandon the rest of our belongings on the shore if we wanted to make it to the opposite side of the lake.

See? I wasn't even thinking about wanting to see Mari's sleeveless dress cling to her fit warrior's body after it got all wet! Not at all!

"Any other options?"

"We might be able to hurry and go back the way we came. How much faster could we go if we took a strength potion, Ganjamary?"

"*Kwee kwee.*"

"It wouldn't make any difference, really," she answered, checking the capsules on her belt. "It takes a while for the effects to kick in if you're not used to taking them."

It still sounded like a better option than trying to swim the lake, though.

"I say we go with potions, it's better than not trying at all. Are there any side effects that keep you from moving after using it?"

"Don't worry, it starts to feel good after a few seconds."

"Yeah, don't worry, Mr. Slave! The Templars use them all the time!"

So it wasn't just a religious cult, it was a junkie religious cult. Great.

Mari set a potion capsule into her applicator and pressed it against her skin before popping another one into me. The muscles in our faces relaxed as the effects of the potions hit our systems, but Mari recovered quickly. She scooped up Yoi into her arms.

Yoi blinked. "Huh? Do I get one?"

"You're still a kid, so you're not ready for this yet. As for you," Mari said as she turned to me, "You've got our stuff to carry, so I'll handle Yoi. If things get dicey, drop everything and get out of there."

"Got it. I can at least slow down anything that comes after us. If that happens, I want you both to leave the dungeon as fast as you can. I've got a duty to protect my master, after all."

"*Kwee!*"

The infant basilisk had wrapped itself around my leg at some point as we talked. Was the little guy warming up to me or something?

"For now, let's just focus on getting out of here," I said. "We'll try taking on this place again once we get some backup."

"You don't have to tell me twice!"

"Roger that!"

We broke into a sprint—but it looked like our escape just wasn't meant to be. A mass the size of a garbage truck appeared before us, seemingly out of thin air.

A basilisk-shaped garbage truck. "Whelp," I said, "it was nice meeting you all."

"GROOOOOOAR!"

The beast's deafening magical roar froze us in our tracks.

• • •

Mari recovered from the basilisk's roar first, probably thanks to having built up a resistance to magical effects after using so many potions. Yoi started to slip from her arms while she was frozen from the roar, so Mari readjusted her hold and gave me a swift kick to snap me out of my stupor. Usually I'd resent that, but I had no problem this time, not with her hands so full.

Finally free from my paralysis, I hoisted our stuff onto my back and got ready to make a break for it. But right then—

"The baby!" Yoi shouted.

"What are you doing?" Mari yelled.

"We can't just leave it here! We have to report it to the guild!"

"Never mind that!" I shouted. "We have to get going! Now!"

When Yoi had almost fallen out of Mari's grasp earlier, she scooped up the cat-sized basilisk hatchling in her arms as well.

The basilisk looming over us completely outclassed the one we defeated earlier. There was a smaller basilisk by its feet, likely a sibling to the hatchling in Yoi's arms.

"I'll force this guy to back off!" Mari shouted.

She conjured up another tennis ball-sized fireball in her free hand and hurled it right into the basilisk's face. There were only about a hundred feet between us and the basilisk, but the absolute size of the thing made it seem so much closer.

I didn't even stick around to finish watching Mari before breaking off at a sprint toward the narrow path we'd originally taken. I was torn between whether or not to abandon our belongings, but I didn't have the luxury to think it over now. In the end, I decided to leave it all behind.

"Pass Miss Yoi over to me!" I shouted.

"I'm already doped up, I've got her."

"You keep that thing at bay with those fireballs, Mari!"

"Fine by me!"

Mari managed to catch up to me at some point, and I took Yoi and the baby basilisk off her hands. The enormous basilisk behind us let out another magic-laced roar of rage, and my body tensed up from its paralyzing effects. Even though I prepared myself for it, I still felt the urge to freeze and fall. I fought it. I kept running.

"Miss Yoi! Some light magic, please!"

"I got it, Mr. Slave. You just make sure not to drop the baby!"

"*Kwee, kwee!*"

"I know, I know!"

We'd already abandoned all our belongings, and to be honest, I was ready to leave the hatchling behind as well. After all, one of the reasons the rampaging basilisk (the father, presumably) was coming at us was because we were basilisk-nappers.

If this monster was anything like dinosaurs, then it was only natural that it wanted to fight to protect its kids. The dinosaur picture book I had as a kid said that this one herbivore called *Maiasaura* was so good at raising its young that its name actually meant "good mother lizard." T-rexes were supposed to be pretty fantastic parents as well, if I remembered right.

I wished giant man-eating lizards weren't such helicopter parents.

"Damn! This thing's a lot faster than it looks!" Mari shouted.

The fact she constantly had to turn around to throw fireballs back at the monster slowed her down a bit, but she always managed to catch back up to me and Yoi. I could hear the basilisk's howls and roars get steadily closer, so maybe the fireballs weren't helping after all. Even retracing our steps and traveling along the same paths as before, it was too dark to see well, and our footing wasn't guaranteed.

We were outsiders in the basilisk's domain. By the code of the hunter, one only becomes the apex predator by fighting on familiar battleground. That presented some obvious problems.

Man, and here I thought I was going to be cautious. I sprinted as fast I could along the path to the midpoint of the dungeon as Yoi gave directions.

"Go left here, Mr. Slave! The other way's a dead end!"

"Understood! Damn it, how's it going on your end, Mari?!"

"It's all right! It's getting narrower here so I think it's slowing!"

"*Kweeeee!*"

Right as the monster was about to catch up to us, the route we were traveling tapered. Since the basilisk pursuing us was even bigger than the one from this morning, it had even less room to maneuver in the cramped passageways. Made you wonder how the thing had gotten down here in the first place, but there must have been some other entrance it used to come and go. Maybe a secret route behind the shrine at the other end of the underground lake or something.

As far as conquering the dungeon went, I'd call this a spectacular failure. We were still alive, though, and that was what mattered.

"We're almost to where we beat that other basilisk this morning!" Yoi shouted.

Suddenly, a violent tremor rocked the entirety of the dungeon. It was the basilisk behind us, slamming into the narrow pathways as it tried to force its way forward. Each quake almost sent me tumbling over. We passed by the corpse of the other basilisk, but—

"Hurry, Mari!" I yelled back. Why was she slowing down?

"The ceiling is super unstable!" Yoi cried. "It could collapse any second!"

"I know that!" Mari called. "I'm going to bring it down on this thing's head!"

Ignoring our shouts, Mari launched a fireball at the ceiling, followed by one more for good measure. It wasn't anywhere close to enough to bring it down, though. Maybe the fireballs could do damage to something more traditionally flammable, but this was solid rock.

"I'll do it! Let me down, Mr. Slave!"

"All right. Get back here if you don't want to get trapped, Mari!"

Earth magic was supposed to be Yoi's specialty, so she was the perfect person to handle a problem like this.

"How long is it going to take?" Mari asked Yoi.

"About as long as you can hold your breath for!"

I nodded. "Let's back up a little further." I grabbed the basilisk hatchling and beat a hasty retreat alongside Mari. Yoi opened her grimoire once more, flipping to a page and sticking her bookmark inside.

Meanwhile, the crashing sound of a very large lizard trying to get through a very cramped passage echoed throughout the dungeon, a sort of thrashing bulldozer noise. If it kept this up, I wouldn't be surprised if it managed to make its own path to the surface.

I tightened my grip on my mace, ready to offer whatever feeble resistance I could muster. The basilisk hatchling trembled in my hold, just like any newborn animal would do. We were really bringing this poor guy along for one wild ride. I wondered, did it even understand that its parent was trying to save it?

"Here we go!" Yoi cried. "Physical, magical, kaboom!"

The basilisk's snout burst through the other side of the passage just as Yoi finished her weird chanting. Enveloped in an aura of magic, the ground quaked—though this time, it wasn't the basilisk making the noise.

Thorns of earth burst from the ground and stabbed the ceiling of the passageway. First five, then ten, then more than I could even count. There were no tentacles this time around as Yoi focused everything on piercing the bedrock above us.

"That should be plenty, Miss Yoi."

"Let's get moving!"

Mari grabbed Yoi from behind and lifted her up before sprinting away, fragments of the ceiling raining down from above and pelting the basilisk with a hail of dirt and rocks.

Mari stopped halfway through running away to unleash one last fireball toward the pillars of spikes Yoi had summoned. "Have a taste of these crimson flames as well!" The ceiling gave way and collapsed as the ball of flame exploded on impact, crumbling the only route between us and the giant basilisk into rubble.

Gasping and panting, we made it out of the dungeon and back into the outside world once more. Strange thinking that it'd taken us two long, careful days to make our way through before but about an hour to sprint back out.

We stumbled back to the ruins of the deserted settlement where we launched our expedition just the other day. We were all run ragged by that point, but the ruins were safe enough. There were no signs of the basilisk following us—for now, at least.

Our escape wasn't without its downsides, though, since we abandoned most of our gear back in the dungeon. If we did end up having to take on the giant basilisk in a proper fight, I wasn't sure how we were supposed to beat it. I couldn't imagine being able to hurt the thing with a mere mace. If we wanted to stand a chance, I was pretty sure we would need those "spike" things the adventurers back at the village used when we fought the wyvern.

Maybe Yoi could burn it using some of her magic? Then Mari could dope up and use one of those spikes against it. Yeah, that could work. Or maybe we could track down Nishka and get her to come up with a plan to take it down.

"I'm dying for a drink here," Mari groaned. "Where's the water, Shooter?"

"I had to leave all our stuff behind when we ran away. If I had to guess, I'd say the canteens are probably back at the underground lake."

"Maybe you should've been protecting those with your life instead of your baby there."

The baby basilisk in question followed along behind us after I let it on the ground, loudly mewling the whole time. It was probably hungry. It wrapped itself around me at first, but it eventually moved over to Mari and started nibbling at her legs.

"Hey, c'mon! That tickles! What's with this thing?"

"I'm guessing it's trying to eat you. You are a juicy, tender-looking young woman, after all."

"Hmph. A toothless baby's trying to eat me. Well that's not something I ever expected to say."

"It'd be nice if we had something to give it to eat," I said.

"Then go catch a rabbit or something. You're a hunter, aren't you?" Mari peeled the hatchling off her leg and thrust it toward me.

"I'll take care of it!" Yoi piped in. "Let's take a quick break before trying to get back to town as fast as we can. Sound okay, Mr. Slave?"

"Perfect. I'll go ahead and try to find something for it to eat, then. You be good while I'm gone, little buddy," I told the tiny basilisk.

"Good luck!"

I patted Yoi on the head, then the baby basilisk before I stood. Unfortunately, I didn't have any of my hunting equipment. And even if I had a bow, it wasn't like I knew how to use it. I would have loved to set a trap instead, but we didn't have that kind of time either.

People in this world really needed to make eating breakfast a thing. We hadn't eaten anything all day, so I was starving.

"Go find a place we can get water from, too," Mari added. "I'm not really getting my hopes up for there being anything we could eat."

"Right, will do."

I looked around at the sparse shrubbery and scatterings of rocks around us. I wasn't going to be able to catch any rabbits or foxes like this. Mari might be right about food; I wasn't sure there was anything edible to find.

Worst-case scenario we could kill the hatchling for some emergency provisions, but we weren't that starving. Not yet, anyway.

It would be easier to explain our failure to the guild with the baby still alive...or that's what I was telling myself. I still couldn't bring myself to kill it, and now we had another mouth to feed.

I started checking for snakes under rocks. Back when I worked at the apparel shop and went roughing it in the woods with my manager, we'd turn over rocks to try and find snakes to eat as part of the survival course. The rat snakes we caught were particularly nasty, probably because whatever they ate was nasty as well. Thank goodness we didn't run into anything like spotted pikes back then.

As I got lost in memory, I finally came across my first snake. It didn't have a triangular-shaped head, so if the rules of my old world still applied, then this little guy wouldn't be venomous. I didn't know what kind of diet it had in this world, but if it fed on mice or something then I was sure it'd be delicious.

I took off my cloak and wrapped it around my hand, moving quickly to grab hold of the snake's neck. It attempted to warp around my arm before I pulled it off and, grateful to my boots, placed my foot on its head. Then I whipped out my shortsword and sliced the snake's head clean off.

Now I had something to feed the baby basilisk, but I still had to find some water for my master and her partner-in-crime. Snakes were edible if you cooked them, so I guess it counted as people food, too.

I let the corpse dangle in my hand as I waited for the blood to drain, scanning the area to see if I could find a stream or something.

I'd considered myself a civilized man so recently, but here I was in another world, living the wild life.

Huh. For some reason, the thought of that brought a smile to my face.

A Letter from My Husband

MY HUSBAND is a very kind person. Yes, he's always naked, and yes, he looks quite cold, but he has never once complained since coming to live with me. I want him to wear nice clothes, but what could I give him with my lifestyle?

The way he stares at me from time to time can be quite frightening, I'll confess. Like when I'm sleeping, changing, bathing, or even using the toilet. Perhaps everything I do seems new and strange to him, customs unfamiliar to his people's ways. That look still frightens me, though.

I married him in the first place at the village chief's behest. I still remember when she called me to her manor in the early afternoon and had me brought to her waiting room for the meeting. She cut right to the chase.

"Y-you're saying that I'm going to be betrothed to a..." I could hardly believe it. "A naked warrior...?"

337

"Correct. I've heard you've been struggling ever since your father passed away last winter. If you were to get married now, it would surely make your life easier. And so, young Cassandra, I would like to congratulate you on your marriage!"

"A n-naked warrior?!"

He was apparently part of some naked tribe from a faraway land and had gotten lost in the Apegut Forest. He was also completely nude when he was found, as was the custom of his strange people. The entire village was suspicious of him, and now this mysterious man was to become my husband.

"Um. Do I have any right to say no?"

"You are aware that marriages are decided upon by me and the other adults of the village, are you not? Or are you saying you are unhappy with my decision?" The village chief's eyes narrowed.

"N-no, I would never say that. I'm thankful for your concern for me, but, um! This is all happening so fast, don't you think? I don't know if my heart can handle it."

She smiled. "Then I want you to try taking deep breaths. Don't you want to be nice and calm for this momentous occasion? Inhale in, exhale slowly out."

The tone of her voice left no room to protest, so I did as she ordered—inhaled deeply in, exhaled slowly out.

"Like that?"

"Perfect. Well, now that your heart is calm and ready for it— congratulations on your marriage, Cassandra!" She clapped three times to celebrate my forced nuptials and moved promptly on, a look of great satisfaction on her face.

"Back to business. According to the older texts, it's said that tribes of people in the nude flourished in the east. I suspect that Shooter is a descendant of those people."

"Shooter?"

"Yes, that's right. That would be what your husband is called."

An odd name.

"It meant 'archer' in the past," she continued, "so we can assume his skills with a bow are unmatched. You're very lucky to find a husband like that, ha ha ha!"

Naked...*completely* naked. The words alone made my head spin. It was true I was the only daughter of a hunter, and my father often told me that I'd likely end up marrying another hunter someday. Still, I never expected to tie the knot with some naked warrior wandering the forest.

"This warrior ended up having a bit of a scuffle with my son Gimul, so at the moment he's in the cell below the watchtower. He wasn't at fault, mind you. It was all an unfortunate misunderstanding."

And my husband was in jail? Innocent or not, any warrior would surely find being stuck in a cell the greatest disgrace.

"Now Cassandra, he might be a touch indignant that he was thrown under the watchtower despite his innocence. That's where you come in."

"What do you mean?"

"You will head to where Shooter is being held and pacify him until I come to explain the rest. That will be your first job as his wife."

I blinked.

"All right, run along, now. ...I said, run along, now."

The village chief was, of course, the ruler of the village, so what could a young village girl do to resist her orders? The prospect of suddenly getting married was surprising enough, but to a nudist from who-knew-where? Thoroughly shocking.

• • •

When I finally arrived at the underground cell of the watchtower, I saw a man lying unconscious on the floor. One of the goblins working for the village chief let me into the cell, then locked the door behind me and left without saying a word.

"Erm...pardon me, then..."

The village chief truly was a cruel person for ordering me to take care of this man for the rest of my life.

"His face is horribly swollen, but he's still breathing, at least. I guess that's good." I was terrified he'd look like a giant apeman when I heard he was completely naked. Thankfully, he was human.

"Should I wake him up? Or would it be better to wait for him to wake naturally, I wonder?"

It was difficult to discern whether he was asleep or just knocked out. Unable to make up my mind on what to do, I took a long, deep breath.

"He really isn't wearing anything at all. He's also much brawnier than my father was. Wounds all over his arms and stomach, too. Perhaps being nude all the time helps show it all off? Some sign of warrior status?"

It wasn't like he was answering.

"I know I may not be the most desirable wife as the daughter of a hunter, but I'm not sure how I'll be able to handle being married to a naked barbarian..."

The barbarian lay motionless on the cell floor. Nakedly.

"I can't hold a grudge against the village chief for doing this to me, but my heart really isn't ready for this..."

Even though there was a man directly on the floor in front of me, I had grown used to talking to myself since my father passed away. It helps the quiet when you're alone. I peered at the naked warrior as I complained to myself, but then—

"Ow! Where am I?"

"Eek?!"

Right when I thought he was out cold, he suddenly stood and began to look around.

"Ah," he said, "sorry about that. Didn't mean to scare you. Where is this? Heaven?"

"Th-this is the cell below the village watchtower."

"Oh yeah? Dang, guess that meant I was overpowered when I was duking it out with Gimul. Oof, that smarts! That meathead really let me have it. Cleaned my clock, I'll tell ya. I must've been out of it for a while."

I watched my new husband raise himself into a sitting position. All I could think was how strange and uncomfortable being around him made me feel. "If we're talking about a watchtower," he said, "I guess that means the big stone tower on the hill I saw. First I get slammed, and now I'm in the slammer. Heh. Eh. Guh, that's not even funny!"

"Eek!" What was he going on about?

"Sorry, my bad, my bad. Got a little carried away. You must have had it pretty rough too, being locked away in this dingy place. Well, I'm also stuck here now, so I guess we should just try to get along as fellow prisoners."

That's what this Shooter thought, did he? He sat cross-legged on the straw on the ground, glancing toward me every now and then.

Where was I supposed to look when I talked to him? He was naked! Still, this was the man who was supposed to become my husband, so I stole peeks at him. Maybe that would help me figure out what sort of person he was.

He had short, jet-black hair, and dark-brown eyes to match. And he had a rugged face with an unkempt beard, but I do believe I saw kindness in his eyes.

"That village chief sure is a nasty piece of work, locking up a girl like you here," he said, laughing as he looked at me.

And that's how I met my husband.

Thinking back on it, I could see a hint of lecherousness in his eyes when he was sneaking peeks at me, but he always worked hard and was unfailingly kind.

"Cassandra," he said, "I know you must be pretty shaken about being married off to me all of a sudden." Those were his words on our first night together under the same roof.

"I know we can't just act like husband and wife right off the bat or anything, so let's try and get to know each other better a bit. Maybe someday we'll be the real deal."

I remembered being grateful that he wasn't a more aggressive man. But still, the fact that this nude man stared at me so intensely made me so uncomfortable that I could hardly look in his direction.

What else could I do but look away, with such an odd distance between us? My newlywed days with Shooter were so strange. It was common for the men in hunter families to stay in bed until late in the morning to make sure their bodies were well rested. It was different when they had to hunt that day, of course, but on their days off they wouldn't start helping out with chores or tending to the fields until the sun was high in the sky.

Shooter was different. I should have been the one waking up early, but he woke up when the sun peeked over the forest and immediately tended to the vegetable patch out front. I would rush to get up as well, and by the time I finished watering the plants and cutting the grass, he'd welcome me back with a smile.

• • •

As soon as Ossandra heard I had been married, he rushed over to comfort me. "I heard that he's some outsider from a tribe of people who stay naked all the time. I'm going straight to the village chief. We need to call this whole thing off."

"No, you can't! You're all I've got left, I don't want anything to happen to you!"

343

"Nothing to worry about. I'll find a way to get him away from you, to divorce you, whatever I can."

"B-but..."

I'd always thought of my cousin Ossandra as a big brother, especially since we were almost the same age. There was something off about him now, though. Ever since my father passed away, he kept talking about how inconvenient it must be for me to be on my own. I was happy for his concern, of course, but he went above and beyond what most relatives did for each other.

I always received strange looks from the neighbors when he was around. Now that I had a husband, those stares were getting even worse.

One day when Wak'wakgoro was visiting the house to drop off some gifts, he gave a warning to Ossandra. "Listen, man. It's time for you to stop hanging around Cassandra all the time."

"But, uh. She doesn't have any family, so I'm here for support."

"No family? What are you, thick? Cassandra's got Shooter! They're married, man!"

"Cassandra and I have been with each other since we were little. We're way closer than some guy she just met the other day!"

Ossandra tried standing his ground, but Wak'wakgoro grabbed him by the beard and gave him a good chewing out. I didn't want any more trouble from Wak'wakgoro or anyone else, so I told my cousin not to come around anymore.

I could see the utter despair in his face after I said that. Eventually he stopped coming to visit me altogether.

• • •

"Then I'm off. I'll bag us a big one, just you wait!"

"Um...be careful, okay?"

That day, Shooter had gone off with Wak'wakgoro to the forest in order to capture a lynx. Lynxes weren't the only big game in the forest, though. It was also home to things like bears...and wyverns.

My father had gone after a wyvern the previous winter, and never came back out. There were so many little risks in a hunter's life. Perhaps my husband would come back empty-handed, or even injured.

Still, when I thought about my late father, I didn't want Shooter to push himself to the point that he met the same fate. He didn't need to go after the most powerful game yet. If he just worked on building his skills as a hunter, then that would be more than enough for me.

Or, well...I knew he was from a clan of nudists, but in this village it was normal to at least wear clothes. All I could offer him was my father's old vest, unfortunately.

Perhaps the reason Shooter wanted to hunt something big was to sell it off and get enough money to buy his own clothes as soon as possible. Or maybe he was concerned about our poverty, and he wanted to do something about it.

As I watched my husband and Wak'wakgoro disappear into the distance, I started to head home to do my housework for the day when I heard a voice behind me.

"So that's the famous naked hunter I've been hearing so much about, then?"

"N-Nishka?"

The voice belonged to Nishka, a long-eared girl living in one of the settlements nearby. She was also from a hunter family, and had grown up alongside Ossandra, Wak'wakgoro, and I.

"Wow, Wak'wakgoro wasn't kidding. The guy's completely buck naked," she continued, watching Shooter walk into the woods.

"Th-that's not true!" I stammered. "He has a fur vest on!"

Nishka folded her arms and turned to look at me. "Vest or no vest, look at that danglin' pork sword and tell me he ain't naked. I heard he became a hunter-in-training, yeah?"

"Wak'wakgoro is teaching him the basics as they hunt together. The plan is for him to eventually become a full-fledged hunter, just like my father."

"Ha! If he's stuck working under someone as boring as Wak'wakgoro, he's never gonna bag himself anything worthwhile."

"It looks like they've been heading out to the forest to hunt lynxes. It's been hard, too—there are days the lynxes just take the bait without springing the trap."

"A lynx, really? Small fry. If it were me, I'd be looking to bag myself a wyvern. I guess it's not wyvern season, but they could at least think about going after deer or bears or something. Put more food on the table for ya."

I swallowed.

"Ah, shit, I'm sorry. Didn't mean to bring up wyverns, I wasn't thinking."

"No, it's all right. I've already come to terms with it."

Nishka was a tall elven girl with an eye patch over her right eye. We practiced archery together when we were little, and now she'd grown into a proper hunter. She put on a confident grin and kept talking.

"Don't worry, I'll keep kicking enough wyvern ass to make your dad proud. I'll be looking after your nudist husband to make sure he doesn't go off and get himself killed, too. Just leave it to me."

"Th-thank you."

"And don't worry, I'm not gonna try to take him away from you or anything! I've hunted as many wyverns as I've seen winters since becoming a hunter, so I can turn any guy into a proper hunter, no matter how useless he might look! Ha!"

Nishka always went into the forest alone to hunt, and she always ended up bragging up a storm about it.

"Actually, how's that deer hide I left you coming along? I reckon the tanning should be nearly finished."

I think this was Nishka's way of consoling me after the loss of my father. She kept coming over to my house and asking me to tan animal hide for her, claiming it was because we were childhood friends. After I married Shooter, she would only show up when he had gone out, and I was happy that she was so concerned.

Still, Wak'wakgoro was a hunter who specialized in lynxes. Shooter was only his apprentice, so I thought there was no chance he would have been able to hunt a wyvern.

I thought wrong.

One day, a wyvern larger than anything I had ever seen before came swooping into the village and attacked Gintanen's cattle. After the battle was over, I found out that Shooter had been injured trying to protect the village chief. Wak'wakgoro and I raced to the church, but (thank goodness) his wounds weren't that serious.

"Don't worry, Cassandra. Some wyvern won't do me in so easily. In fact, I wish all those other amateurs could've just stayed out of the way. Flailing all over the place, making it so much harder for the real professionals."

I nodded gravely. Shooter may have been an apprentice hunter, but he had once been a warrior. A warrior from a tribe of naked people, mind you, but a warrior nonetheless. He wasn't the kind of person to let a wyvern get the better of him.

I wanted to tell him I was glad he was safe, but he was still extremely naked. I ended up looking at the ground. "No, that's all right. More than that, what happened to your clothes?"

"Oh, you mean the vest? The deacon said it was unsanitary and tossed it. I'm sorry," he said with an apologetic bow.

"It's just a vest," I whispered softly. "I'm glad it wasn't you."

Shooter looked shocked at my words, for some reason. "I came in out of nowhere and just...wrecked everything for you, didn't I? I'm sorry."

"No, it's all right. I'm fine with this."

"Don't worry. Once we're finished with all this wyvern stuff and things start going back to normal, I'll make a better living for us. Put in some real work this time."

"Um. Please, just don't overdo it, all right?"

I just wanted him to stay safe, but he was utterly committed to slaying this wyvern. When it was our turn to take watch at the top of the village watchtower, that very wyvern came hurtling back across the skies.

"No, it's not that! Look, over there—that black cloud of seeds in the air!"

"Where? Oh, huh...that does look like a bunch of black seeds. Is that a stealth bomber?"

"I can see it clearer now—it's the wyvern!"

"Ah crap, seriously? It's started!"

● ● ●

After ringing the alarm bell at the top of the watchtower and alerting the village to the wyvern's arrival, Shooter turned to me, tension tight in his face. "I'm pretty sure it's safe up here, so stay and keep a lookout. If this thing tries to fly off, tell us where it's going."

"A-all right. What are you going to do, Shooter?"

"I'm going down with the rest. I'll show them what I can do with this here spear, yeah?"

"Um, all right, but don't do anything too reckless."

"What, are you worried about me?"

"I, uh..."

"Okay, I can't even deal with how cute that is, it's amazing, but how about we do this after we kill the ruler of the skies?" He flashed me a smile and ran down the stairs. I watched him as he sprinted to his position. The wyvern landed in the village, and it made its way to the open space toward the forest where the trap had been set for it.

A breath caught in my throat as it tore into the bait that served as the lure for the trap. Some kind of signal was given then, and the hired hunters and adventurers charged it together. I could see my husband among them, wielding a spear and keeping himself low to the ground as he ran toward its underside.

"Shooter!"

I couldn't hold myself back from shouting, but surely no one could have heard me over the wyvern's ferocious roar. Shooter found an opening as the monster writhed and thrust his spear deep into its underbelly.

He truly must have been a warrior among warriors in that fierce nudist tribe. He didn't once falter, and was courageous enough to get closer to the wyvern than any of the other hunters or adventurers. Only when I was sure my husband dodged the wyvern's attacks and retreated could I breathe a sigh of relief.

The wyvern limped away from the battle, beating its wings until it could finally lug itself from the ground and fly away. Even though it wasn't finished for good, I was overjoyed to see my husband fight well and come out without a scratch. What a nightmare it would've been, being a widow after only ten days.

As I rushed down the tower to where the others were, I came just in time to hear the hunters and adventurers talking about Shooter.

"He's one of our village's hunters, and was a warrior before he arrived here, too."

"But he didn't finish it off," someone pointed out. "Wounded wyverns are way worse. It's gonna be pretty much impossible getting to it now." That complaint came from Nishka, whose blunt words utterly killed the village chief's mood. Nishka was probably sulking over the fact that they hadn't killed it, which must have been even more grating given her reputation as a wyvern hunter.

All the hunters in the village knew just how dangerous an injured wyvern could be, especially after what happened to my father last winter. Even if Shooter was a warrior, going after it now would be incredibly dangerous.

Before I knew it, I found myself squeezing his arm just to hold him for a moment.

"It's all right," he said, "the adventurers are gonna be there to help, too."

"Just don't push yourself too hard, all right?"

"I won't, but I've gotta make sure and show everyone I'm doing my part."

"I know, but—"

"You don't want people whispering behind your back all the time about how you got stuck with the naked guy, right?" he said, grinning. "I'm going to get out there and show them what I can do with a spear. Get you the kinda life you deserve."

351

As the village chief was talking with the others about how to divvy up the teams, Nishka took the chance to sneak over to me.

"Hey, Cassandra. Can I borrow ol' pork sword for a bit?"

"Wh-what do you mean?"

"The wyvern's injured, yeah? Your husband's just going to end up shredded if he stays on the frontline."

"Yes, I was worried about that as well."

"Yeah. Goddess, I'm sure you'd never get over it if he croaked the same way as your old man, so I'll be there to keep an eye on him."

Which meant...what, exactly? Nishka wrapped an arm around me as I wondered.

"I'll take him and go on ahead. At this rate he's gonna end up getting stuck with the most dangerous, rough-'n-tumble team. I'm not gonna wait around for that, so I'll just nab the guy and we'll take care of it ourselves."

"Y-you can't! The village chief will be furious with you if she finds out."

"Cassandra, we're not gonna hunt anything by hurling ourselves at it in droves. It's way better for just a few people to come at it from downwind and finish it off before it sees us coming. As long as we take it out, the village chief's not gonna complain." She had a point.

"But I don't think Shooter has hunted a wyvern before."

"Don't worry, I won't let him bite off more than he can chew. And I'll use wind magic on his arrows, so all he'll have to do is let 'em loose. Then it won't matter if he's inexperienced or not." Nishka flashed me a smile, but I could tell by the look in her eye (the one not covered by her eye patch) that she was dead serious. She left as quietly as she came, making her way to Shooter without a sound.

"Are you talking to me?" I heard my husband ask.

"You see anyone else around?" said Nishka. "You're the one who ripped right through that thing's wing, yeah?"

"Yeah."

"Get over here, I've got a plan..."

Nishka pulled Shooter away from the crowd, turning back to give me a wave as they left. Shooter the brave warrior and Nishka the wyvern killer...maybe they'd really be able to hunt down the wyvern. With my biggest fear assuaged, I could finally relax and wave back at Nishka.

That feeling was short-lived, though.

"And who would you be waving to, Cassandra?"

"Oh, M-Miss Alexandricia! It was, erm! No one. No one at all."

"How very eccentric. You know, I seem to have lost track of your husband. Do you know where he is?"

"I-I don't know anything about that. I haven't been paying attention. Perhaps he's over there somewhere?" I gestured vaguely.

"Scalesplitter seems to have vanished as well. Ha. I see. So that's what's going on."

She spoke slowly, as if tasting each word. A smile crept over her face as she looked at me; she must have enjoyed watching my reactions. "Ha ha ha! Delightful! There's no need to hide it. Scalesplitter and Shooter already went on ahead, did they? I'm sure it was Nishka's idea to split off in the first place, which means she thinks she has good odds. Very well, I saw nothing, heard nothing. Let's let them do as they please."

I certainly wasn't about to say anything more.

"It's true," she continued, "that our village isn't very accepting of outsiders, but your husband may be thinking he can change that if he can prove his skills with his spear."

"Y-yes, I believe he said something along those lines before."

"Then he made the right choice, pairing up with Nishka. We lost many in our fight, but that warrior may just be the one to bring good tidings to our village."

How I hoped so. "You must be glad to have such a good husband. I'm almost jealous, ha ha!"

• • •

The search parties who entered the forest to pursue the wounded wyvern made a real fuss after the shrill whistle of the messenger arrow came from deeper in the woods. It seemed Nishka and my husband managed to take down the wyvern once and for all. The gossip went on and on...

"That outsider warrior finished off the wyvern with Nishka the Scalesplitter!"

"What, seriously? I thought he was just some naked weirdo, but I guess they don't call him a warrior for nothing. That signal must be the sign they took the wyvern down!"

"Heh, not bad for a guy who doesn't even wear clothes. It sounds like the arrow came from the lake to the west. Someone report this to the village chief and we'll send search teams right away! Let's get this wyvern sliced and diced!"

I didn't know if Nishka really kept Shooter from biting off more than he could chew, or if she found a way to get them through something way, way tougher than they expected. What I did know was that I had her to thank for Shooter's success.

It hadn't been more than two weeks since we were married, yet all the hunters from the village rushed over to me to celebrate my husband's accomplishment. Of everyone, no one was happier to hear the news than the village chief.

"Brave and gallant, just as one would expect from a warrior. I couldn't be prouder than to have one of our own slay the wyvern—and to do it before the adventurers we hired from town! You must be even prouder to have a husband such as him."

"Y-yes. Thank you for your kind words."

At this rate, Shooter was going to graduate from his apprenticeship much sooner than I thought. When that happened, he would be able to take over my father's work as a full-fledged hunter.

"Seems like your life has taken a turn for the better with him around."

"It has."

"I will make sure you are the first to receive the meat from the kill. Meat is more important than ever with summer approaching, and I've heard that hunters love the taste of wyvern. It will be my reward to you."

"N-no, I couldn't!"

And I didn't particularly want to either. In truth wyvern meat was tough and dry, and though I was thankful for the kind words and free food, I wasn't happy at the thought of having to eat it for weeks.

"What, you don't want it? Nishka has told me it gets more flavorful the longer you chew it, making it the ultimate feast for a hunter. Is this not true?"

"I received plenty of the meat from the wyvern my father hunted, and I'm...more than, um, fine with...eating it."

The village chief nodded. "Well if you're so satisfied, then I suppose I'll have to find a different reward for you and just eat it all myself..."

And with that, the village chief walked away from me, her shoulders slumped. As she did, the other members of the search squads hooted and hollered, racing after the direction of the whistle-arrow.

They originally intended to overwhelm the wyvern with sheer numbers—I saw some of the adventurers pushing carts full of hunting nets and strange spears. I joined in to help, pushing the carts through the dense forest just in case we needed the weapons after all. Finally we came to a grassy clearing near a lake, and there lay the once intimidating wyvern, limp on the ground as Nishka and Shooter worked to gut it.

It was one thing to hear about it, and another to see that they really pulled it off. What's more, Shooter was unharmed. The moment he saw me, he ran to me, beaming. Before I knew it, I had taken my hands off the cart and started running toward him too.

"Shooter!"

"Hey, Cassandra! Over here!"

All the other villagers around me gave me sly grins as they heard me shout out to my husband; it flustered me. When I finally caught up to him on that grassy field, though, I could see the gentle smile on his face. Though I could feel my cheeks getting hotter, I checked him over from head to toe and found that he had truly made it through this ordeal without a scratch.

"No need to rush over like that! As you can see, I'm still fit as a fiddle."

Our eyes met, and I hurried to look away. I could see Nishka grinning at us out of the corner of my eye, much to my chagrin. There was something I needed to say to Shooter first, though.

"I was afraid you might have been hurt," I said.

"Huh? O-oh, yeah! Sorry, I didn't mean to worry you. Thanks to Nishka, we took that wyvern down clean and quick. Maybe that means I got revenge for your dad as well? Heh."

"I don't care about that. I'm...I'm just glad you're all right. Welcome back, Shooter."

"Yeah. Glad to be back."

More waves of embarrassment flooded over me. I fought them off and looked up at him. My husband smiled right back at me.

● ● ●

Just when things were finally calming down after the battle against the wyvern, my husband was to be sent to town by order of the village chief.

357

We'd been married for a couple weeks, and I still didn't know how to act around him. I was prepared for whatever "marital duties" I had to take on now, but none had yet happened. Maybe he was just as unhappy with the village chief telling us to marry as I initially had been.

Though he told me that we should take our time trying to become husband and wife, he was so worked up when we first met that I was terrified he might actually try and push me down and have his way with me, then and there. But he never did, and never even tried to lay his hands on me. If anything, I worked hard to close the gap between my husband and I.

Before Shooter left for town, on a day he had gone out to hunt, I asked Nishka for advice on the matter.

She said, "It's not like it's all that unusual for a hunter to head out by themselves into the forest for a long hunt, just married or not."

I stopped cleaning the beast hide I was holding and turned to face her. "That's true, but he's not going hunting this time. He'll be heading to a huge town."

"Oh yeah, that's right. I've never been, but I know Gimul goes tons of times throughout the year to buy gifts, party, all that fun stuff."

"Does Gimul...party?" I simply couldn't picture it, and I was sure Gimul would've yelled his head off at the accusation.

"C'mon, don't be dumb. You know that momma's boy is always buying presents for the village chief." Nishka crept in closer and whispered to me. "Back when we were kids, I stole some box from him, right? He came back from town with it, and he was treating it like a puppy, a baby—a baby puppy. When I looked inside, he'd bought some fancy scarf for the village chief, something you could only get in town!"

It was a fun enough story. I didn't feel much better.

"Hey, Cassandra."

"Hm?"

"If you're that worried about him, how about I go along with him to make sure he stays safe?"

"Oh, no! I couldn't ask you to do that. If the village chief found out, you'd get far more than a scolding!"

"Don't sweat it, there isn't anything worth hunting in the summer, anyway. I've still got enough savings tucked away to keep my sister fed, too. Keep it a secret from Shooter and the village chief, though, got that? I'll tail 'em all sneaky-like and force them to let me come along for the ride!"

A mischievous grin crept over Nishka's face, the same look I had seen her make when we were kids and she had come up with a new prank.

And so my husband left me again on a journey to town, a brave warrior acting as Gimul's escort. Together they were to sell the parts of the slain wyvern. All very well, but despite my husband's strength, I still worried. He didn't know this place.

No one knew, either, that Nishka would be stealthily following them, but I could tell she could hardly wait to go to the big city.

Once the day of departure was decided, Wak'wakgoro dropped by the house to give us some potatoes and clean cloth.

It was a wife's duty to support her husband, so I used the cloth to make Shooter a new pair of underwear. I gave them to him right before he was to head off into town, and he was ecstatic to receive the present.

"So, um, there's food and a change of clothes wrapped in the cloth I gave you."

"Thank you, thank you so much! I'll make sure to keep it all wrapped up at night."

Odd that I finally felt so much closer to my husband, and now he was going to leave. Odd and unfair. Neither the village chief nor Shooter told me when he would return, so I stood outside our house and waited so I could at least see him off.

Though I was a little embarrassed, I couldn't help but start waving once I saw him on his way. When he saw me as well, he waved back at me in kind.

"Have a good trip, Shooter."

• • •

After my husband left, the old silence returned to my house, a familiar animal that had curled up in the space left by my father's death and always waited for opportunities to stretch and fill my home. Though I may have been the daughter of a hunter, I didn't have the strength of one, which left me with limited things to do. I could tan animal skins along with the other hunter wives, perhaps, or tend to our crops.

At the very least I wasn't going to let Shooter's vegetable patch wilt. I could do that much by myself. Despite my best efforts, though, I piled my limited options too high and wore myself out, winding up with a hurt back and an earful from Wak'wakgoro as I lay in bed recovering.

"You don't have to do everything, all right? I can have my dumb brothers take care of stuff like this, so just let me know anytime and I'll send them over."

"Thank you...thank you so much."

"Hey, you're starting to sound a bit like Shooter there. Wonder if he's doing all right?" he said with a grin.

Ha. I hadn't noticed. "Yes, he does tend to go overboard when he's gracious, doesn't he?" I smiled at the thought.

One day, for the first time in a long while, Ossandra came to pay me a visit. He'd heard about my back, and apparently couldn't keep himself away. I was happy to see him, of course...but things were different now. Relative or no, it was strange for an unmarried man to pay me a visit when my husband was gone. People could get the wrong idea.

I tried my best to gently persuade him to leave, but to no avail.

"I heard from Shooter that you were running low on apple cider vinegar, so I came to bring you some more. Vinegar makes for good medicine as well, so drink up and feel better."

"You have to understand, Ossandra, I don't want any strange rumors spreading among the neighbors. This is a little...you know?"

"Go on, you can tell me anything. We're family, aren't we?"

"Y-yes, and you're dear to me, but we're only cousins."

Ossandra's lips tightened. Something felt wrong; he was starting to scare me. "I'm coming in."

"G-Gimul?"

At that moment, the village chief's son Gimul just happened to stop by.

"Ossandra," said Gimul. He looked at him, looked at me. "What, exactly, are you doing?"

"I'm Cassandra's cousin. She's family. This is a visit. Nothing more."

Gimul nodded. Then he unsheathed the sword he kept on his waist. For a second he stood there, pointing the blade at Ossandra...and then Ossandra ran.

Well. At least things hadn't gotten *too* serious.

"I'm just glad you're all right," said Gimul. "Or doing well enough, I suppose. I heard from the village chief that you hurt your back."

"It's nothing major, thankfully."

"I see. Good to hear."

Did he come all the way here just to say that? He did happen to protect me from Ossandra just now, so it's not like I was ungrateful for his presence, but...

Anyway, my cousin was a good person—really, he was—but when he got a thought in his head, everything else tended to fall away. Sometimes I worried about him.

"Actually," Gimul continued, "I just returned from Bulka."

"Ah. Thank you for all the hard work you do for the village. Does that mean that Shooter is here, too?" My heart started pounding at the thought...but that joy couldn't last.

"No, sorry to say. He's going to be staying in Bulka for a while longer."

"Oh...I see..." More silence, then.

"It was on my orders, so if you want someone to hate, then hate me."

"N-no, I would never..."

And anyway, Shooter would tell me I had a duty to protect the house, even if he was taking a bit longer than expected to get back home.

Gimul sighed, then rummaged around in his breast pocket before pulling out something and handing it to me. It was a letter, as well as one other thing: a hand mirror.

"These are for you. A present and a letter from Shooter."

"I'm so terribly sorry Gimul, but..." I glanced away. "I can't read."

"I already know you're both a couple of illiterates, so I'll go ahead and read it for you. Ahem..."

Dear Cassandra: I hope all is well with you. Bulka is a regular metropolis, dotted with faint midnight streetlamps, and though the city can overwhelm the senses and leave one flailing in uncertainty, at times I recall the comfort that your magnificent cooking brings me after a hard day's work. Upon Gimul's orders, I have agreed to stay longer here. I want to see you again, but this is part of my duty to the village.

"That should be everything he said, if I recall correctly."

"'Said'? Didn't he write a letter?"

"The only thing he wrote was the bit at the end—that he was staying longer and how he wanted to see you again. Everything he couldn't write down, I just memorized for you."

"And the mirror?"

"He picked it out personally for you. Make sure you take care of it."

"Th-thank you...thank you so much."

"Hmph. If you want someone to thank, thank him. Also, please don't become just as ingratiating as him when you thank people. I can deal with one of you at the most."

"O-oh, yes. I'll be sure to do that."

When I looked in the hand mirror Gimul gave me, I saw a girl with blushing, bright red cheeks staring right back at me.

I pray every day that you will stay safe, Shooter.

Please come home soon.

Electra's Diary

As I scanned the bulletin board inside the adventurer's guild, I spotted a pretty tasty job. Some village out in the sticks was looking to hire adventurers like me. The pay wasn't the greatest, but it guaranteed whomever they hired would have food, housing, the whole shebang. High pay was nice, but stability? Priceless.

Besides, all the men in town were just pretentious pricks who liked to show off, and none of them fit my tastes. A nice boy from the countryside sounded more like marriage material to me.

Not that I'd have much luck anywhere if I kept to the adventuring life.

"Oh?" I said. Someone else seemed interested in the posting as well. "You planning on taking this job, too?"

"Sure am," said the guy. "If I get hired by a village on the edge of the frontier, then I'll probably get to face off with some huge monster. Add that to my list of accomplishments and I'd be able to charge a higher price for whoever hires me next, maybe for years."

The guy was a hulking specimen of a man with a shiny bald head, and it seemed like he had the exact opposite reasons for wanting the job.

"Name's Dyson," he said. "I like using a broadax to get the job done."

"Electra. I'm more about one-on-one sword work, and I'm damn good at it. Judging by your looks, I'd guess your specialty is taking out monsters?"

"Taking them out? I turn bandits and wild animals to mulch!"

"The posting says the village is somewhere out in the middle of the wilderness, so I wouldn't worry about bandits."

"Then I guess there'd be nothing else to do but get to know the girlies there better and settle down! Gah ha ha!" Dyson's gigantic pecs wiggled as he laughed heartily.

He sure talked big, but he went down without much of a fight when he went up against the village interviewer. It was pretty pathetic, too—I mean, the interviewer just used a pole.

And then the interviewer took me out with the same pole. He may have been naked, but this "Shooter" guy really was strong.

● ● ●

"So, Mr. Gimul," I said, "what, exactly, are we expected to do at Apegut now that you've hired us?"

The cart trundled shakily down the road as Dyson and I made our way to the village with our new employer. The village itself was supposed to be as idyllic as they come, without much chance of a bandit attack and everyone farming and tending to livestock. But in that case, why hire adventurers?

"The village is a peaceful place. That much is proof of the talents my mothe—ahem—village chief brings as a governor. We have another problem, though."

"And what'd that be?" Dyson asked, throwing a puzzled look my way. "It's gotta be one helluva problem if you're gonna be setting up another guild there in addition to hiring me 'n Electra here."

Gimul grimaced from the driver's seat of the cart before continuing. "Just beyond the village lies a vast and untamed wilderness. There are mountains just beyond the forest where wyverns make their home."

"W-wyverns?!"

"We were actually just attacked by one the other day. We had to hire adventurers from town to help take care of it."

Even talkative Dyson was quiet now. That definitely explained why the village wanted adventurers staying in their village. I had expected nothing more than steady pay and free meals out of the deal. How naïve of me.

"What's wrong, Electra?" Dyson stammered. "You aren't s-scared, are you?"

"Ha, y-you're one to talk! You look even more freaked than before."

"Hah! Flying lizards? Nothing! You're, uh, looking at the...the great Dyson!"

The great and definitely not terrified Dyson.

369

Gimul kept calm throughout the whole conversation, so maybe that meant he was used to wyvern attacks. Which did not bode well.

"Then did those adventurers from Bulka end up killing the wyvern?" I asked.

"No. It was a naked barbarian and a drunkard who ended up dealing the final blow."

What were their names? "Shooter and Nishka, then?"

"Right."

Shooter could use a pole to beat other adventurers without even breaking a sweat, so I could easily imagine him charging in close to a wyvern and taking it down with one well-placed stab. I wasn't as well versed on what Nishka was capable of, but she was Shooter's partner. Anyone like that had to be the real deal.

"Both of them are hunters, so they end up away from the village to head into the forest often. There's no guarantee they'll be able to respond to threats immediately. That's why we need you. Adventurers are supposed to be experts when it comes to hunting monsters and the like, so I'm expecting good work from you two."

Dyson forced a laugh. It took a couple tries. "Y-yeah, you can count on us! Right, Electra?"

"Y-yes, of course! I can handle anyone that comes our way!"

When we asked for more details, we learned that the wyvern had also just-so-happened to be much bigger than most, and the adventurers from town hadn't stood a chance against it.

Stability, huh? What a delusion on my part. Settle down in a peaceful village, find myself a good man...it was all too good to be true. Still, there was some part of me that thought Gimul was bluffing in order to make Dyson and I think this wasn't going to be an easy job.

It didn't take long to realize that he hadn't been exaggerating. Once we arrived in the village, we were led to the manor of the woman in charge.

"Welcome to the village of Apegut! What do you think? Disappointed that it's just a quiet place in the middle of nowhere?" The village chief laughed at the thought.

The village chief greeted us in her personal study, the head of a wyvern mounted on the wall behind her. I had never seen one in real life, but the fact it looked big enough to swallow a person whole made it hard to think about anything else. I wasn't exactly looking forward to seeing what village life had in store for me.

At the very least, I had to find a good man to marry. I was going to end up single forever if I did nothing but fight off all these wyverns. Just a good man, somewhere! I'd be fine with Shooter, for instance!

Huh. Yeah. I guess I *would* be fine with Shooter. Now there's a thought...

BUCK NAKED in ANOTHER WORLD

Yeah, It's an Afterword

HEY, ALL, thank you so much for picking up the first volume of *Buck Naked in Another World*. The story you just read was an enhanced version of what I originally wrote and first posted online starting back in summer of 2015, and it goes all the way up through the end of 2016.

Trying to get everything ready for publication turned out to be a lot harder than I first thought, and the first volume of this series ended up going on sale at the same time as the second one. Not only that, but Ashimoto★Yoi-sensei started on the manga for this series with Takeshobo, and MAG Garden started publishing another one of my series in comic form. I couldn't be happier as an author for all that to happen.

Thank you...thank you so much (the author said, prostrating in the nude).

When I read the manga and reread everything I posted online before as I got ready to fix up my original draft of the story, I was surprised at how Yoshida Shuta practically overflowed with stamina and vitality! Seeing how positive his character was drawn in the manga was also a happy rediscovery of what kind of person he was. The second volume of that manga came out the same day as this book, so please pick it up and give it a read if you find it in a bookstore or something!

By the way, the very first day I started penning this story, I just happened to visit a local restaurant with some of the richest, most delicious ramen imaginable. As I was eating, I got a text from my friend saying that if I wrote a story about a fish-out-of-water story about a guy being reborn in another world, it would definitely rack up views online. I thought he was crazy, but posting this was really the start of something great. Thinking back on it now, I have nothing but gratitude toward them. Thank you...thank you so much!

Now whenever I'm coming back from a meeting, or something bad happens to me, or I just want to rediscover why I got into this story in the first place, I go back to that restaurant and order the same thing I ordered back on that day.

I hope you think about this series whenever you have yourself an amazing bowl of ramen, too!

It's thanks to all the editing and publishing staff that this book exists as it does today, and I'm happy to be able to share it with all of you, the readers.

I hope you continue to enjoy the *Buck Naked in Another World* series for a long time to come!

—MADOKA KOTANI, AUGUST 2017